DEAT
HARI

THE
BOYS
ARE
BACK

The Best Short Thrillers
From Today's Best Authors

ISBN 0956159281
EAN-13 9780956159281

To our readers everywhere,
without you we'd be talking to ourselves.

Death Toll 2: Hard Targets

Praise for DEATH TOLL

"Nothing excites me more than discovering new writing talent, and this book is bursting with it!"

- **Stephen Leather**, International bestselling author of the Spider Shepherd & Jack Nightingale thrillers.

"Some of the best short, sharp offerings on the delights of physical elimination. Welcome to the art of great fiction in compressed form."

- **Seumas Gallacher,** Blogger of the Year & bestselling author of VENGEANCE WEARS BLACK

"Meet the boys! And these boys are good. Some of my favourite writers offering thrilling entertainment in short bursts. "

- **Harlan Wolff**, bestselling author of *BANGKOK RULES*

"I'm delighted to share the pages with some of the most exciting and talented thriller writers around. Death Toll 2 rocks!"

- **Matt Hilton** International bestselling author of the Joe Hunter thriller series.

DEATH TOLL 2: HARD TARGETS

THE BOYS ARE BACK

The Best Short Thrillers
From Today's Best Authors

THE ABLE MAN
Matt Hilton

A man walked into a bar…

But that was where the joke ended.

He took himself a stool at the far end of the bar, beneath a plasma screen playing MTV with the sound muted. He could see the entrance door, and the short corridor to the restrooms, without having to turn his head. In the mirror behind the bar he could check out the patrons. There weren't too many this early in the day, only a couple of grizzled old men sitting apart at separate corners of the room. They'd probably sat in those same chairs over many years, but had yet to acknowledge the presence of the other. There was a young couple huddled in a booth. They weren't lovers, they were united in their addictions, and the weak beer they supped didn't stop them fidgeting. They had suspicious eyes, but they barely checked out the newcomer. He was no cop, no drug dealer, and he wasn't a mark, so they weren't interested. Two skinny youths, enough alike to be twins, played pool at a table where the green baize was stained brown from old spillages.

'What will I get ya?'

The man looked across at the bartender who hadn't moved from his place at the opposite end of the bar counter.

'Got a Corona?'

The bartender nodded and pushed away from the counter to dig in a cooler. He snapped off the top, handed over the bottle.

'You need a glass?'

'The bottle's good, thanks. Got a slice of lime?'

The bartender only looked, and the man shrugged. The man chucked a few dollars on the counter top. He pulled the bottle close but didn't sip from it. He swept droplets of condensation onto the counter, watched bubbles rising up the neck to gather as a pale froth.

'It ain't like a good wine where you gotta let it breathe,' the bartender pointed out as he deftly spirited the dollars into his pocket.

Now the man just looked. The bartender shrugged and walked away. He leaned on the counter, his previous place, and watched the cavorting of some nubile popster on the TV screen. Occasionally his eyes flicked over the man, but his curiosity went no further.

The man was unremarkable. To look at he was your usual guy down on his luck and killing part of another dreary uneventful day working his way to the bottom of a glass. But that was only on outward appearance. His battered leather jacket and jeans hid a tight body, and the ball cap covered his high and tight cut that would equally mark him as a military man. The cap also served to conceal a recent wound to his skull. It still itched and wept beads of blood, but the sweatband kept it from trickling down his face. His jaw was lean, but there was nothing weak about it. There was an old scar on his right cheekbone that ended at the corner of his deep-set eye. Other scars showed white on the backs of his hands and fingers, stark against the suntanned skin. He wore no rings or other jewellery, though a pale band around this second finger showed that hadn't always been the case. The only adornment he wore was a watch on his left wrist, a leather cover over its face, snapped down with a press-stud. It was a diver's watch if anyone could have seen it. A Breitling given him as an anniversary gift by his late wife.

He tipped the Corona towards himself, but still didn't drink.

The motion didn't elicit a response from the bartender. He'd been forgotten until next he ordered. Good enough. He allowed the beer to settle, again seemingly absorbed in watching the bubbles rise to the top.

Nobody could have imagined his thoughts while watching the bubbles dancing. He gave no hint of the dark place to which he'd sunk in those brief seconds of recollection.

He nursed the bottle some more. He glanced from the beer to the mirror, then laid his left elbow on the bar top. His position was languid, but purposeful. He could check out the four newcomers entering the bar without seeming to do so.

They'd taken longer to come inside than he'd anticipated. He'd followed them to the roadside bar, and with no other destination in sight had took it that they had elected for a beer stop after their long drive. While they'd sat in their truck, one of them taking a call on an iPhone, he'd slipped by them unnoticed, concealed by the trail dust hanging in the air from where they'd come to an abrupt halt in the unpaved lot. They came into the dimness of the bar in the same herky-jerky manner as they drove their truck. The same herky-jerky way they'd each taken a go at his wife. The only time to his knowledge where they hadn't been pushing and shoving at each other was when one of them cleanly wiped a blade across Trisha-Mae's throat then dumped her over the dock into the river.

They were brothers, or maybe cousins. Family at least. They were all big-boned, raw-faced men with the inbred stamp all over them. Motherfuckers was the least of aspersions that could be thrown at these guys. One of them had a turn in his eyes. In the pecking order he was lowest, and the one sent to the bar while the others headed for a booth. There was only the one booth, but the junkies knew to vacate it. They left the dregs in their glasses and staggered out: wise for such crack-addled brains.

The trio in the booth was noisy, laughing, swearing, scraping the table further out to make way for their bulk. A glass fell on the floor and shattered. The bartender studiously ignored the willful destruction of his property.

The man didn't look at Squint Eye. He didn't have to look to know where he was: the sour stink of the red neck was enough to pinpoint him in the darkest of rooms. Squint Eye waved the bartender over, gruffly made his order. There was no please or thank you. He left without paying the tab, and returned to the booth. He had to pull up a spare chair and sit with his back to the bar. The bartender delivered four glasses and the remainder of a bottle of sour mash to their table. The biggest of the bunch in back of the booth snatched the bottle and told the bartender to fuck off. He came back to his usual place at the counter, making sure his frown was turned from the men in the booth. They noisily set about downing their first round.

The man tipped his Corona towards him, same as before, then flipped it away, onto the bar top. He made a grab for it, but some of the amber liquid splashed across the walnut counter. The motion was akin to the accidental fumbling of a drunk and didn't get a reaction from the family in the booth. But it caught a scowl from the bartender.

'Got a cloth?' the man asked.

The bartender lifted a bar towel from a shelf and came over. It was bleached out, showing holes from much use. He made to swipe the spillage, but the man placed his hand on top of the tender's hand and said, 'There are some messes you just gotta clean up yerself.'

4

HARD TARGETS

The bartender glanced once at the family, back at the man and got the message. But he didn't like it. He sighed through his clenched teeth, said, 'I gotta go an' check the barrels.'

The man looked at him, and the bartender looked back. Then the bartender came out from behind the counter and went through the passage towards the restrooms. Maybe there was another room back there for barrel storage. Maybe there was a phone and the bartender was going to call the law. It wouldn't matter. Things would be over before the cops made it to this out of the way place. They'd be as slow to respond as he assumed they were when the man had called them after the family brutally raped and then murdered his wife.

The man sopped up the spilled beer, then held the wet towel in his fist. The bottle was still half full: optimistically he chugged it down in one long pull. He reversed his left hand on the neck and slid from the stool. He didn't approach the booth. He went to the pool table. The twins saw him coming and stepped back. Their large Adam's apples bobbed with unspoken questions as the man draped the wet cloth over the cue ball, then scooped it up. 'Maybe now would be a good time to get on home, boys,' said the man.

The twins shared a look, like they were staring in a mirror, then nodded in unison. They put away their cue sticks, and headed for the exit.

The man checked out the two old guys. Parked in their respective corners they were out of harm's way. Maybe they knew what kind of establishment this was and chose those seats for sound reason. They could watch the action without having to play any active part in it. The man caught a knowing wink from one of the oldsters. He gave only a subtle nod in acknowledgement, then veered towards the booth. As he walked, he wound the cloth tight, letting the cue ball hang heavy in the bag made of the wet towel.

5

Trisha-Mae gave Jerrod the Breitling on their fifth wedding anniversary. He gave her a gold necklace with a solitaire diamond on a locket. Neither could afford such extravagance, but that was the way they had ever been. The Breitling cost more than the car that Jerrod drove, but Trisha-Mae had wanted to mark their anniversary as something extra special.

He admired the watch, checking out the black dial with three inset sub dials in white, not quite sure what each was for.

'It's a Navitimer Chronograph watch,' Trisha-Mae beamed at him. 'Waterproof to thirty metres.'

'I'm an army Ranger,' Jerrod smiled back. 'Not a Navy SEAL. You know I can't swim worth a lick.'

The watch cost her around eight thousand dollars, and his gift felt measly in comparison. But she loved it and wore it to bed that night. It was all she wore.

That night he gave her a baby, the real gift she'd been longing for.

The following day Jerrod reported to Fort Benning, and from there shipped out to Afghanistan for his third tour. He didn't get to test its water resistance, but had purchased himself a leather cover to keep the mountain grit out of the Breitling's workings. Daily he'd checked the countdown on his watch till he could get home to his pregnant wife.

When he arrived home six months later, Trisha-Mae had swelled up nicely. The kid was growing big and strong inside of her, but she was taking no harm. Her pregnancy suited her. She'd blossomed like a rose and was prettier than ever.

They lived on a small plot adjacent to the levee road between Lake Chicot and the Mississippi River, down in the southeast corner of Arkansas. It was a good place to live, a safe place usually. Neighbours were neighbourly. Doors weren't always locked at night. It made their home ripe for invasion by the group of men on their way back from a drugs deal up in Pine Bluff, as they wended their way back to Louisiana. The men, all of the Cheighnier family, Cajun red necks from some bayou outside of Baton Rouge, entered their home in search of something the cocaine they snorted and booze they swilled couldn't satisfy. They were looking for a woman, and, despite being heavy with child, Trisha-Mae was just what the doctor ordered.

It was after two in the morning. The old clapboard house ticked as it cooled, and outside the frogs and insects made a racket. Normally the ambient noise wouldn't have covered the sound of the engine as the Cheighnier's pulled up the dirt drive and parked on the lawn outside their house. It wouldn't have hidden the whispers as the men inspected the house, then let them in through the front door. But both Jerrod and Trisha-Mae were exhausted, his first night home on furlough had been a full one. The first hint that the family was inside was when one of the Cheighnier's placed the barrel of his gun against the man of the house's head and ordered him to get the fuck outta the bed.

Jerrod felt like a kicked dog. He was a goddamn Army Ranger, had survived three tours in Afghanistan, one in Iraq, taking on the best the mountain and desert fighters could field against him. Yet here he was, caught napping in his own bed by a bunch of drugged up red necks. He was ashamed, but more than anything he was fearful for his wife. Trisha-Mae was in bed beside him, and if he fought then and there, she would get hurt. Their baby would get hurt. Jerrod allowed two of the ugly guys to drag him from the bed, his mind feverishly weighing the odds, figuring a plan to take the fight back to them.

One of them held Trisha-Mae on the bed. Sleep had befuddled her, but now she was fully in the waking nightmare. She screamed silently as she beseeched Jerrod with her eyes.

Jerrod tried to move towards her. A squint-eyed man punched him in the gut, and he folded.

'Don't get stupid now, boy,' said the cockeyed man.

They stood Jerrod in his boxer shorts. The two that held him pushed and shoved, and not always at him. His arms were twisted behind his back. One of them got a cord from the bedside lamp and tied it tight round his wrists. He was kicked to his knees.

'Take whatever you want,' Jerrod said. 'Just don't hurt my wife. Don't you see she's with child.'

One of the others leaned in close, a bearded man with a faded tattoo on his right cheek. It was a star, the black ink now fading to blue. His stink washed over Jerrod. When he opened his mouth his teeth were the colour of caramel and his breath sickly sweet. Jerrod tried not to squint at the vile stink when the man spoke. 'Ain't she just a pretty one? Even with that fat belly she's sweeter than any of the whores we got back home.'

'Don't touch her.' Jerrod stared at the tattoo.

'You're in no position to give orders,' said Tattoo.

'I've some cash,' Jerrod said.

'I'll take it thanks. But it ain't gonna make no difference.'

'My watch. Take it and leave.'

One of the two behind him studied the old leather, pitted with scuff marks and sweat stains. 'Piece of shit ain't worth the trouble of taking it off your arm.'

The fourth man, the one holding Trisha-Mae, hooked the gold necklace in his fat fingers. 'Lookit what we got here, boys! This'll look pretty hanging round the necka the next whore we fuck.'

He pulled the necklace over Trisha-Mae's head, yanking out strands of her long hair with it. Trisha-Mae wailed as the man dangled it before her. He slipped it into the pocket of his jeans. Trisha-Mae wailed louder.

Jerrod looked at her, tried to import the need to stay calm. Give them a reason and he didn't doubt the brutes would resort to violence. But Trisha-Mae was growing frantic. The man who'd stolen her necklace jammed his dirty hand over her mouth and forced her down. Trisha-Mae kicked and squirmed for air. The man laughed at her feeble attempts, and inserted a hand up the hem of her nightgown.

'Get your fucking hands off her!'

Jerrod could feel the blood in his skull. It pounded. His eyes bolted from their sockets.

'Shut him up, why don'tcha?' said Tattoo.

'Without warning, Jerrod was clubbed on the back of the head. Gun butt, or something else, he didn't know. It was heavy, split his scalp and sent a wave of black through his vision. He blinked hard to stay awake.

Squint Eye ducked down close to him.

'You gonna keep your peace, boy, or am I gonna have to cut out your tongue?'

Jerrod knew there was no way out of this. Shit! Why didn't he fight before? He was hoping for a peaceful resolution, safety for Trisha-Mae and their baby, but now things had gone too far. The drug-fueled red necks weren't going to leave them alone unmolested, or even alive.

Jerrod got a foot under him and tried to rise.

'Nuh-uhh!' said the second guy holding him. He was the clubber. He struck Jerrod a second time, right on the same sore spot and blood poured down Jerrod's nape and over his collarbone. A new wave of nausea swept over Jerrod and he went back to his knees. Squint Eye grabbed him by an ear and twisted his head to the side.

'You get to watch, but you do it in silence, boy.'

He shoved Jerrod to the floor, using the twisted ear as a fulcrum. Jerrod went on his chest and Squint Eye kneeled between his shoulders. Jerrod craned up, yelling furiously as the necklace thief ripped off Trisha-Mae's panties.

The blackness descended over him as Tattoo pushed aside his kinsman. 'I ain't taking no sloppy seconds.'

'Where you off to, Bobbie?' Squint Eye demanded of the man who'd split Jerrod's scalp. 'You leaving me sitting here like this all on my lonesome?'

9

'You'll get your chance soon enough,' said the man called Bobbie. 'Last in the queue as usual.' He went to help the necklace thief hold Trisha-Mae down as Tattoo clambered between her thighs. The trio were on top of her like hyenas round a carcass, pushing and shoving, hooting and laughing, goading Tattoo to a quick finish.

To Jerrod, Squint Eye said, 'Motherfucker, you see the fun you're making me miss?'

In Jerrod's vision all now was a scarlet mist.

They were laid on the rickety dock. Here the Mississippi made a wide turn, the river broad and dark and mist hazed the distant shore. Less than a mile to the south the interstate spanned the river, but there was no traffic on the bridge at the early hour. Nobody nearby to hear their shouts for help. Jerrod was still bound. There was snot in his nostrils and the back of his mouth. Blood had poured across his cheek, pooling in an old shrapnel scar and directed to the corner of his right eye. The blood had congealed and matted his lashes. He tried to see Trisha-Mae with his one good eye, but his wife was lying down near his feet and she had turned her face away from him. Shame, or disgust at him, he wasn't sure.

All four of the men had taken their turn at her. Tattoo had done it twice, the violent rape of the woman by the other Cheighnier's getting him up again. Then they'd ransacked the house for anything worth taking. They'd been high on the violence and had whooped and hollered, pushing and shoving in their exuberance. More than one of them had come to kick Jerrod where he lay. The necklace thief set the house on fire, and Jerrod hoped they'd leave, and he'd at least get an opportunity to get Trisha-Mae out of the house alive. He didn't know what he could do for their unborn. But the Cheighnier's had other plans. They dragged first Trisha-Mae, and then him out of the house and across the front lot of their home to the levee. They

10

hauled them down the far side to the river and threw them down on the warped and muddy planks of the old dock.

Tattoo crouched down so Jerrod could see him. Jerrod focussed on the blue star on the man's cheek. Seeing only through one eye, Jerrod thought the star jumped and shimmered.

'I have the feeling that you're a vengeful man,' said Tattoo.

Jerrod only looked.

'Hmmm. I can't afford to have no able man come looking for revenge, now can I?'

Tattoo stood up and held out a hand.

Bobbie handed over a large hunting knife, and the butt was still clotted with Jerrod's blood and a tuft of short hair torn from his scalp.

'The cops round here don't need to find no DNA to bring 'em to our door,' Tattoo said. 'Pretty sure them gators and snapping turtles in the river are as hungry for a pretty girl as we were.'

Tattoo crouched and made a swiping motion.

Jerrod screamed inside as he heard Trisha-Mae gag and the blood bubbling out of her.

Two of the Cheighnier's lugged Trisha-Mae away and there came a solid splash as she went in the river.

'Give him a new mouth, too,' Squint Eye encouraged, but Tattoo came back to crouch before Jerrod. He held the knife down by his side. It was so sharp it didn't hold a bead of Trisha-Mae's life on its steel edge. Tattoo shook his head. 'Nah, more fun if we watch this one drown.'

The men manhandled Jerrod to his feet. He hadn't the strength to stand. They lifted and shoved and pulled him to the edge of the dock. His wrists were still bound behind his back. Jerrod looked for his wife but she'd sunk without trace, but for a few dirty bubbles that popped at the surface of the river.

'Who wants to make a bet on how long he can hold his breath?' Tattoo asked to a round of laughter.

Who kicked him in the river wasn't important. Jerrod had already decided that they were all going to die.

11

Jerrod saw bubbles. The river was so muddy that his vision was filled with brown froth, as he fought to get his feet beneath him. His bare feet slipped and twisted in the deep silt, and he could feel the mud pulling him down. He couldn't swim, had never swum more than a couple of ungainly yards in his life. But strangely he didn't panic. His overriding emotion was rage, and he fought the river as much as he demanded repayment from those who'd destroyed his life. He got his foot on something, and in some distant corner of his mind he knew that it was Trisha-Mae sunk into the silt. His reaction was to jerk away, but then he realised that it was his only way out of this. He had to accept his wife's helping hand if ever he was going to avenge her. He placed his foot squarely on her, got the other up. He closed his eyes when he realised he was standing on her swollen belly –their unborn babe demanded vengeance from him too – and pushed up.

His head broke the surface and he sucked in lungful's of air.

Beneath him, Trisha-Mae was pressed deeper into the silt, and he felt himself dip under again. He pushed against her and found her knee and a more stable leverage point and threw himself for the bank.

The sluggish undercurrent had taken him a dozen yards from where he'd gone in. Already the family was a clot of shapeless silhouettes retreating over the levee to where they'd parked their truck. None of them looked back as Jerrod rolled onto his back, kicking with his feet until his shoulders butted onto the sloping embankment. He wedged himself in the mud there, breathing hard, sucking in life giving oxygen. He heard laughter and it made him madder than ever. He dug in with his heels and pushed himself further on to land. An engine growled and the truck peeled away, accompanied by hooting and hollering. The Cheighnier's were pleased with their night's fun.

Finally in a position to sit up, Jerrod got his hands beneath him. He twisted and squirmed and the cord that had been looped around his left wrist felt slack. Squint Eye had tied it over his watchstrap, and now that it had slipped off it gave him and extra half inch of freedom. Jerrod twisted and pulled, and lost a bit of skin, but he yanked out his left hand. He pulled the remainder of the cord from his right. Then sat, looking at the river. Bubbles still popped and fizzed at the surface. Their house was now fully ablaze, and the glow from the furnace hot flames bathed the river. Jerrod thought the amber colour on the water the same as his favourite brand of beer.

He should get Trisha-Mae out of the water, but didn't know how.

He turned and looked at the house, and then pushed to his feet.

'I love you,' he said towards the river then turned and trotted as best he could up the slope of the levee.

The house was an inferno.

But his car was parked on the bed of crushed oyster shells across the yard.

He went to the car and popped the trunk.

He was still in service, his furlough apt to be cut short at any time, and he had prepared for such an eventuality. He 'd left a rucksack in the trunk packed with a spare set of clothing should he have to leave home in a hurry.

He dressed in jeans and T-shirt and pulled on an old battered leather jacket. He settled an old ball cap on his head. His time in the water had washed off most of the blood, but the cap would do to hide the raw wound. He laced up his spare boots. He smelled of the river, but that didn't matter. In the glove compartment was a small roll of emergency money, which he pocketed. Pity he hadn't thought to bring home a gun.

He got in the car and started it, and pulled out, following the levee road south, after the Cheighnier family.

As he drove his mind was numb to anything but vengeance.

Up ahead he could see the taillights of the truck, but it was madness to try to push them from the road and take them on barehanded. He required weapons to go against their guns and knives.

The Cheighnier truck pulled over at a gas station on the outskirts of Tallulah. Tattoo paid for the gas Squint Eye pumped with the cash stolen from Jerrod. Jerrod contemplated heading on in and striking a match and chucking it at the nozzle Squint Eye wielded. But he didn't have a match. Nothing was dry about him. Except maybe one thing.

He checked his watch. Waterproof to thirty metres. Trisha-Mae had been right. It was a little after 7 a.m. None of the family had seen him dressed, and they certainly wouldn't expect him to be the same man who went to a payphone on the corner of the gas station and called 911. Jerrod got the cops but didn't tell them where he was. He asked them to go pull his wife and unborn out of the river.

'This some kind of nasty joke, son?' asked the operator.

'Do I sound like I'm fucking joking?'

He hung up.

Maybe he should have told the police where the Cheighnier's were, but then he'd miss his opportunity for vengeance.

"I can't afford to have no able man come looking for revenge, now can I?"

Tattoo had that right.

Jerrod followed them south, through Tallulah and on. They took a left at Ferriday, crossed the Big Muddy at Natchez and took Route 62 towards Baton Rouge. When road markers indicated that St Francisville was only two miles ahead they left the main route and got onto a strip of crumbling asphalt leading to some other ass-end collection of dwellings, and another mile on the roadside bar. It was nearing ten in the morning, and it looked like the family was almost home. They were familiar enough with the bar to know it was open for service.

Squint Eye had his back to Jerrod.

14

Jerrod would have preferred to look him in the eye when he killed him, but he wouldn't know which one to focus on anyhow.

He smashed the Corona bottle against Squint Eye's head, then reversed the broken glass and jammed it deep in the man's carotid.

'Just think of all the fun you're gonna miss now,' Jerrod growled as he shoved over the dying man. Squint Eye hit the planks grabbing at the bottle's neck embedded in his throat. He made the mistake of pulling it out and blood spurted in the air.

Only seconds had passed, but already the tableau had changed. The other three Cheighnier's had erupted out of their seats, but instead of going for their weapons they gawped at the living dead man standing on the opposite side of the table.

'You?' Tattoo gasped. 'What are you doing here?'

'You should've made sure I was dead.'

'We can change that now!'

Tattoo was wedged between Bobbie and the necklace thief. They kind of squashed against him, maybe looking for protection from the Alpha dog.

Tattoo pushed with his elbows, going for the gun in his waistband.

Jerrod ignored him. He swung the cue ball in the cloth and smashed caramel chunks out of Tattoo's mouth. The big man fell back in the booth and Jerrod turned on Bobbie. The man had slipped out his knife, the one that slit Trisha-Mae's throat. Jerrod swung the cue ball and smashed the hand holding it. The same hand that had pawed at Trisha-Mae, held her while the others had their way with her. The hand that he'd used to invade her when checking she was wet enough to accommodate him.

Jerrod whipped the cue ball into his head, and it left a deep dent. Bobbie fell over the table. His weight broke the legs and it crashed down with him on top. Jerrod stamped on the back of his neck for good measure.

15

The necklace thief apparently had no weapon to speak of. But he came for Jerrod with his clawing hands, perhaps hoping to throttle him. Jerrod back swiped the cue ball into his right elbow, then the left and the thief made a pitiful sound as his clawing hands folded towards his chest.

'You broke my arms,' he moaned.

'I broke your elbows. Your hands still work just fine.' Jerrod snapped the fingers of his left hand. 'You have something belonging my wife. Give it to me.'

The thief tentatively dipped his hand in his pocket, wincing and moaning at the agony, but he pulled out Trisha-Mae's necklace. The solitaire diamond winked and it was all the approval Jerrod needed. He snatched the necklace from the thief then brought the cue ball back over his shoulder and down, and battered it between the thief's eyes. Eye sockets and nose collapsed, and the shards drove in deep enough to make liver pate of his brain.

Jerrod had not yet taken a step back. Once committed a Ranger always moved forward. He stepped over Bobbie, and looked down at Tattoo. He concentrated on the blue star on the man's cheek, while he took out his wedding ring and placed it on the gold chain next to the diamond. Deliberately he fed the chain in his jeans pocket for safekeeping.

Tattoo had both hands over his mouth. Blood poured down his chin, collecting in his beard, making his dull shirt even dirtier. His eyes went to the cue ball in the cloth.

Jerrod knew what he was thinking: could he get to the gun in his jeans before that ball smashed his head to pulp?

The answer was no.

He didn't resist as Jerrod leaned in and yanked free the revolver.

Jerrod could tell by weight alone that there were no rounds in the chambers. Why else had Tattoo used Bobbie's knife to murder Trisha-Mae? In the dark, in the confusion of strangers invading his home, and his fear that a stray round could hit

Trisha-Mae, Jerrod couldn't know the gun was empty. If only he'd known then...

'You asked me if I was a vengeful man.' Jerrod eyed Tattoo. 'Stand up.'

'What you gonna do?' Tattoo's voice was wet with blood and mucus.

'Something you should've done.'

Jerrod stood behind Tattoo at the edge of a bayou. He'd walked the man there, having noted it a few hundred yards west of the roadhouse on the way here.

He'd secured Tattoo's wrists behind his back.

A small gathering had come out to watch. The two old men and the bartender. Even the twins had stuck around, wanting to know the outcome of what was going down in the bar. Only the crackhead couple had gone off elsewhere, seeking their next fix.

The small group didn't interfere. Maybe they'd been waiting a long time for Tattoo and his family to bite off more than they could chew.

'Please, mistuh,' Tattoo begged. 'Don't do this to me.'

Jerrod said, 'Your pleading is falling on deaf ears. The way mine did when I begged you not to harm my wife. Do you remember Trisha-Mae? She was the pregnant lady you and your scumbag family raped and murdered.'

'Jesus freakin' Christ! You've killed three of my brothers already. How much vengeance does any man need?'

'I need it all.'

'Please?'

'You said you couldn't afford to have no able man come looking for revenge. Can I?'

Jerrod swiped Bobbie's knife across Tattoo's throat.

The blade bit so deep it opened him up almost to the vertebrae. Jerrod wasn't taking chances.

'Try holding your breath, fucker.'

He kicked tattoo into the bayou.

It wasn't deep, but it was enough to flood over the top of Tattoo.

All Jerrod could see was where his bound hands twitched and his heels kicked feebly at the water, churning up bubbles.

He sure could drink that Corona now.

But he waited.

Only when tattoo was still and the mud at the bed of the bayou claimed him did he turn away and walk back towards the bar.

One of the old men – the one who'd offered the wink earlier – slow clapped him every step. The other old man neither clapped, smiled nor nothing else. Just watched Jerrod as he approached. Then he turned and went inside the bar, obviously seeking out his favourite corner.

'Did you call the cops?' Jerrod looked at the bartender.

The man was fearful, but Jerrod dipped his head, said, 'You had to. I get that. And it's OK. I need to speak with them about another murder any way.'

The bartender nodded. He indicated the bar. 'It'll be a while till they get their asses out here. Come inside. As I recall you spilled your drink. Let me buy you a fresh one.'

Jerrod walked for the door. Yeah, he guessed once the cops got here it'd be a while until he had himself another beer.

KILL ZONE
Stephen Leather

October 2002.
Afghanistan.

Spider Shepherd squatted on his heels outside his tent, drinking his first brew of the day from a battered mug as he watched the wind stirring dust devils from the dirt floor of the compound. The dust covered every surface, leaving everything as brown and drab as the wintry Afghan hills that surrounded him. Unshaven and wearing a tee-shirt and fatigues worn and sun-faded from long use, Shepherd drank the last of his brew and tossed the dregs into the dirt. 'Why does a brew never taste right out here?' he asked.

Sitting next to him with his legs outstretched was Geordie Mitchell, an SAS medic who was a couple of years older than Shepherd. 'That'd be one of those rhetorical questions, would it?' said Geordie. He had a floppy hat pulled low over his head. His hair was thinning and his scalp was always the first area to burn under the hot Afghan sun.

Shepherd stood up and stretched. 'It just never tastes right, that's all.'

'It's because we use bottled water, plus the altitude we're at affects the boiling point of the water, plus the milk is crap. Plus the sand gets everywhere.' Geordie stood up and looked at his watch, a rugged Rolex Submariner. 'Soon be time for morning prayers,' he said.

The two men strolled across the compound, their AK47s hanging on slings on their backs. They heard raised voices at the entrance to the compound and headed in that direction.

They found a young SAS officer, Captain Todd, in the middle of a furious altercation with the guard at the gates. Like all the Regiment's officers, Harry Todd had been seconded to the SAS from his own regiment for a three-year tour of duty, and was on his first trip with them. He'd only been in Afghanistan for two months and he was finding it tough going. As if his Oxford, Sandhurst and The Guards background was not already enough to raise hackles among the men he nominally led, Todd's blond hair flopped over his eyes like a poor man's Hugh Grant and, despite his youth, his nervous habit of clearing his throat made him sound like some ancient brigadier harrumphing over the Daily Telegraph in the Army & Navy Club.

Shepherd had managed to avoid the Captain so far, which suited him just fine. The Major had realised that Todd was going to be an awkward fit and soon after he'd arrived he had detached him from the Squadron to the Intelligence Clearing Centre, largely with the aim of keeping him from getting under everybody's feet. The Clearing Centre was where all the intelligence received was collated and evaluated. It came from a variety of sources; satellite and drone surveillance imagery, communication intercepts from GCHQ, and humint – human intelligence – in all its varied forms, from "eyes on" information from SAS observation posts right down to tip-offs of often dubious value from assorted spies, grasses and ordinary Afghans with grudges against their neighbours.   Todd's job was to sift the intelligence as it came in and then brief the OC - the Boss - at the morning prayers held at 0800 every day. Like documents passing across some bureaucrat's desk, the intelligence was divided into three categories: "For Immediate Action" that might be acted on within hours or even minutes; "Pending", for events that might be coming up in the near future; and "File For Future Use". Documents in the latter category often disappeared into the back of a filing cabinet and never saw the light of day again. Much of his work was humdrum and routine, but Todd had clearly been looking for an opportunity to show his worth and by the look of it, he had decided that today was the day.

Todd was standing next to an Afghan in a black dishdasha, with an AK 74 slung across his back. Initially Shepherd was more interested in the weapon than the Afghan - its orange plastic furniture and magazine made it easy to identify as the updated and improved version of the ubiquitous AK47, and it was an unusual weapon for an Afghan to be carrying.

As Shepherd and Geordie walked over, the Afghan turned to look at them. He had the hook-nosed profile, sun and wind-burned skin, and dark beard and hair of a typical Afghan, but he had a distinguishing feature that Shepherd noticed at once - though his right eye was hazel, the pupil of his left one was a strange, milky white, almost opalescent colour.

Todd was haranguing two armed guards at the entrance who appeared to be refusing to allow the Captain and the Afghan into the compound. 'I'll have you on a charge for this, I'm warning you!' said Todd.

'What's the problem, Captain?' Geordie said.

'This guard is refusing to let us into the compound,' Todd said, flicking his hair from his eyes.

Geordie grinned. 'That's probably because you've got an armed and unknown Afghan with you,' he said. He didn't call the officer 'sir.' That was the SAS way. No saluting and no honorifics, though the Major was always referred to as 'Boss'.

'This man is Ahmad Khan, a Surrendered Enemy Personnel,' said the Captain.

'Well, that doesn't carry too much weight in these parts,' said Geordie. 'I can tell you from my own experience that SEPs are like junkies - they're only with you long enough to get their next fix: cash, weapons, whatever, and then they're gone again. With respect, Captain, no experienced guy would trust an SEP as far as he could throw him.'

Todd glared at the medic. 'This man has vital intelligence I need to put before the Boss and I am not going to exclude him from the compound just because of your prejudice against SEPs and perhaps Afghans in general.'

Shepherd could see that Geordie was close to giving the officer a piece of his mind, and while he preferred not to get involved, he figured that he should at least try to defuse the situation. 'It's not about prejudice,' he said, choosing his words carefully. 'It's based on bitter experience. We've had more than our fair share of green on blue attacks out here.' He pointed at the Afghan's rifle. 'One: He's carrying a loaded AK74. Only the top guys in the Taliban carry them. So he's not some tribesman picking up a few extra dollars for fighting the faranji invaders, he's one of their leaders. Two: This is a secure compound. Not even a Brit would get in here without being vetted or vouched for, and yet you're trying to bring an armed Taliban fighter in here.'

Geordie pointed a finger at the officer. 'The thing is, Captain, you're not only jeopardising the safety of everyone here, but you'd better watch your own back, because I'd take odds that he'd rub you out if he thought he could get away with it.'

'Your comments are noted,' Todd said, barely keeping the fury from his voice. 'Now step aside, the OC needs to hear what he has to say.'

The two guards – both paratroopers – stood their ground, their weapons in the ready position.

'With the greatest of respect, Captain, they're not going to let you in while your SEP has a loaded weapon,' said Shepherd. 'But if he unloads his weapon and leaves the magazine and his ammunition belt with the guards, he can probably be allowed into the compound. He can pick them up again on his way out.'

Ahmad Khan looked to Todd for guidance, then shrugged and began unloading his AK 74, but he glared at Shepherd, clearly unhappy.

'Do you speak English?' Geordie asked the Afghan.

'Enough,' said the man, handing his ammunition belt and magazine to one of the paratroopers.

'What's your name?'

'Ahmad Khan.'

'Well, Ahmad Khan, you'd better be on your best behaviour while you're here because we'll be watching you.'

The Afghan smiled. 'Do I scare you, soldier? Is that it?' He nodded slowly. 'Yes, I can see the fear in your eyes.' He chuckled.

'You don't scare me, mate,' said Geordie. 'I've slotted more than my fair share of guys like you.'

The Afghan gave a mirthless smile. 'Tread carefully, my friend. We Afghans are a proud people. We don't give in to threats, nor tolerate insults to our honour.'

'Leave it, Geordie,' said Shepherd, putting a hand on the medic's shoulder. 'He can't hurt anyone now.' He nodded at the Captain. 'Morning prayers are about to start,' he said.

Shepherd and Geordie walked away from the entrance as the two paratroopers stepped aside to allow the Captain and the Afghan to enter. They caught up with Jim 'Jimbo' Shortt, an SAS trooper who had been on selection with Shepherd four years earlier.

'What's up with Goldilocks?' asked Jimbo as Shepherd and Geordie fell into step with him. 'Porridge too cold?'

'He's come in with an SEP,' Shepherd said. 'And because the guy speaks English, Todd thinks he's some sort of Deep Throat in a dishdasha.'

Jimbo gave a weary shake of his head. 'Typical fucking Rupert,' he said. 'They always think locals who can speak English must be trustworthy.'

They walked up to the HQ - a grandiose name for the mud-brick building shielded by berms and banks of sandbags, that served as camp office, briefing room, and sleeping quarters for the officers. They filed through the doorway and along a corridor with a series of small, dark rooms opening off it, lit only by narrow windows high up in the walls. There was no furniture in the rooms, just mattresses on the floor with personal belongings kept in plastic bags hanging from nails hammered into the walls. At the far end was a larger space, the office and briefing room, with two trestle tables pushed together in the centre of the room and the walls and every available surface covered with maps, documents and surveillance photographs.

There were already half a dozen troopers there and the three men flopped down into empty chairs. Major Allan Gannon appeared and took his place at the head of the table. He was a big man with wide shoulders and a nose that had been broken at least twice. The Major looked at his watch just as Captain Todd appeared. The Captain nodded at the Major. 'Sorry, Boss,' he said.

'No problem,' said The Major.

The Captain led the morning prayers, giving his intelligence briefing including outlining possible targets on satellite surveillance photographs. When he'd finished, he folded his arms and looked at the Major. 'I have some very interesting human intel that I want to take advantage of,' he said to the Major. 'I have access to an SEP who has just defected. He's on the compound as we speak. But Ahmad Khan has not only defected himself, he has persuaded the rest of his group of

24

twenty Taliban fighters to surrender as well. I need an escort. All his fighters want is five hundred US dollars each and the guarantee of safe conduct that your presence will provide.'

The Major raised his eyebrows. 'Where has this come from?'

'He walked up to an Afghan Army patrol and gave himself up. He said he wanted to speak to the Brits.'

'And not the Yanks?' said The Major.

'He says he doesn't trust the Americans.'

'Is that so? And what is he exactly? A Taliban fighter?'

'He was a sniper, but he's been trained in explosives and IEDs.'

'Has he now?'

'Boss, this stinks to high Heaven,' said Geordie. 'If this was genuine then his men would have come in with him.'

'He thinks there is a risk to their safety if they come in on their own. His men fear that the Afghans might be trigger-happy. They want an escort to bring them in.'

'Boss, I wouldn't trust this raghead as far as I can throw him,' said Geordie. 'I certainly won't be taking a trip up the road with him.'

'That sort of language is unacceptable,' said the Captain.

'What sort of language?' asked Geordie.

'You know what I'm talking about,' said the Captain. He looked over at the Major, obviously hoping for his support.

'I think we do need to tread carefully,' said the Major.

'Talk about into the lion's den,' said Jimbo. 'For all we know, he could be setting up an ambush.'

'I've spoken to the man, I can vouch for him,' said Todd.

'Then you can go and bring in his men,' said Geordie.

'You can't trust these guys,' said Jock McIntyre, his voice a Glaswegian growl. Jock was a twelve-year veteran of the SAS and had been a Para for eight years before that. In all he had five times as much experience as the Captain, and both men knew it. 'If they switch sides once, they'll do it again. And I wouldn't want them in the compound with guns in their hands.'

25

Captain Todd was faced with a row of nodding heads and his lips tightened into a thin white line. Although he outranked them, Todd had already discovered that in the SAS, respect was given only to skill and battlefield experience, not to stripes on the sleeve or pips on the shoulder.

'And I'm certainly not going to be volunteering to ride off into the middle of nowhere with this Ahmad Kahn,' said Jock. 'No matter who vouches for him.'

The Captain glanced at the Major for support again. 'Ahmad Khan has already proved his worth by identifying a previously unknown Taliban commander,' said Todd. 'B Squadron are dealing with him.'

'If he's previously unknown, we've only the SEP's word that the guy really is a Taliban commander,' said Jock. 'He could just be some local warlord or the leader of a rival faction that he wants to get rid of. And even if the SEP's men seriously do want to switch sides, why would we take the risk of providing them with an escort, when they could just come in themselves?'

'Because they're afraid that they'll be walking into an ambush,' Todd said.

Jock shrugged. 'The same fear that we'd have about going to an RV in the mountains with them, then. I've not heard anything to change my mind.' There was a rumble of agreement from the other SAS men. Jock was one of the most experienced men in the Squadron and one of the most highly-regarded.

Todd looked over at the Major but Gannon just shrugged. It wasn't the sort of mission that he could force on his men. 'Right,' Todd said, after a lengthy pause. 'I'll see if the members of the Para Support Group are less mule-headed.'

Todd strode out of the room.

'Tosser,' said one of the troopers.

'Bloody Rupert,' said another.

'Give the guy a break, lads,' said the Major. 'He's still wet behind the ears.'

'I know he's keen, Boss, but this has all the makings of a trap,' said Shepherd. 'We've seen this guy and something doesn't smell right.'

'Yeah, and it's not just the fact that he hasn't showered for a month,' said Geordie.

'No one's forcing any of you to go,' said the Major.

'Someone needs to tell him he's playing with fire,' said Shepherd.

'Let's see how it plays out,' said the Major. 'If he's right then it could be an intel coup for us. He could ID a lot of local bad guys for us.'

Shepherd wasn't convinced but knew better than to press his luck with the Major. He walked out of the HQ with Geordie. Shepherd saw Lex Harper running around the perimeter of the compound with a large rucksack on his back. The young Para had already watched Shepherd's back while serving as his spotter on a couple of previous ops and Shepherd realised he had the chance to return the favour.

'He's keen,' said Geordie.

'He's a good lad,' said Shepherd. 'He's wasted in the Paras. I'm going to suggest he puts himself for Selection when he gets back to the UK.' He waved over at Lex and the Para sprinted over to them. He'd clearly been running for a while and he leaned forward, hands on his knees, his chest heaving and sweat dripping from his brow into the dust.

'Sure you're cut out for this line of work?' Shepherd said with a grin. 'Special Forces never sweat.'

'Is that right?' Lex said, grinning back. 'They talk a lot of shite, though. So what's up?'

'Todd's looking for volunteers for a job,' Shepherd said. 'Make sure you're not one of them.'

Lex gave him a curious look. 'Any particular reason why?'

Shepherd shrugged. 'We've just got a bad feeling about it.'

Geordie hawked and spat. 'He's wanting the Paras to take his new Taliban boyfriend up country,' he growled. 'And on a good

27

day, they'll be bringing back another twenty SEPs, Pied Piper style.'

'And on a bad day?'

'On a bad day it could all turn to shit,' said Shepherd. 'So no volunteering, okay?'

Lex nodded. 'Okay, got it,' he said. 'Thanks. I owe you one.'

'What's in the rucksack?' asked Geordie.

Lex grinned and shrugged the rucksack off his back. It hit the ground with a thud. 'Just some gear. Dirty laundry, mainly.'

Geordie laughed. 'Bricks, mate. That's what you need. Bricks wrapped in newspapers.'

'That's a wind-up, right?' said Lex, looking at Shepherd.

Shepherd grinned. 'Nah, it's Gospel,' he said. 'Geordie got me into it years ago. You need something heavy, really heavy. That's what builds muscle and stamina. The harder you train, the easier it is when it's for real.' He pointed down at Lex's dust-covered Nikes. 'And lose the training shoes. You want to run in boots.'

'Bloody hell, you want to make it difficult for yourself, don't you?' said the Para.

'That's the point,' said Shepherd. 'Train hard, fight easy. The times in your life when you'll need to run like the devil are probably the times when you're not wearing your Nikes.'

Lex nodded. 'Thanks,' he said.

'And remember – no volunteering.'

* * *

An hour later, Shepherd and Geordie saw a Landrover pull out of the compound. Two Paras sat in front, with another one alongside Ahmad Khan in the back. There was a Gimpy - a General Purpose Machine Gun - mounted on the bonnet and the three Paras all carried M16s. The Afghan had his AK74 cradled in his lap.

'I see Captain Dickhead isn't with them,' said Geordie.

28

'No back up, either,' said Shepherd. 'I tell you, this is going to go tits-up.'

'You're preaching to the converted, mate.'

Jock walked over, carrying two green ammo boxes. Shepherd gestured at the disappearing Landrover. 'No back-up? What's the story?'

'Todd reckons the RV with the Taliban fighters is in an area that had been pacified and was largely peaceful, at least by day. Says one vehicle is all they need.'

'Bollocks,' said Jimbo. 'There are Taliban insurgents everywhere, staging hit and run raids, extorting money and supplies, or assassinating village elders suspected of collaborating with the British and Americans. Where does he come up with "pacified?" The man's a bloody idiot and he's going to get people killed.'

'Are you volunteering to go with them?" asked Jock.

'It's too late anyway,' said Shepherd. The Landrover had just disappeared around a bend in the road.

* * *

According to Jock, it should have taken the Landrover just over ninety minutes to reach the RV. Assuming it would take half an hour to muster the Taliban fighters, and a maximum of two hours to get them back to the compound, they should have returned by two o'clock in the afternoon at the latest.

At one o'clock Shepherd wandered over to the entrance of the compound. Half an hour later he was joined by Lex. 'No sign?' asked the Para.

'We don't know what transport the Taliban guys have,' said Shepherd.

'I don't suppose they'll be walking.'

'Anything on comms?' asked Shepherd.

'They said they were approaching the RV but nothing since,' said Lex. 'That's not good, is it?'

'No, mate. Not good at all.'

The two men paced up and down under the hot Afghan sun.

'You married, Spider?' asked the Para.

'Yeah, why do you ask?'

'One of the guys was saying you had a wife and kid. But you don't wear a ring.'

'Never been a big fan of jewellery,' said Shepherd. 'But yeah, I've been married for going on five years. And my boy's four. You?'

'Nah, had a girlfriend but that went south when I signed up.'

'Yeah, it's not easy being involved with a soldier. My wife's forever nagging me to hand in my papers.'

'Serious?'

'Dead serious. She reckons that it's too dangerous.'

'Bless her,' said Lex, and the two men laughed.

'She's got a point, though,' said Shepherd. 'It was different when I was based in Hereford and could get home most nights. I could help around the house and be a dad for Liam. I've missed two of his last birthdays and it's looking like we're going to be here over Christmas.'

'That goes with the job, though,' said Lex.

'She's a Hereford girl so she understands that. But when she married me she had no way of knowing how crazy the world was going to get.'

'And will you do it? Hand in your papers?'

'And do what?' said Shepherd. 'I'm a soldier, that's what I do. I can't go back and work in an office.' He shrugged. 'I've told her to wait and see how this works out. I can see us being here for ever.'

'I'm not sure about this,' said Lex. 'It's a right mess here. The Russians couldn't control this country and I don't see that we'll do a better job. And I don't know about you but I'm getting a bad feeling about Iraq.'

'In what way?'

'I think the Yanks want to invade. And if they go in Blair will have us in on Uncle Sam's coat tails.'

Shepherd smiled ruefully. 'I hope Sue doesn't start thinking that way,' he said.

'I'm serious, Spider. Since 9-11 the Yanks have been on a mission.'

Shepherd nodded. 'You might be right.'

Geordie jogged over, his round face bathed in sweat. 'Boss wants you in the briefing room,' he said.

'Problem?'

'He reckons they've been gone long enough. And there's been nothing on comms for a while.'

'Can I come?' asked Lex.

'Don't see why not,' said Shepherd. The three men hurried over to the briefing room where the Major was huddled over a map with Jimbo, Jock and two other SAS troopers. There was no sign of Captain Todd.

The Major looked up. 'I'm getting a bad feeling about this,' he said. 'I'm asking Jock to put together a Quick Reaction Force, a small group with a big punch if it's needed.' He nodded at Jock. 'Don't take a heap of men with you though, but you'll need a Forward Air Controller and a Royal Engineer Search Team, in case of mines or booby traps. And take a couple of Laser Target Markers. I'll make sure there are fast jets with Paveways in the air and in the area the whole time that you're on the ground.'

'Okay Boss,' Jock said. 'We might be best with B-52s out of Diego Garcia. You know what the Bagram jet jockeys are like, they hate being too close to the ground because it puts them within range of the muj SAM-7s. If they're flying low and one of them is launched, they've got to go on the tail and race the missile up to 15,000 feet, hoping it'll run out of fuel before it blows their arseholes out through their nostrils. The B 52s'll just cruise out of sight, well above the SAM-7's height ceiling, and if we get an LTM on a target, they can just drop the iron bomb and let the laser detector on the Paveway's nose and the fins on its tail do the rest.'

'Okay,' the Boss said. 'And I want you to take Todd with you. He caused this fuck-up. Make sure that he sees the consequences of his pig-headedness and learns from it'. He looked at his watch. 'Let's get moving.'

The SAS troopers headed out of the briefing room. 'Spider, can I tag along?' asked Lex.

'Is that okay with you, Jock?' asked Shepherd.

'Better than okay,' growled Jock. 'In fact he can bring half a dozen or so of his mates. I'll get a one-tonner sorted.'

'Off you go, mate,' said Shepherd. 'We'll clear it with your boss. As much firepower as you can carry.'

Lex nodded and ran off.

'Right Spider, we've got work to do,' said Jock, patting him on the back.

* * *

With sunset less than three hours away, Jock led a convoy of three SAS Landrovers and a one-tonner full of Paras and Engineers out of the compound to search for the missing men, though only the most optimistic of them expected to find the three Paras alive. They were armed with Gimpies, assault rifles and grenade launchers.

Shepherd sat next to Jock and Captain Todd sat in the back. The officer didn't speak during the drive over the rough and shell-cratered road towards the mountains.

The place where Ahmad Khan had taken the Paras to RV with his Taliban fighters was a dead-end valley with steep-sided hills surrounding it. Jock called the convoy to a halt near the valley entrance, where the road narrowed to little more than a dirt track running alongside the bed of a dried up river. He ordered four of the Paras to set up a perimeter around the vehicles then gathered the SAS and the rest of the Paras around him. 'Right,'

32

he said. 'It's been the same old story in Afghan warfare since Adam was a lad: whoever controls the high ground controls the battle. So, two groups of four - Jimbo, you take one, Geordie the other - one either side of the valley, picketing the high ground. Spider, you stay with me. Each group, carry an LTM. We've no mortars, unfortunately - too heavy for this job - but we've got all the air support we need, so if there are muj heavy weapons or concentrations of fighters up there, get an LTM on them and we'll call in the cavalry. We'll give you thirty minutes to get into position and then we'll begin moving up the valley floor at 1520.'

The two groups formed and moved off, Jimbo and Geordie leading the way, Geordie's short steps contrasting with Jimbo's rangy, ground-eating stride, but both men covered the ground equally fast, moving up the sides of the valley as smoothly as if they were on an escalator.

The rest of the men waited on the valley floor with Jock and Shepherd. Shepherd walked over to the Forward Air Controller. 'Keep the jets high,' Shepherd said. 'Out of sight and sound. We don't want to spoil the surprise for any muj who might be here, now do we?'

Todd appeared at his elbow. 'The REs look jumpy,' he said.

Shepherd looked across at the engineers, huddled in a group near the back of the one-tonner. They looked painfully young, white-faced and twitchy with nerves. 'Not surprising, is it?' he said. 'They're the poor saps who have to find the devices before the Bomb Disposal guys can deal with them. Wherever they're serving, none of them last more than a couple of tours. Once they realise the risks, they leave the Army PDQ, or at least those of them who are still alive do. Worst job in the army, pretty much.'

He glanced at his watch and spoke into his throat mic. 'In position?' There was a double click in his ear-piece, followed a moment later by another as Jimbo and Geordie acknowledged.

'They're ready, Jock,' said Shepherd. Jock nodded and signalled to the others to move out and began to lead the advance along the road, his gaze never still, raking the road ahead and the ground to either side. Todd followed a couple of paces behind Shepherd. They had been moving forward slowly but steadily for some twenty minutes when they cleared a low rise and saw the Landrover some way ahead of them, nose down in a ditch at the side of the road. Two figures were visible, still in their seats, though both sprawled at odd angles. Another lay in the dirt a yard or so away. Shepherd felt a surge of anger and wanted to lash out at once at the officer who had sent them to their deaths, but there was no time for recriminations - they were all in danger until the job was done. He tried to put the cold focus of his anger on the enemy, not the man behind him.

When he saw the Landrover, Todd let out a sound that was somewhere between a gasp and a cry and began to stumble towards it. 'Freeze!' Shepherd barked. Todd stopped dead, his gaze still fixed on the Landrover. 'There may be an IED or a booby-trap,' Shepherd said. 'We wait while the REs clear the area.' He nodded to the engineers and they fanned out into a line and began inching their way forward, some sweeping mine detectors in arcs over the ground ahead of them, while others probed with thin steel prodders.
'They're not probing for mines are they?' Todd said, nervously. 'If they hit a mine with one of those rods, they'll blow themselves to pieces.'
'They're looking for command wires,' said Shepherd. 'Our AWACs and Nimrods can suppress the wireless initiation of devices but the Taliban usually prefer the old-fashioned methods.' They watched in silence as the REs continued the search, moving steadily away from them and towards the Landrover. Suddenly there was a "Pop" sound in the distance.
Shepherd recognised the sound immediately. 'Mortar!' he shouted.

'Take cover,' Todd yelled, throwing himself flat and worming towards the ditch at the side of the road. Up ahead the REs searching for command wires had also flattened themselves to the ground.

Shepherd smiled despite the seriousness of the situation. 'No rush,' he said, strolling over to the ditch and squatting down alongside Todd. 'Time of flight for a mortar is a good thirty seconds and after that all you can do is hope for the best.'

The seconds ticked by with agonising slowness. There was no way of predicting where the mortar shell would fall nor, if it landed close by, any way of avoiding its murderous shrapnel. The jagged fragments of steel, white hot from the furnace of the explosion, would blast outwards with devastating force and if it landed on top you it was game over. After half a minute of stomach churning tension, there was a loud "crump!" sound that Shepherd felt in the pit of his stomach as dirt and smoke erupted into the air. The mortar round had exploded about fifty feet away from the engineers. 'They're not after us,' Shepherd said. 'They're after the Search Team.'

A cloud of smoke and dust dispersed slowly on the breeze and the REs got to their feet, unhurt, and resumed their slow, methodical search.

Shepherd spoke into his throat mic. 'Pickets, keep your eyes peeled for that mortar crew.'

Again there was the double-click of acknowledgement from Jimbo and Geordie. Shepherd glanced up towards the ridgelines on either side, and saw a faint movement as the pickets moved further up the valley, hunting for a position from which they could spot the hidden mortar crew.

At random intervals a handful of mortar rounds dropped into the valley, bracketing the search team as they moved towards the Landrover.

'Any sign of them?' called Jock.

'They're well hidden,' said Shepherd.

'Why can't the pickets spot them?' Todd asked.

'Because the Taliban are being very cautious,' Shepherd said. 'Weapons are ten a penny but good mortar crews are precious. Takes a long time to train a crew so they make sure they're protected.'

There was another popping sound off in the distance and half a minute later another mortar round exploded. This time it was much closer to the Search Team and one of the REs, lying prone in the dirt, was picked up and flung sideways by the blast. He lay on the ground screaming in pain and fear as a Paratrooper medic ran to him. The medic crouched over him and pressed a trauma pad onto a wound on his thigh.

'This is a bloody nightmare,' said Todd.

'He's probably all right,' Shepherd said. 'Geordie always reckons that if they're making that much noise, they're going to be okay. It's the ones who make no sound at all who have serious trauma.' Shepherd didn't feel half as calm as he sounded. The mortar strikes were ranging in on the Search Team, and though that round might not have been fatal, the next one might well be.

A moment later, Geordie's voice crackled in Shepherd's earpiece. 'Spotted them - three muj with a mortar.'

'Bingo,' Shepherd said. 'Mark them with the LTD.'

'Laying LTD now.'

Once Geordie had aimed his laser at the mortar crew the bombers would be able to take it out with pinpoint accuracy.

'LTD laid,' said Geordie. An instant later, Shepherd heard the Forward Air Controller on the net to the AWACs, calling in an airstrike.

'How will we know when it's going to happen?' asked Todd.

Shepherd shrugged. 'We won't. The first news we'll get is "Bang!" You ever seen a five hundred pound bomb go off? It's quite a show. The LTD doesn't have to be anywhere near the target; as long as it's in line of sight with it, that's enough. We'll not see or hear the jet. The pilot doesn't even aim, he just drops

36

it blind and the detector in the nose cone homes in along the laser light track emitted from the LTD, and steers itself onto the target with the fins on its tail.'

'Sounds like a video game,' said Todd.

'It pretty much is,' said Shepherd. 'Except you only get the one life.'

The minutes ticked by in a silence broken only by the now muted cries of the wounded RE when suddenly there was vivid flash from the ridge to the north-east. Red-orange flame and oily black smoke boiled upwards while fragments that might have been rock, metal - or body parts - were flung out, black against the sky. A moment later the sound of the blast rolled over them like a clap of thunder, and the shock wave swept through in a storm of fine dust and debris. As Shepherd dusted himself down he heard Geordie's laconic voice in his earpiece: 'Target neutralised'.

The REs showed less signs of nerves as they resumed their work and five minutes later there was an excited shout as one of them reached down into the dirt and held up a length of a command wire. 'Got it!' he shouted. He used a pair of wire cutters to sever the wire before moving towards the Landrover with the rest of the REs. Lex and a group of Paras tracked the wire in the other direction, weapons at the ready. The wire extended to a clump of wind-stunted acacia trees that had provided cover for the bombers, but they had already fled and the Paras returned empty-handed.

The REs had followed the command wire to a device buried by the wrecked Landrover. It contained enough explosive to blow up the Landrover and anyone near it.

'It's safe!' shouted one of the Res.

Shepherd, Jock and Todd walked over to the Landrover. Jock checked the bodies for life signs one by one, even though there was no doubt that they were all stone dead.

They had all been shot at close range with a semi-automatic weapon. None of their weapons had been fired. Two of the men were still in their seats. The one who had been sitting behind the driver had a bullet hole above his left ear and a much larger exit wound on the other side of his head. The front-seat passenger had been shot in the back of the head; his blood and brains covered the windscreen. The driver had had time to jump from his seat, but had then been cut down by a burst of fire in the back before he had gone a yard. There was no sign of Ahmad Khan and no blood on the seat he had been occupying, but the floor around it was littered with ejected 5.45 cases.

The Captain stared at the cases.

'That's right, they're from an AK74,' said Shepherd.

'Khan shot them, is that what you're saying?'

'What do you think, Captain? Seriously?'

Todd put a hand up to his face, covering his eyes. 'I had no idea.'

'We warned you,' said Jock. 'You can't trust these ragheads.'

Todd's face had gone white. He began to shake and then he threw up over the offside front wheel. Jock shook his head in disgust.

Shepherd waved over at the Paras and they came over and began to load the bodies of their dead comrades into the truck.

Todd walked away from the Landrover and stood staring at the ground, cradling his carbine.

'Part of me wants to give him a piece of my mind, part of me wants to tell him that we all make mistakes,' Shepherd said to Jock.

'Yeah, but not all mistakes end up with three dead Paras,' said Jock. He cursed under his breath. 'I should've stopped them going. I knew it was a mistake. I should have told the Boss to stop them.'

'Could have, would have, should have,' said Shepherd.

'I'm just saying, this is partly my fault.'

'Don't be a prick, Jock. You told them it was a bad idea and you were overruled by a Captain and a Major.'

'Ours not to reason why, eh?'

'Something like that.' Shepherd spat at the ground. 'We do our best, it's just sometimes our best isn't good enough.' He nodded over at the Captain. 'He knows what he did was wrong and he'll never make that mistake again. What we need to do is find the murdering bastard and sort him out.'

Jock nodded. 'Amen to that.'

* * *

The body bags containing the dead Paras were heli-ed out later that day, beginning the long journey home that would end, not with a silent procession through the streets of the Para Support Group's base at St Asaph, but in near-anonymous funerals attended only by their family and close friends. In common with other Special Forces deaths, the casualties would be acknowledged but the regimental affiliations of the dead men would be concealed to preserve the secrecy of SAS operations.

Anyone who bothered to study the small print of combat deaths would have been surprised at how many men from the Royal Anglian Regiment had apparently lost their lives in Afghanistan. It had become so noticeable that in recent months the Mercian and Yorkshire Regiments had also been used as cover for the deaths of Special Forces soldiers.

Todd kept a very low profile over the next few days, but though he was censured, he was allowed to remain with the SAS Squadron, to Jock's undisguised disgust. 'If we'd pulled that kind of fuck up, we'd have been RTU'd toot sweet,' he said in his trademark Glaswegian growl. 'But as it's a Rupert, they just put it down to the learning curve and let him carry on.'

Shepherd nodded. 'I know, but look, he knows how badly he fucked up and to be honest when we were young and keen most of us caused cock-ups that could have been just as disastrous. I don't know about you, but I certainly thought I knew it all when I passed Selection.'

'You've got that right,' Jock said. 'I've never seen such a cocky bugger.'

Shepherd grinned. 'I had my moments, didn't I? Anyway, we're stuck with Todd for now, and however hard we are on him about it, I'm sure he'll be a hell of a sight harder on himself, so let's give him a break, okay?'

'You're too soft sometimes, you know that?'

'Yeah, so I've been told.'

* * *

For the next week Spider was engaged on routine surveillance, intelligence gathering and their trademark hearts and minds work, with Geordie dispensing drugs and dressings and carrying out minor operations on the local villagers. It was work that had won the SAS local allies in every campaign in which they'd fought but it was hard going in Afghanistan as Geordie ruefully remarked as they made their way back to the FOB after another long, tiring day in the field. 'Hearts and Minds is fine when we're operating on our own. But it only takes the Yanks to fire one Hellfire missile into the middle of an Afghan wedding party to fuck up six months of patient work.'

Shepherd enjoyed meeting the local Afghans and he got some satisfaction from actually being able to help. Antibiotics were in short supply and infections often went untreated. It was amazing to see the difference that a few tablets could make.

After seven days in the field, they were recalled to the main base at Bagram. As the heli landed on the sprawling base, shared with U.S. forces and awash with American personnel, vehicles and kit, they could see that the mountains of military equipment were still being added to, as forklift trucks shuttled between giant C5 transports on the concrete hard standing and the supply dumps ringing the base. It was clear that the

Americans were in Afghanistan to stay – for the foreseeable future at least.

As the heli came to a stand and the rotors wound down, Shepherd jumped down and glanced around. 'Do you know what?' he said. 'After a few weeks in that fly-blown dust-bowl we laughingly call an FOB, even Bagram is beginning to look quite civilised.'

'Don't get too excited,' Jock said. 'The Boss has set up a briefing for seventeen hundred hours today. So we may not be here for long.'

The briefing room was a windowless, air-conditioned room, set below ground in a building shielded by concrete blast walls and berms bulldozed out of the sandy Afghan soil. As Shepherd, Jock, Jimbo and Geordie and the other members of the Squadron filed into the briefing room, they found Todd already there, adjusting a laptop projector and spreading a series of maps and documents on the table. He waited until they had all seated themselves before speaking. 'Before we get the briefing under way, I have something I need to say.' He took a deep breath, then turned to face Shepherd and Jock directly. 'I owe you all an apology. I screwed up badly over Ahmad Khan. I was an idiot and three men paid the ultimate price for my stupidity. I know nothing can bring those men back, but I want to make what amends I can, and to do so I'm claiming "Droit de Seigneur". I want to be in at the kill.'

Shepherds eyebrows shot skywards and he could see several of the troopers frowning in confusion.

'Twat what?' said Jimbo, and Spider threw him a withering look.

'How do you know about that?' Shepherd said.

There was a tradition within the Regiment that the murderer of any SAS guy killed in cold blood would be hunted until he was found and killed. Any man claiming Droit de Seigneur because of his personal involvement with the original incident or

41

friendship with the dead man, had the right to be involved in any operation to kill the murderer.

The Captain saw that several of the men were confused so he struggled to explain himself. Droit de Seigneur goes back to the Middle Ages, when feudal lords claimed the right to deflower the local virgins. In the Regiment it refers to the right for revenge. One of the "old and bold" SAS guys told me about it. He said he'd claimed the right in Oman, after his best mate was killed, but it had also happened as far back as Borneo in the 1960s, when a captured SAS man was tortured and murdered by an Indonesian Army Sergeant. The Squadron offered blood money to the local highland tribes to kill the man responsible and it was paid after the tribesmen produced the head of the Indonesian sergeant as proof that he had been killed.'

Jock raised a hand. 'You're confusing me, now. This is about Ahmad Khan?'

Todd flicked his fringe away from his eyes. 'Very much so.'

'You know where he is?'

'That's the purpose of this briefing. Yes.' He looked over at the Major who was sitting at the back of the room, his arms folded across his chest. The Major nodded, letting Todd know that he should get on with it.

'Right,' said Todd, his confidence returning. 'We've received very credible intelligence that a mud brick building in the tribal areas across the Pakistan border is a money clearing house, where some of the proceeds of the Taliban's opium trafficking, protection rackets, etc, etc, are being paid out to the local fighters to keep them loyal. We believe there are around a dozen Taliban there. I've spent a lot of Intelligence funds tracking Khan, and a fair bit of my own money too. Like I said, I screwed up and I'm doing my best to put it right. Anyway, I have good humint, that's been assessed by the Boss as well as by me, that Khan is at the clearing house.'

'Right enough,' Jock said. 'Spend enough money, you can always get humint.' Jimbo murmured in agreement.

Todd took a deep breath. He was clearly uneasy about speaking in public. 'According to the reports, one of the Taliban there has a curious eye defect - one brown pupil, one milky-white one. The source got close enough to see a group of men in Afghan dress outside the building. Most were holding AK47s, but one had an AK74 slung over his shoulder. I'm ninety per cent sure that we have identified Ahmad Khan.' He shook his head. 'Correction, I'm one hundred per cent sure. It's him. And we need to take him out.' He nodded at the Major, who had his chin on his chest and seemed to be staring at his boots. 'I've asked the Boss for the chance to lead the group to do the job.' He paused again, staring unseeing at the wall at the far end of the room. 'As you all know, I have a personal debt to repay, but if you're willing to be part of the team, I'd like you men alongside me when we do the job.' He looked directly at Shepherd and Jock.

Shepherd nodded immediately. Jock flashed him a sideways look. 'Seriously?' he whispered.

'Why not?' said Shepherd.

Jimbo held up his hand. 'Count me in,' he said.

Jock sighed and slowly raised his hands. 'In for a penny,' he said.

'Just like the three musketeers,' said Jimbo.

'Make that four,' said Geordie.

'We're all in,' said Shepherd, and the Captain smiled gratefully.

The Major stood up. 'Five should be enough,' he said. 'We'll leave you to it. Considering this is over the border, the less we know the better.'

The Major left the room, followed by the rest of the SAS troopers. The Captain walked over to a table that was overflowing with maps, surveillance imagery and intelligence data. Jock, Spider, Jimbo and Geordie joined him.

'What's the plan?' Jock asked Todd.

'We take out anyone in the building and destroy any money that's there,' said the Captain. 'That alone will make the mission

43

worthwhile. But there are some very heavy hitters going in and out of that building and every one of them is a viable target. But what I want is the chance to take out Ahmad Kahn. That's the mission, but obviously you guys have the experience so I'm going to be relying on your know-how.'

As the most experienced man there, Jock took the lead but standard practice was for every man to chip in if he had any suggestions or reservations. 'Usual rules,' Jock said. 'If you've anything to say about the plan we're putting together, say it now. If it all goes tits up, and you've said nothing at the planning stage, you don't get to whine about it afterwards.' All the men nodded, including the Captain.

'Okay,' continued Jock, studying the map and frowning. 'Insertion will be by Chinook and, given the distance to the target and the time we're going to need there, it's going to be close to maximum range even with an extra fuel tank in the cargo bay. So we're going to have to strip out everything inessential from the heli and make our own kit and equipment as light as possible. It's going to be a long and not particularly comfortable flight, because the only place left for us and our kit is going to be the tailgate, so we'll either have to stand or lie on the floor. I think six is the maximum we can take which means we can take one more.'

'Who do you suggest?' asked the Captain.

'I'll grab Billy Armstrong,' said Jock. He's around somewhere.

'It's a long flight, Jock,' said Shepherd. 'To save weight we could cut back on the crew.'

Jock nodded. The Chinook would normally be crewed by four men - two pilots and two crewmen, with the second pilot acting as navigator. 'We can take three pilots and use one of them as a navigator. But Spider's right, with all the fuel and equipment we'll need, it's going to be a heavy flight.' He looked across at Captain Todd. 'You've not been on one of these super-heavy flights before, have you? Just so you know, when it's fully loaded - and on this flight it'll probably be overloaded - the

Chinook pilots achieve take off by rolling along the runway until they've built up enough momentum and sufficient lift to get airborne. It can be a bit scary if you're not expecting it.'

'What about the landing zone?' asked the Captain.

'The best type of LZ is a dome-shaped feature because then the wind will usually dissipate the sound of the heli, making it very difficult for Taliban spotters or sentries to pinpoint where it is,' said Geordie. 'We've often found that it's impossible to even detect whether a heli is there at all until you can get visual on it, and since we'll be night-flying without navigation lights, the Taliban will probably have to be sitting on the same hilltop to spot us.'

'It also gives us a further advantage,' Shepherd said, 'because with a feature that's accessible from all directions, even if we're observed landing, it's impossible for anyone to predict in what direction we're going to move away from there.'

The Captain nodded. It was clear from his expression that this was all very new to him.

They began pouring over a large-scale map of the area around the target. 'For us to be absolutely certain that the Chinook won't be detected by anyone at or near the target, the LZ needs to be a minimum of ten kilometres away,' said Jock. 'Let's say twelve clicks for safety.'

'Which might make this,' Todd said, tapping the map at a point where the contour lines indicated a roughly round-topped hill with steep, but usable slopes on all sides, 'a very plausible LZ.'

Shepherd glanced at it. 'Looks good to me,' he said. 'What about getting to the site? We're going on foot?'

Jock shook his head. 'With the extra fuel tank filling the load space, we don't have the room or the weight allowance to use quad bikes. And because it's a cross-border op, all our kit and particularly anything we're leaving behind, needs to be non-attributable. I'm thinking 50cc mopeds.'

Geordie laughed out loud. 'You're taking the piss, right?'

'I'm serious, mate,' said Jock. 'They're small, quiet and relatively light, and they're similar to the ones the Taliban use. That'll be a big plus if we get spotted by the muj. The heli will land on the Afghan side of the border and we'll cross on the bikes.'

'It's not a great distance,' Todd said. 'As you'd expect, the clearing house is very close to the border.' He rubbed his chin thoughtfully. 'It works for me.'

Jock nodded. 'Now, Comms. Because weight is an absolute premium we will not be taking any comms kit other than our Personal Locator Beacons. Once activated, the PLBs send out a pulse signal which will be picked up on a pre-determined frequency by a Nimrod or AWACs aircraft. Activating a single PLB at the selected time will indicate that everything is OK. If more than one PLB is activated at any other time, it will be an emergency signal and the Nimrod will send the Chinook back to the area. It will do a linear approach along the route we are exiting for an immediate pick up. All we have to do is hit a valley and go along it and the Chinook will find us. For short range comms to the Chinook there is a voice capability to talk the heli in to the LZ.'

Todd cleared his throat. 'Yes, Captain?' Shepherd said.

'I understand that weight is at a premium, but I'm wondering why we're leaving ourselves so light on comms equipment and yet taking half a dozen mopeds for what is only a relatively short distance. We could walk in to the target in a couple of hours.'

'True,' Jock said. 'We could, but when we detonate those charges, every muj within fifty miles is going to come running. So we need to be in like Flynn, do the job and get out again. Okay?' He waited for a nod from Todd before continuing.

'Right, I'm thinking all we need is six, four to form a defensive cordon around the building and stop our one-eyed friend, or anyone else for that matter, from escaping, and a two-man assault group. Geordie will be the team medic for emergencies.'

He looked across at the Captain. 'Spider's got explosives experience, so I suggest that he and you form the assault group. That gives you the chance to be in at the kill.'

'That's fine by me,' said Todd.

Jock looked at Shepherd. 'Sure,' said Shepherd.

'All good,' said Jock. 'Now, arms. All of us will carry AKS 74s, the ones with the folding butts, that can be slung across the chest ready for immediate use. We're using them because weight restrictions are going to be very tight and the 5.45 cal ammo the AK 74 uses is very light, so we can carry a lot of it. Each man will also carry a three foot length of a sectional ladder, for the assault on our friends' hide-out.' He glanced at Todd. 'Don't worry, we often use them. They're standard kit for Counter-Terrorist teams, short enough to carry in vehicles - or on mopeds - and obtainable from most heavy lift aircraft. In theory you can make a ladder as long as you want it, but, judging from the description of the target, we'll not need more than eighteen feet. It's a three-storey building and like all assaults we'll be doing it top down, because it's impossible to clear a building by going up the stairs. Even a kid with a catapult can be enough to stop a highly-trained team of experts.' He nodded at Shepherd. 'Explosives?'

'I'm thinking of using shaped charges of standard issue, PE4 to effect entry by blowing holes through the walls.' Shepherd paused. 'Have you done any demolitions, Captain?' Captain Todd shook his head. 'Well, the shaped charges are PE4 plastic explosives held in triangular-shaped sections of plastic material. Because the charge is shaped, it will go through any material: metal, brick, concrete, whatever, without a lot of collateral damage. Provided you protect your ears, you can stand quite near to it, even as close as one or two yards if you're feeling really lucky, although you're a lot safer if you're around a corner when it goes off. Obviously it requires an initiation set to get it to explode and we'll be using a Number 33 electric detonator - a length of cable and an initiator, either battery or exploder.'

Todd frowned. 'There may be twelve or even more Taliban fighters inside the building. Are you confident that an assault team of two will be enough? And, apart from the AK74s, what weapons we'll be using to clear the rooms inside the building of the Taliban?'

'A dustpan and brush would be handy,' Jock said, provoking a burst of laughter from the others.

'There won't be any Taliban to deal with because anyone inside that building will be dead,' explained Shepherd. 'What kills anyone inside a room when a shaped charge detonates is not the debris blown in by the explosion but the sudden increase in air pressure. It's known as "over-pressure" and it instantly destroys most of the organs in the human body.' He showed Todd a well-thumbed booklet full of columns of figures. 'Normally SAS demolitions work with a precise amount of PE4, calculated using these tables in response to the thickness and materials of the walls to be breached and the estimated size of the rooms beyond. You then fill the plastic form that holds the shaped charge with just the right amount of PE4 to breach the walls.'

'So what form will we be using for this?' Jimbo asked.

Shepherd shrugged. 'Well, we've got what are probably double-skinned mud-brick walls, and rooms of around two hundred square feet, but knowing that a rat's nest of Taliban are going to be hiding inside those walls, including the bastard who killed three of our guys, I'm not too worried about precision, so screw them, let's just go for P for Plenty and pack in enough PE4 to destroy a reinforced concrete wall, never mind a mud-brick one. Any objections?' No voices were raised in protest. Jock patted him on the back.

'Lastly, RVs,' Jock said. 'First RV here.' His finger jabbed at a point on the map. 'Emergency RV here,' he pointed to another, 'open until daybreak. The war RV is here,' he said, moving his finger to another point further from the target. 'That'll be good until midnight the following night. After that, anyone separated from the main group will have to make their own E and E. Okay, that's it. Sunset's at sixteen-fifty hours local time today. Final briefing at fifteen hundred hours, take-off at sixteen hundred.'

The briefing over, the men filed out of the room. Jock and Shepherd stayed behind until they were alone with the Captain. Todd looked at Jock. It was clear that the trooper had something on his mind.

'Permission to speak frankly,' said Jock.

'Of course,' said Todd, frowning.

Jock nodded. 'We all fuck up somewhere along the way, Captain, and it takes balls to admit it when we do. But only a total twat fucks up twice. With that proviso, we're with you all the way, but if we are going to work together on this job, there is one other thing we also need to get clear. As you may already have noticed, this isn't the green army; when we're at work, experience counts more than rank. If I or Spider or Geordie or Jimbo or any of the others tell you to do something, we don't expect to have a fucking discussion about it. If one of us tells you to fire, all we ever want to hear from you is "Bang!" Got it?'

Todd nodded. 'Understood.'

Jock smiled. 'Then we're good to go,' he said. 'Let's go get that bastard and give him the good news.'

As they left the room, Lex hurried over to Shepherd. 'What's the story?' he asked.

'What have you heard?' asked Shepherd. Jock walked away but Shepherd called him back.

'Nothing much,' said Lex. 'Just that there's something up.'

'It's Ahmad Khan. We think we know where he is.'

'And you're going after him?'

'That's the plan,' said Shepherd.

'Spider, I want to come.' He put a hand on Shepherd's shoulder. 'I need to be on this mission.'

'It's SAS only,' said Jock. 'Sorry, mate.'

'Guys, please. It could have been me in that Landrover. If you hadn't had a word, I'd have volunteered. So one of those guys died in my place.'

Shepherd nodded at Jock. 'He's got a point.'

'So he's claiming Singing Twat like the Captain?'

'Droit de Seigneur,' said Shepherd. 'Look, a bird in the hand, right? We're not even sure where Billy is. Lex is here and ready to go.'

'What the hell are you talking about?' asked Lex, totally confused.

Jock ignored him and continued to stare at Shepherd. 'If he comes with us, he's your responsibility,' he said.

'Not a problem.'

'Okay. I'll tell the Captain.'

'I can go?' asked Lex.

'Get your kit,' said Shepherd. 'No overnight gear. Grab an AK74. And lots of ammo. All you can carry.'

* * *

Just before four that afternoon, the six-man team jogged over to the concrete hard standing where a Chinook waited, its twin rotors already turning idly. The cargo area of the massive helicopter, normally big enough to house two Land Rovers, was almost entirely filled by a huge additional fuel tank. It gave the Chinook the range and the time in or near the target area to complete the mission and make the long return flight back to Bagram. Six mopeds were already lashed to the tailgate and the SAS men clambered up with Lex, each with an AK74 carried on a sling around his neck with the folding butt closed. Their pockets were jammed with spare clips for their weapon and their bergens were loaded with more ammunition.

As the Chinook's crew completed their final checks before take-off, the SAS settled themselves, sitting or lying on the tailgate among the mopeds. Lex sat down next to Shepherd. He grinned and nodded at Shepherd but there was no disguising the apprehension in his eyes. Shepherd winked at him.

The din of the rotors increased to a nerve-jangling roar and the Chinook shook and rattled as it began to move, almost invisible inside the fog of dust and dirt stirred up by the groundwash. As Jock had predicted at the briefing, the heli did not rise vertically into the air but began to rumble down the runway like a fixed wing aircraft, so heavily laden that its only means of getting airborne was to build enough forward momentum to generate the necessary lift.

With the engines screaming and the whole airframe vibrating and rattling like a boiler about to explode, the Chinook finally lumbered into the air, its dispensers punching out clouds of chaff and flares to deflect any missiles that might be launched at them. Even above the most fortified and heavily protected military base in the country, the threat of terrorist attacks was never underestimated.

The Chinook rose high into the sky as it cleared the immediate area surrounding the base, and set a course heading due west. Once safe from the prying eyes of the Taliban spies - who watched all air traffic in and out of the base and reported the heading of any troop carrying helicopters - the Chinook descended to low-level and swung round on to its true course, making for the tribal areas.

The first part of the flight was in the low sun of the remaining minutes of daylight. To the north, Shepherd could see the aquamarine ice fields and glaciers high on the slopes of the mountains of the Hindu Kush, with spindrifts of snow spilling from the ridges in the ferocious winds at those heights. He tapped Lex on the shoulder and pointed at the beautiful but forbidding snow-capped peaks as they caught the last rays of the setting sun, turning gold and then deep blood-red as it sank to the western horizon. 'Wow,' mouthed Lex. 'That's awesome.'

The Chinook flew on, so close to the ground that the wash of the rotors shook the trees. Its course twisted and turned as the pilots skirted every town and village and used every natural feature to screen their flight from view. It almost doubled the distance to the target but was the best way of ensuring that they would reach it undetected. The Chinook skimmed a ridge and flew up a narrow valley, following the course of the braided river channels, the turquoise green meltwater from the glaciers in the mountains constantly finding fresh ways through the moraines of rock and gravel washed down by the ferocious spring floods.

Night had fallen and the soldiers put on their Passive Night Goggles. The heli was in total darkness with the pilots also using PNGs to steer and navigate. Through his own goggles, Shepherd could see the starlight reflecting from the surface of the river below them, tracing its course as clearly as if it were floodlit. The wash of the rotors stirred blizzards of dead leaves from the scrub willows and the poplars along the banks, and in the yellow-tinged world view through the goggles, the leaves shone like flakes of gold, circling in eddies around the bare trunks before the river carried them away.

He glanced around him and saw that, true to form, indifferent to the beauty of the natural world over which they were passing, Jock and Geordie were cat-napping. Not for the first time, Shepherd marvelled at their ability to fall asleep anywhere, even on their way to a job that might see them killed, riding in a bucketing Chinook with the thunder of the rotors so loud it was rattling their teeth.

They had been flying for over five hours, when he heard the pilot's voice in his earpiece. 'LZ in fifteen minutes.'

Jock and Geordie were instantly as awake and watchful as the others, their weapons at the ready in case the LZ was compromised. A quarter of an hour later, the Chinook cleared a low ridge, dropped to the floor of a plateau and then rose again, following the steep slopes of the round-topped hill they had identified from the map. The heli came to a hover and landed as the groundwash stirred up a storm of dust and debris.

Jock, Geordie, Jimbo and Lex jumped down and went into positions of all-round defence while Shepherd and the Captain unloaded the mopeds. They remained crouched and watchful as the Chinook took off, rolling forward and plummeting off the hill-top, building speed to generate additional lift. It crawled into the sky, then wheeled away to fly a circuitous holding pattern twenty or thirty miles away, far enough away to avoid any risk of compromise to the operation but near enough to make a fast return when a signal on the tactical beacon called it back to the LZ to extract the team once their job was done.

The team took a few more minutes to watch and listen, allowing their hearing to become attuned to the quietness of the night after the din of the heli. They scanned the surrounding countryside for any movement or sign that might suggest they had been spotted. All was dark and quiet, and eventually Jock signalled to them to move out. He led the column of mopeds down the hill before looping around to make their way to the target.

Jock and Shepherd rode at the head of the column, with Lex, Todd and Jimbo behind them and Geordie as "Tail-end Charlie" at the rear of the line. They rode without lights, their Passive Night Goggles allowing them enough vision to avoid potholes and obstacles in the path. They passed through fields of opium poppies. Milked of their sap, the remaining seed heads had withered and dried brown and hard under the fierce Afghan sun and as the mopeds passed between them, they made a rattling sound that Shepherd could hear above the sound of the moped engine.

Jock led the way up a ridge, following the ghostly line of an animal track and passing the skeleton of a long dead goat. Stripped by vultures of its flesh, patches of skin still clung to the

53

bleached bones, mummified by the sun and the dry cold wind that was constantly blowing through the mountains.

The night was icy, the wind stinging their faces as they cleared the top of the ridge. Jock checked his GPS, signalled to the rest of the team, silenced his engine and freewheeled down the slope, towards the dark, indistinct shape of a tall building set into a fold of the hills.

They hid the mopeds in a clump of trees a hundred yards from the target and moved forward on foot, carrying the sections of ladder and the prepared charges, and leaving a faint trail of their boot-prints on the frost-covered ground. Shepherd caught a whiff of woodsmoke on the breeze as they approached from downwind, and a moment later, the tall shape of the target building loomed out of the surrounding darkness, the wall facing them glowing an eerie yellow through the goggles as it caught and reflected the moonlight filtering through the clouds.

There was a straggle of huts and outbuildings surrounding it and a pile of rubble that might once have been another house. While the others kept watch on the main building, Jimbo and Geordie made sure that all the outbuildings were deserted.

They dug in and watched the main building. In the early hours of the night, two small groups of men arrived and left again. Another hour passed and then a solitary figure, shrouded by a black cloak, emerged from the door and disappeared into the darkness. After that, there was no more traffic, and the faint glow of a lantern inside the building was extinguished well before midnight.

Eventually the area was in darkness, the cloud cover masked the starlight. They waited another full hour before assembling the ladder. Shepherd and Todd crept silently towards the building while the others set up a cordon and covered them. Even if any of the Taliban managed to escape before the charges were detonated, they would not avoid the deadly crossfire from the waiting soldiers.

54

Shepherd and the Captain placed the ladder against the wall and, after listening for any sound from within the building, Shepherd climbed up and began to place shaped charges against the wall on each floor. He allowed the cables of the initiators to trail over his shoulder as he moved up. When he'd finished, he slid back down the ladder without using the rungs, slowing his descent by using his hands and feet on the outside of the uprights as brakes. He glanced at Todd and mimed protecting his ears.

Todd slipped round the corner and Shepherd followed him, pressing his fingers into his ears to protect them from the shock wave as he triggered the charges. The blasts of the three shaped charges came so close together that they could have been a single explosion.

Within seconds of the detonation, Shepherd was on the move, rushing up the ladder with Todd hard on his heels. The two men stormed through the gaping hole that had been blown in the top floor wall. A thick fog of dust and debris still hung in the air as they swung around their AK74s. Four Taliban lay on the floor, killed as they lay sleeping, their internal organs pulverised by the devastating concussive force of the blast wave. They moved slowly through the building, clearing the rooms one at a time.

The top two floors were sleeping areas, littered with Taliban dead, but the ground floor was where the cash was stored and disbursed. As they blew in the walls, the shaped charges had created a blizzard of hundred dollar bills. The cash was all in US dollars, traded for drugs in Pakistan, extorted from businesses in the areas they controlled, or plundered from the avalanches of cash that the Americans had been pouring into the country in their attempts to buy the loyalty of warlords and tribal elders. Stacked on the floor were crates of ammunition, a few rocket-propelled grenades and a rack of AK 47s.

They turned over the last bodies, three men killed as they slept around the fire on the ground floor. Their faces were contorted in their death agony, but none of them had the distinctive milky white eye of Ahmad Khan. 'He's not here,' Shepherd said. 'We missed him. Bastard.' He looked over at the Captain. 'No point in leaving what's left of the cash and weapons and ammo for any Taliban who turn up later,' he said. 'Flip your goggles up or turn your back while I get a nice fire going for them. The flare in your goggles will blind you for ten minutes if you don't.'

He dragged a few bits of bedding, rags and broken chairs and tables together in the centre of the room, kicked the embers of the fire across the floor and then stacked boxes of the Taliban's ammunition next to the pile. He surveyed his handiwork for a moment, then scooped up a stray $100 bill and set fire to it. He dropped it onto the pile of debris and waited until it was well alight before murmuring into his throat mic, 'Coming out'.

Todd climbed out through the hole in the wall first. As Shepherd moved to follow him, he heard the whiplash crack of an assault rifle and saw Todd fall backwards. There was a second crack as the Captain dropped to the ground, gouts of blood pumping from his throat. Shepherd had seen no muzzle flash but heard answering fire from the SAS cordon and swung up his own weapon, loosing off a burst, firing blind just to keep the muj heads down before he slid down the ladder and ran over to Todd and crouched next to him.

Todd lay sprawled in the dirt, blood still spouting from his throat. The first round had struck his head, close to the left ear, gouging out a chunk of skull. The second had torn out Todd's larynx. Either wound might have been fatal, the two together guaranteed it. Shepherd cursed under his breath, took a syrette of morphine and injected him, squeezing the body of the syrette to push out the drug like toothpaste from a tube. He began fixing a trauma dressing over the wounds, even though he knew he was merely going through the motions, because

56

nothing could save the Captain now. Death was seconds away, a minute or so at the most.

Once the dressings were in place he cradled Todd's head against his chest, listening to the wet, sucking sound of the air bubbling through his shattered larynx as blood soaked his shirt.

The Captain grabbed at his arm as his body began to shudder. There were more bursts of fire off to Shepherd's left. Todd was staring at Shepherd, his eyes fearful. 'You did good, Captain,' Shepherd said. 'You did good.'

A fresh spasm shook Todd, his eyes rolled up into his head and he slumped sideways to the ground.

As Shepherd looked up, he saw a movement in the shadows by a pile of rubble at the edge of the compound. A dark shape resolved itself into a crouching figure and Shepherd saw a milky-white eye staring at him, though, seen through his goggles, it glowed an eerie yellow. Shepherd grabbed his weapon and swung it up but in the same instant he saw a double muzzle flash. The first round tugged at his sleeve, but the next smashed into his shoulder, a sledgehammer blow knocking him flat on his back, leaving the burst of fire from his own weapon arcing harmlessly into the sky.

A further burst of fire chewed the ground around him, and his face was needled by cuts from rock splinters, though they were no more than gnat bites compared with the searing pain in his shoulder. From the corner of his eye, Shepherd saw Jock swivelling to face the danger and loosing off a controlled burst of double taps, but Ahmad Khan had already ducked into cover behind the rubble.

Shepherd looked down at his shoulder. There was a spreading pool of blood on his jacket, glistening like wet tar in the flickering light of the muzzle flashes as his team kept up a barrage of suppressing fire.

Jimbo ran over, pulling a field dressing from his jacket. 'Stay down,' he shouted and slapped the dressing over the bullet wound. Shepherd took slow, deep breaths and fought to stay calm. 'Geordie, get over here !' shouted Jimbo. 'Spider's hit!'

Geordie sprinted over, bent double. He looked at Todd but could see without checking that the Captain was already dead. He hurried over to Shepherd. 'You okay?' he asked.

Shepherd shook his head. He was far from okay. He opened his mouth to speak but the words were lost as he coughed and choked and his mouth filled with blood. Helpless, he saw the dark shape of the Taliban killer move away, inching around the rubble heap and then disappearing into the darkness beyond. He tried to point at the escaping Afghan but all the strength had drained from his arms.

'I'm on it,' said Jimbo, standing up and firing a burst in the direction of the escaping Afghan.

Spider tried to sit up but Geordie's big, powerful hand pressed him flat again. 'Keep still and let me work on you,' he growled. Geordie clamped the trauma pad over the wound, compressed it and bound it as tight as he could. 'Oboe! Oboe! All stations minimize,' said Geordie into his mic, SAS-speak ordering all unnecessary traffic off the radios. Geordie looked down at Shepherd and slapped him gently across the face. 'Stay with me Spider.'

Shepherd nodded. 'I'm all right,' he said, though each word was a strain.

Geordie spoke into his mic again. 'Oboe! Oboe! We have casualties: Alpha 1, Alpha 5. One KIA, one serious trauma of the right shoulder and chest. He needs fluids fast and we've no plasma or saline because of weight limits. We have to get him out of here. Request immediate casevac. Repeat: one serious trauma of chest and shoulder, request immediate casevac.'

Geordie was leaning over Shepherd again. 'I can't give you morphine yet, Spider, we need you alert for this. We're going to have to take you out Red Indian style.'

Jock rushed over with a section of the ladder that Shepherd had used to gain access to the building. Jock and Geordie lifted

Shepherd onto the ladder and tied him to it with a nylon tac line.

Jock nodded over at the body of the Captain. 'We're taking him with us,' he said.

Geordie nodded. Todd was dead but the SAS made a point of not leaving its people behind, no matter what the circumstances.

Covered by fire from Jimbo and Lex, they ran with their makeshift stretcher to the first RV point where they'd left the mopeds. Geordie began lashing the end of the ladder to the back of one of them, leaving the other end and Shepherd's feet trailing in the dirt. Jock ran to get another section of ladder and lashed Todd to it before dragging it back to the mopeds.

Shepherd heard a voice in his earpiece. 'Speed it up. They're round us like flies on shit.' He couldn't tell if it was Jimbo or Lex.

Drawn by the noise of firing and explosions, tribesmen and Taliban fighters were pouring from their scattered huts and houses and racing over the fields towards the burning building. They fired from the hip as they ran so their bullets went wide. Jimbo and Lex fired methodically, taking out more than a dozen of the Taliban fighters with carefully-placed shots.

Geordie fired a short bust at the wheels of Shepherd and Todd's mopeds, disabling them so that the Taliban couldn't use them to give chase. Jock attached the ladder with Todd's body to the back of Geordie's moped, then checked it was secure. 'Let's get out of here!' he shouted.

Jock climbed on to the moped attached to Shepherd's makeshift stretcher. 'This is going to hurt, Spider, but we've got to get you out of here.'

Shepherd nodded, using his hand to keep the pressure on the dressing. Jock kicked the engine into life.

As Jimbo and Lex continued to give covering fire, Jock and Geordie sped away. Shepherd gritted his teeth as the improvised stretcher bumped and jolted over the rough terrain.

Jimbo and Lex fired final bursts, climbed onto their mopeds and sped after Jock and Geordie.

Behind them, they heard a barrage of explosions and saw the sky light up with tracer as the fire in the burning building reached the Taliban's ammunition store.

Every bump and jolt caused Shepherd agonising pain but he clamped his jaw to stop himself from crying out and tried to focus on the column of flame shrinking behind them as they sped towards the heli landing site. They had covered only half the distance when Shepherd heard Geordie's voice in his earpiece, 'We'll have to stop. The jolting's loosened his trauma pads, he's bleeding like a stuck pig.'

'Roger that,' said Jock, applying his brakes. 'Alpha 3 and 7 drop back and set up an Immediate Ambush. Buy us a little time.'

The bikes slewed to a halt as Jimbo and Lex peeled off and circled back before jumping off their bikes and diving into cover.

Jock stayed on his moped as Geordie hurried over to Shepherd.

Shepherd felt the fierce pressure on his chest as Geordie slapped on a fresh trauma pack and tightened the bindings with a savage jerk.

'Are you okay, mate?' asked the medic.

Shepherd nodded and grunted. He could feel blood still oozing from the wound and it hurt like hell, but he didn't feel weak and he wasn't going numb so he figured that the injury was survivable, so long as they got him back to base without delay.

A moment later the agonised bumping and jolting began again as the moped sped on towards the LZ. Behind them there was the chatter of firing as Lex and Jimbo let rip with their AK74s, cutting down three of their pursuers and sending the rest diving for cover. Moments later the SAS men were mobile again, gunning their mopeds as they sped over the dusty terrain towards the hill where the Chinook was already landing, its rotors thundering in the night air.

Lex and Jimbo took up defensive positions while Jock and Geordie manhandled Shepherd's improvised stretcher onto the tailgate. The helicopter's six-barreled M134 Minigun, operated by the co-pilot from the side window, unleashed a further torrent of fire at the Taliban pursuers as they closed on the hill.

Geordie checked Shepherd's dressing while Jock ran back for the Captain. He threw the body over his shoulder and ran back to the Chinook. Lex and Jimbo fired final bursts at the Taliban fighters and then threw themselves into the belly of the helicopter.

There was a shout of 'Go! Go! Go!' and the Chinook's still-bellowing engines wound up another octave and the airframe juddered and shuddered as the heli lumbered forward.

Shepherd felt a sudden drop in the pit of his stomach as, engines screaming, the Chinook plunged off the hilltop and dropped. The whirling rotors fought to generate lift and then the helicopter started to climb. It climbed higher, swinging away from the pursuit, the tinny rattle of a few last rounds against its armoured fuselage fading as it climbed higher and set a course for the distant base at Bagram.

Shepherd felt the stab of a morphine syrette in his arm. At once his agony began to fade into a hazy blur and he heard Geordie's voice as if it was coming to him from the bottom of a well. 'I need to get the bullet out and tie off some of these bleeders.'

Jock shouted over the roar of the engines. 'We're airborne. Geordie, do what you need to do.'

Geordie loomed over Shepherd. 'Spider, I'm going to have to take the bullet out now so I can stem the bleeding.'

'Just do it,' said Shepherd, and he gritted his teeth.

Shepherd saw the glint of steel and felt the bite as the scalpel opened the wound further and Geordie began probing for the bullet.

61

Shepherd grunted and turned to the side to see Lex looking at him, clearly concerned. Shepherd forced a smile. 'There's one good thing to come out of this,' he said.

'Yeah?' said Lex. 'What's that?'

'At least I'll be back with my family for Christmas.' He closed his eyes and grunted as Geordie dug deep for the bullet.

KYIV RULES
Alex Shaw

Kyiv, Ukraine

Vitaly Blazhevich and Ivan Nedilko, agents of the Security Service of Ukraine (SBU), sat stiffly in an unmarked Volkswagen on the side of Prospect Peremohy - 'Victory Avenue'. Cold morning air drifted in through their part open windows as dawn arrived and the city started to awaken around them. First the old women sweeping the pavements with twig brooms, then the man who searched the bins for empty beer bottles had ambled past. Now the highway behind them had started to fill with trucks and soon the city would be busy with commuters.

Living in Kyiv's Sviatoshyn district in an apartment block directly overlooking the busy avenue, wasn't glamorous but it was where their suspect had set up shop. It was barely six a.m.

and the SBU agents had been static since they'd followed their target back home four hours earlier. The SBU had reason to believe the target was running a protection racquet on the local kiosk owners and paying off the Sviatoshyn militia. It wasn't his business that was the target of the investigation, rather the trail that led back to the militia officers who were accepting the bribes.

"This is the longest I've ever sat in a parked car." Nedilko said.

Blazhevich frowned. "Didn't you have stakeouts with SOCOL?"

"We were usually on our bellies in fields. This is too comfortable."

"If you like you can get under the car."

"I think I'll pass."

Blazhevich liked his new partner, a recent recruit from Western Ukraine where he had been a member of the Elite Border Guard unit. "How's your flat?"

"Near the metro, next to a bar. Great."

"Kyiv's different to Ivano-Frankivsk."

"True, more Russian spoken here."

"And that's just the politicians!" Blazhevich liked his own joke.

"Seriously, if there's anything you need just let me know."

"There is one thing. Has your wife got a sister?"

Blazhevich smirked. "No, but her mum's available."

"Again, I think I'll pass."

"So would she."

They fell into silence again until Nedilko said, matter of fact. "Movement."

Blazhevich nodded. "Time to rock and roll."

Nedilko exited the Volkswagen Passat and walked away casually.

As Blazhevich looked on, the hulking, tracksuited figure of former boxer turned bandit Victor Krilov bounded down the five steps from the building's entrance and onto the pavement. He turned left and started to jog towards their position, heading for the expanse of forest beyond that marked the edge of the city. Taking Nedilko for a commuter, he passed him on the pavement without a second glance.

Blazhevich retrieved his phone, got out of the car and pretended to be in the middle of a heated conversation. When Krilov was within touching distance Blazhevich abruptly blocked his path.

"I'd like a word with you Victor."

"Who the hell are you?" Krilov barked as he towered over Blazhevich.

"You need to know 'what' I am not who."

"Eh?" The giant frowned.

Blazhevich flashed his ID "SBU."

Krilov shook his head and held up his long arms in a mock show of incomprehension before he forcefully shoved Blazhevich against the Passat and broke into a run. Blazhevich swore, struggled back to his feet and started after the big man. Krilov moved quickly and was pulling way. Blazhevich pumped his legs. He wasn't out of shape and wasn't short but Krilov had twenty centimetres on him, longer legs and a head start.

Thundering downhill, Krilov ran blindly across a turn-off, causing a bakery van to brake sharply and fishtail. Blazhevich negotiated the vehicle and as he did so Nedilko caught up with him. They entered the forecourt of the Soviet era petrol station that bordered the forest. As Blazhevich glanced sideways at Nedilko, he was conscious of the painted image of Misha the bear from the 1980 Moscow Olympics, still proudly present on the old brick wall. Nedilko increased his pace and left Blazhevich behind.

After starting out too quickly, Krilov was tiring. They were closing the gap. Seconds later, Nedilko launched himself at Krilov. Caught mid stride, the giant tumbled forward and threw his arms out to break his fall but momentum and the weight of

Nedilko on his back drove his face into the damp grass. Dazed but not fazed Krilov jerked his elbows back viciously, frantically. A left connected with Nedilko's chest as he rolled sideways and delivered a quick jab to Krilov's right kidney. Both men scrabbled to their feet. Krilov grunting, fists up and ready.

"Good morning." Nedilko said, rotating his shoulder loose.

"Come on, little man!" Krilov lunged, his right fist exploding towards Nedilko's face. Without a word the smaller SBU agent stepped around the attack and delivered a high knee to the boxer's exposed groin. Krilov snorted, folded forward and fell to his knees.

"Enough!" Blazhevich panted as he arrived. "Why did you run Victor?"

"I didn't know who you were." Krilov replied red faced.

"You can't read?" Nedilko asked.

Krilov glared up at them. "You've got nothing on me?"

"Assaulting two SBU agents is a start."

"What do you want?" Krilov hissed as he attempted to stand.

"It's not very good for your business to be seen out here with us, is it?" Blazhevich stated.

The large man grinned through his pain. "I don't need to talk to you. I have a Krisha! Ask any of the local militia!"

"That rhymed." Nedilko stated.

"Eh?"

"That is what this is all about, Victor. Your 'insurance'." Blazhevich paused for a moment to watch the wave of realisation roll across Krilov's face. "Let's go and have a little chat. How about your place?"

"What? No. I've got a girl there."

"I know we saw here go in with you." Nedilko said.

Krilov's expression changed into a dirty grin. "What, you've been sitting outside all night playing with each other and imagining what she's been doing to me?"

66

"Actually I was thinking about you." Nedilko said tugging the man's arms.

"What? Ergh!"

"Back to the car."

With a strength that surprised Krilov, Nedilko wrestled the giant's arms behind his back and cuffed him. Blazhevich led the trio to the car. Krilov walked bent forward to both hide his face and alleviate the ache in his groin. Two silent minutes later Blazhevich opened the rear door.

"Get in."

Krilov glared again, at Blazhevich but said nothing as he bent at the waist and squeezed into the back of the Volkswagen. Nedilko pushed in next to him. Blazhevich got into the driver's seat, started the car and they pulled away into the early morning Kyiv traffic.

"You've really got nothing on me." Krilov stated for a second time.

Blazhevich kept his eyes on the road but spoke to his detainee. "Don't you worry about what we have, worry about what's going to happen if you don't cooperate."

Krilov shook his head. "What? Am I supposed to be scared of a pair of blue-boys? I make a call and it's you two queers that get scared."

"Ivan, please hit our guest."

Before Krilov could react Nedilko backhanded him in the mouth.

"You fuck!"

"Yes I do," Nedilko said. "Lots, and I don't pay for mine."

"Now Victor," Blazhevich admonished. "Let's all be nice and friendly."

"I'll report you! I want to see a lawyer."

"I can do better than that, what about a judge? We'll go now and wake up judge Ostryzniuk."

Krilov sighed. "What do you want? A cut? Is that it?"

"Who's running your little enterprise, Victor?"

67

"Me of course. What? You think I can't take care of my own business interests?"

"Yes." Nedilko replied.

Krilov looked around. "Where are we going?"

"Sviatoshyn district militia headquarters, I hear that they have a great anti-corruption squad."

"They'll kill me!"

"We'll kill you twice." Nedilko said.

"OK! Ok. The name you want is Pastushak, Ok? Leonid Pastushak."

Blazhevich pulled the car over to the side of the road. With his eyes on the immense form of Krilov via the rear-view mirror he asked. "Leonid Pastushak, the Lieutenant Colonel of the Militia?"

"That's what I said."

"Shall I hit him again?"

"No Ivan, not yet." Blazhevich turned in his seat. "Victor. Stop playing games. Give me the name of your contact. The real name."

"I just did." Krilov jutted his chin forward proudly. "I deal with Lieutenant Colonel Pastushak, we are partners!"

Blazhevich nodded and got out of the car. He opened the passenger door and hauled Krilov up by his tracksuit collar. Nedilko alighted on the other side. Blazhevich pushed Krilov towards the curb. "Un-cuff him."

Nedilko frowned but followed his partner's instruction.

"So that's it?" Krilov asked as he rubbed his wrists.

"Yes."

"How am I going to get home?"

Blazhevich pointed at the giant's sports shoes. "Try running."

Krilov stared at both men for a long moment before turning, taking several steps and then breaking into a run. Both SBU agents got back into the Passat. Nedilko waited until they were underway again before he spoke. "Can I ask why we let him go?"

"Yes."

"And?"

"Now that Victor knows he is on our radar he's going to do one of two things. Either pack-up and go home or carry on and keep quiet about the fact that he gave up Pastushak."

"But Vitaly, I don't understand why you believe him?"

Blazhevich smiled. "Victor is from Kamyanka. It's a village to the south of Donetsk."

"And?"

"And so is Lieutenant Colonel Pastushak."

SBU Headquarters, Volodymyrska Street, Kyiv

Dudka looked up from his papers, the double doors to his office opened. As the Director of the SBU's Anti-Corruption & Organised Crime Directorate the only person who ever entered Dudka's office without knocking was his boss, Yuri Zlotnik.

The Head of the SBU marched across the room and took a chair on the opposite side of Dudka's desk. "There has been another incident."

Dudka took his time to reply, as he always did to annoy his visitor. "I am aware of this fact."

"An armoured cash in transit truck was attacked on the Odessa to Mykolaiv highway. The money it was transporting was taken; the guards were beaten and left tied up."

Dudka nodded slowly and patted his papers into a neat pile. "Terrible news."

"This is the fifth such attack on an interbank vehicle in two months!" Zlotnik nostrils flared, they always did when he was annoyed. He was annoyed a lot of the time. "So what is your directorate doing to find those responsible?"

"Everything we possibly can." Dudka replied evenly to the much younger plutocrat.

"Explain."

"Do I really need bore you with all the details Yuri Ruslanovich?"

Zlotnik's right eye twitched, he opened his mouth to speak then thought better of it.

"We have several avenues of investigation," Dudka continued. "The cash in transit vehicles that have been targeted belonged to three different banks so we do not think that it is a personal matter. Perhaps it is a business dispute or just bandits lining their pockets?"

"Look, Gennady Stepanovich, we have to stop these raids. The President has taken a personal interest in this matter."

"Really?" Dudka raised his eyebrows in mock interest.

"Yes, really. Have you forgotten that the conference with the Vice-President of Interpol is scheduled for next week? The President is well aware that all arms of Ukrainian law enforcement have been working up to this moment for over a year. We must be seen as ready to fully cooperate with our western and international colleagues. I thought you for one would understand this Gennady Stepanovich? Ukraine must be seen as a bandit free zone, but what do we have? A new spree of organised crime! Unless we can show the President some quick results I am afraid that there will be consequences."

Dudka narrowed his eye. "I am afraid that I do not understand you, Director. Can you please elaborate?"

Zlotnik became noticeably more agitated. "Do I have to spell it out?"

Dudka smiled, pleasantly. "Please."

Zlotnik leaned forward and placed his palms on the table. If that was his attempt to look menacing, thought Dudka, he had failed. "You are a relic, the President told me so, and now with your directorate failing to prevent the spread of this crime wave you have become an embarrassment."

Dudka sat back in his chair "You don't look embarrassed."

Zlotnik's hands became fists. "Dudka! Will you listen to me? Solve this or...or else."

"I see." Dudka folded his arms.

Zlotnik pushed himself to his feet and started to pace. Dudka imagined he was trying to give the illusion that he was 'conflicted'. He willed Zlotnik to trip on the rug.

"Don't you see; I have no choice? I'm giving you this warning because I respect both you and the work you have done here. You are the longest serving Director in the entire SBU, but unless your directorate's results improve I am afraid that the President..." Zlotnik took two more steps before shaking his head. "Most people your age would be happy to retire."

"You want me to collect my pension and play chess in Shevchenko Park?"

"No. I want you to catch the bandits who are targeting the armoured trucks."

"Agreed." Dudka stated.

There was a silence as Zlotnik stared at Dudka. Dudka held his gaze and raised his eyebrows.

"Very well Gennady Stepanovich." Zlotnik said, breaking the silence.

"Very well what?"

Zlotnik's nostrils flared, not a pretty sight from where Dudka sat. "Very well I shall leave you to continue your investigation. I will expect a report by the day after tomorrow and that report must show me some real progress. Do I make myself clear?"

"Occasionally."

Zlotnik blinked. "Don't you forget whom you are speaking to Gennady Stepanovich."

"I am not senile, Yuri Ruslanovich."

Zlotnik left the room, muttering to himself.

Dudka picked up his desk phone and spoke to his secretary. "Please have Blazhevich come to see me immediately. He may as well also bring the new recruit."

Dudka leaned back in his Director's chair, his hands in his lap and fingers interlaced. It helped him think. So was Zlotnik again

71

trying to be rid of him? Was that it? Or was it really the man above him - the President of Ukraine? Dudka couldn't see the reason, or more importantly the timing of the reason. One day he would leave, he would retire and Zlotnik or whoever was in charge would then be happy. But he would go on his terms, and at a time of his own choosing. So silly-season had once again commenced. Dudka leaned forward and pulled a magazine out of a desk drawer. He flicked it open to the four page spread on the President he'd started to read the day before. The magazine 'Olympic Arena', published by the Ministry of Sports, stated that the President was 'the tenth best tennis player of his age in Ukraine despite having only taken up the game for a bet'. Maybe he should launch an investigation against the magazine Dudka mused and allowed himself a small smile. There was a knock at the door.

"Come." Dudka put both the smile and magazine away.

"Good morning Gennady Stepanovich." Blazhevich stopped in front of the desk.

"Is it?"

"Sir." Nedilko stated as he all but came to attention.

Dudka waved them both into chairs before he again interlaced his hands. There was a silence as the two SBU agents waited for him to speak. "So? What have we got?" Dudka flicked his right index finger at Blazhevich.

"Krilov confirmed that his orders come from Leonid Pastushak, the Lieutenant Colonel of the Militia."

"Yes I know who he is."

"I think we need to put tighter surveillance on Pastushak."

"Place a team on it. Who do you suggest?"

"Rizanenko, Mishkin and Nykyforuk."

"I agree. Tell them." Dudka looked at Blazhevich, then Nedilko. "Good work."

"Thank you, sir."

"Now on to something else, cash in transit vehicles or 'CIT', to use the accepted industry abbreviation."

72

HARD TARGETS

Premier Palace Hotel, Kyiv

KGB General Valeriy Ivanovich Varchenko (retired) was again in residence at the luxury penthouse of Kyiv's Premier Palace hotel. When in Kyiv it was the base he used to mix with the international business elite. Varchenko was a prominent public figure from the time of the USSR, having been awarded the title of 'Hero of the Soviet Union'.

He had also been Dudka's boss, and was one of his oldest friends. Twenty years on Varchenko was now one of the 'Nedotorkany' - 'the untouchables', a new business elite of oligarchs who played both sides of the law and as such believed themselves above it. He had been the friend of Presidents and bandits alike, if there was anyone who knew what was happening in the corridors of power it was Varchenko.

As always two of his personal protection detail stood outside the suite and an armoured Maybach 57S sat nearby in a secure garage. Varchenko took his security very seriously, this amused Dudka who lived alone, walked mostly and when forced to use a car drove himself. Varchenko sipped Italian mineral water from a crystal tumbler. Dudka bit into a complementary peach and added another stain to his tie.
"So?" Varchenko asked.
Dudka mopped his lips on a linen napkin and placed the peach stone on a silver tray. "Armoured cars."
"Like my Maybach?"
"No the type banks use to transport cash between banks – cash in transit vehicles."
Varchenko raised his eyebrows and pretended to look uninterested. "What of them, Genna?"
"I have been told to stop the bandits who are robbing them."
"Is the amount of money involved so great that a Director of the SBU need get involved?"

"According to Zlotnik, yes. According to our beloved President, absolutely."

"Ah, I see." Varchenko quaffed more imported water. "You have been told to stop them, and want to know why?"

"Apart from robbery being illegal, yes."

"Well, believe it or not I do have some information regarding the next 'heist'."

Dudka frowned. "You have been told that another truck is to be hit?"

Varchenko was proud. "In my position it is very hard not to hear things."

"So why have they not targeted your bank?"

"There are many banks in Ukraine apart from my little venture."

"So?"

Now Varchenko frowned. "So what?"

Dudka reached for another peach. "Tell me what you know."

Varchenko wagged his finger. "Not so fast." He sensed an unusual urgency in his friend's voice. "What is really happening here?"

"The President wants me out."

"Again?"

Dudka nodded "If Zlotnik is to be believed."

"Fools, the both of them."

"So the real question Valery is do you know what is going on?" Dudka ate his peach.

"Yes I do." Varchenko stood and walked to the window theatrically, his hands clasped behind his back. "There is growing pressure on the President from both the wild east and the EU."

"As ever."

Varchenko turned. "He needs to sure up his army, that includes you – the SBU."

"I am apolitical, everyone knows that."

"Ah, therein lies the rub Genna. You are not a party supporter."

"I support Ukraine." Dudka dropped the second peach stone abruptly. It made a loud clang as it landed on the tray.

"I know. We know."

"We?"

"And believe me old friend. The men from Donetsk may want to push you out, but we do not. Zlotnik wants results, so you will get them."

"I always get results Valery."

"You don't need to tell me that."

"Look, I didn't come here for a favour. I am not to be owned by anyone."

"Oh Genna, Genna." Varchenko sat again. "Where would it all end? First you, then who else would they target?"

Dudka nodded. "I thought you were being too sincere. You are after saving your own skin?"

Varchenko brushed a piece of invisible lint from his designer Italian cardigan. "My skin is perfectly safe, thank you very much. It is at times like this that men, such as us, must do what we can to keep our country from falling from the tightrope."

Dudka grunted. "Who is the acrobat holding us as he walks the wire? The President?"

Varchenko let a smile crease his face. "Could you imagine?"

"I'd rather not."

"Of course you are aware of the conference with the Vice-President of Interpol?"

"Of course. Yet another reason why the President must not wobble on the wire! These new organisations Interpol, Europol think they wrote the book on intelligence and law enforcement. This Vice-President should meet with me, he may learn a few things."

"It is I who currently wants to learn something new!"

"Ah yes Genna, as I said, I have information on the next 'heist'."

SBU Headquarters, Volodymyrska Street, Kyiv

Dudka and his desk were bathed in the afternoon sun as it reflected off of the windows across the street. Blazhevich squinted and asked. "How was General Varchenko?"

"Rich and pompous, as always."

"I see."

"But informative. Here." Dudka leant forward and handed Blazhevich a note written in Varchenko's flowery hand. "That is the next target. The address of the bank and the time and date of the interbank shipment."

"This is tomorrow. Have you informed the bank?"

"No."

"And you are not going to because?"

"You tell me, Vitaly."

"All banks are already on high alert. They have been briefed, but this bank has not been targeted before. Do we inform this specific bank of this specific threat? No. There are two reasons for this. First they may cancel 'the run' and secondly the bandits may run if they get wind that we know of their plans. Correct?"

"Correct, as always."

"Are you going to give this to Director Zlotnik?"

"Should I?" Dudka raised his eyebrows.

"Yes. It would show progress."

Dudka nodded. "No."

"Oh?"

"I do not have to justify myself and my directorate to Yuri Ruslanovich Zlotnik. I was chasing hoodlums when he was still chasing paper aeroplanes. I am going to act on this information, as I feel fit. Vitaly, you are going to brief Major Bodaretski of our ALPHA assault unit. He has a troop on standby and will meet you in the briefing room in an hour. Due to the secrecy of this mission Bodaretski will personally lead it. Ask the Major, but I suggest you assign a team to tail the truck, and a second to form a cut off group further along the route to intercept if needed."

"And when the truck is hit?"

"ALPHA will apprehend the crooks of course."

Blazhevich frowned and looked again at the note. "So if the shipment is leaving this bank in Rivne where is it heading, Kyiv?"

"Correct. It is a little over 327 km if they take the M06 highway, and they will."

"That's a lot of road to cover."

"Yes."

"Do we have any idea of where they'll make their move?"

"No. Again I suggest you consult with ALPHA on this. They are highly experienced; ask them where they would assault the truck if they were so inclined. Is everything clear?"

"Yes Gennady Stepanovich." Blazhevich studied the note again.

"Something is troubling you, Vitaly, besides the sunlight? Tell me, I won't bite."

"Why am I not to be included in the actual mission?"

"Do you know how many agents I have in my directorate? Quite a few; and you are my most trusted."

"Oh?" Blazhevich was surprised that Dudka had been so frank.

"I need you to take Nedilko and look at something else for me. Something 'covert'."

Blazhevich supressed a smile. "And that would be what Gennady Stepanovich?"

"Bread. Follow the crumbs and you will find the loaf." Dudka wrote an address down on an envelope. "Set up an OP here, tonight. Man it in four hour shifts."

Puzzled, Blazhevich took the envelope. He felt a key inside. "Ok."

"Good. That is all Vitaly."

Dudka waited for Blazhevich to leave and then looked at his watch. He nodded to himself, time for a late lunch. It was a pleasant enough day, he'd walk back downhill to his flat and eat at home. He saw no point in patronizing the canteen when he had meat in his fridge and had just that morning collected a bag of his favourite fresh bread.

Lvivska Street, Kyiv, Ukraine

Located in a leafy side street amongst apartment blocks and two schools, the bakery was originally a small former state run business which had been bought out by the management soon after Ukrainian independence.

'Khlibko' now produced bread and cakes to be sold in the grocery shops and kiosks throughout Kyiv's Sviatoshyn district, and were particularly renowned for their Ukrainsky bread and poppy seed croissants.

It was seven a.m. and the bakery should have been busy, but it was silent. From his OP in the dressmakers shop across the street Nedilko observed a dark blue Mercedes glide to a halt, and captured the process in HD. Whilst the video recorded he snapped stills of the same scene.

He saw the man known to be Lieutenant Colonel Pastushak climb out of the driver's seat, it was his personal car, and extend his hand to the older man awaiting him on the pavement. A parabolic microphone recorded the audio; Nedilko listened to this via an earpiece and continued to film.

"Thank you for meeting me, Sergey."

"Did I have a choice, Leonid Andreyevich?"

"Come now Sergey, there is always a choice in business and you have made the right one. How is the family, your wife and two daughters?"

Nedilko saw the man called 'Sergey' stiffen before he replied.

"They are very well. Thank you."

"And your grandson?"

"Very healthy."

"That is important. In life the family must come first. Do you agree?"

"Yes of course."

"Do you have my papers?"

"Inside, in my office."

"Then let us go inside. And I hope you have something to drink for me also? To toast our agreement?"

"At this hour?"

"What does time have to do with anything?" Pastushak snapped.

"I will have a look." Sergey answered wearily.

Both men climbed the steps into the building. Nedilko lost visual contact and pushed himself back from the surveillance equipment. He retrieved his phone and dialled a number. "Vitaly, Pastushak has just arrived."

At the other end Blazhevich smirked. "And are you surprised?"

"Yes I am. How did Dudka know?"

"The old man has been in the game for a very long time and has his sources. Nothing gets past him."

"So what do you want me to do?"

"Wait until Pastushak leaves then RTB."

"O.k."

"And Ivan, try not to be seen."

Nedilko ended the call, stretched and then returned to the equipment.

M03 Highway, Poltava Region, Ukraine

The armoured CIT van was a based on a Mercedes Benz Vario design and was standard for banks in the West. It had a crew of three, two in the cab and one riding in the back with the cargo. The job was a simple transfer of funds from a smaller branch to a larger one. Still in this electronic age real money had to be ferried around, even if fewer and fewer people actually used it.

It was a regular journey and as such a known route, as such insecure. But the driver had faith in his team and in his boss. They had been trained in exactly what to do should they ever be targeted. Former military, each man knew how to use a weapon and would not hesitate to use it.

Inside the cab both driver and 'shotgun' felt an odd sense of safety, cocooned as they were behind armour plated panels and glass that had been uprated to B6 'High Power Rifle' B6 Ballistic Protection. The sound of the outside world was somewhat muffled and their vision was fractionally distorted by the thickness of the glass.

This was however an illusion. Undetected from inside the cab, an armoured .50 cal round shredded the offside front 'run-flat' tire and tore through the steel wheel beneath. Travelling at what had been a steady 80 km/h, the heavy, squat truck lurched sideways and onto the grass verge where its momentum made it slalom towards the trees. As the ruined wheel gradually embedded itself in the soft muddy earth, the van pivoted the rear rising up and fell on its side lodging against several trees. There was eerie silence inside the van. Driver and shotgun hung by their belts, bruised, bloodied but alive. Neither of them could twist to open the viewing slot to check up on their colleague in the back. Just as the driver started to regain his senses there was a loud thud from behind.

In the hold and lying awkwardly on his back, the third security guard started to berate himself for not wearing his helmet during transit. He raised his head and tried to sit up just as the rear doors fell off of their hinges. A pre-sized and pre-cut explosive charge had been used to blow open the van like a heavy tin of sardines. There was a loud popping sound and as the guard's vision started to grey out he was aware of a shadow standing over him.

HARD TARGETS

SBU Headquarters, Volodymyrska Street, Kyiv

"Pastushak." Nedilko had a large smile on his face and an A4 envelope held by his side.

Blazhevich finished his mouthful of soup. "Sit."

Nedilko handed Blazhevich the envelope and got comfortable on a canteen chair. "We need to give these to Dudka."

Blazhevich glanced around the SBU canteen, it was mostly empty. He twisted and put his bowl on an empty table before opening the envelope and pulling out the contents, a series of 8 X 10 surveillance photos taken by Nedilko. "Did the technician see these?"

"Of course, aren't we meant to be transparent in the Anti-Corruption Directorate?"

Blazhevich frowned. "Really?"

"No I made the prints myself."

"Good." Blazhevich fanned the prints out on the table. They showed the Militia Lieutenant Colonel arriving, greeting his contact, heading inside and finally emerging again with papers clutched in one hand and a black loaf in the other. "He certainly likes his bread."

"I know, but I think it's the 'dough' he likes more."

"Funny. So tell me what's going on Ivan?"

Nedilko wasn't sure. "Pastushak was talking about papers and a deal. Could be anything, but I think I'm safe in saying that it's not militia business."

"Of course. He's getting something from Khlibko that's for sure."

Nedilko nodded and leant across the table. "Dough..."

Blazhevich swiftly butted the prints together. "Sit. Zlotnik."

Nedilko turned and saw the Director standing at the door of the canteen flanked by two suited men he didn't recognise. Zlotnik did a double take when he noticed Blazhevich and Nedilko, but then proceeded to walk over. The two men in suits followed him a step behind.

81

"Where is Director Dudka?" Zlotnik enquired.

"I believe it is his lunch break, Yuri Ruslanovich."

"I know that Vitaly Romanovich. What I am asking you is if you know where he is?"

"I'm sorry I do not, Director."

"Very well. When you see Dudka tell him to report to my office."

"Yes, Yuri Ruslanovich."

Zlotnik shifted his gaze to Nedilko. "You are the new recruit?"

"Yes, sir."

Zlotnik smiled at the use of 'sir'. "From the west I hear?"

"Ivano-Frankivsk."

Zlotnik smiled vanished. "I've never been." He turned and left the room followed by the suits.

"Doesn't Dudka like to eat at home?" Nedilko asked.

"Yes." Blazhevich replied. "But he also likes to not be disturbed, least of all by Zlotnik."

Zankovetskaya Street, Kyiv

The radio was old but in perfect working order, the problem was finding a radio station that played real music and not noise. But Dudka had found one and ate contentedly as an orchestra somewhere played a tune that reminded him of his youth.

His thoughts turned to his late wife. Irina had loved to dance, that was how they had met. Dudka was the young KGB officer who fell for the ballerina. His friends laughed at him, but abruptly stopped when the couple were married a month later. That had been fifty years before, when the world was different. Their daughter Katya was born and she too loved to dance.

They had all danced together in the flat on Zankovetskaya street; the flat where he now lived alone with his memories. Katya had moved to Cyprus with her daughter but Dudka preferred Kyiv, he preferred his flat. He continued to eat, the music was very relaxing, aided his digestion or it had until there was a loud rapping sound. His mobile phone vibrated against the kitchen table. The LG was on silent but nevertheless the vibration annoyed him.

Dudka frowned, ignored it and continued to eat. The tapping stopped and then almost immediately his landline started up. The shrill ringing screeched at him from across the kitchen. Dudka sighed, clicked the radio off, got to his feet and shuffled in his slippers to the phone. There was no caller ID on the twelve year old device, he didn't need it. Five people had this number, and two of those lived in Cyprus.

"Yes?" He carried the phone back to the table, making sure he didn't trip over the cord.

"Genna have you heard? One of my armoured trucks has been attacked!" Varchenko sounded furious.

"Really, Valery, are you sure?" Dudka bit into his Ukrainsky bread.

"Yes I am sure; I have just gotten off of the phone with my head of security. It is outrageous."

"I quite agree." Dudka slurped his black tea and then again bit into his bread.

"Are you eating?"

"What else would I be doing at lunchtime?"

"I don't know how you can sit there and eat whilst my trucks are targeted!"

"Simple. They are not my trucks."

"Genna!" Varchenko barked. "Will you please take this seriously? Don't you see what is happening? All of this has been a rouse to get at me. They have been carefully coming at me from the side, the other attacks were diversionary and the tip off was a sham."

"Perhaps."

Varchenko paused and took a breath. "Genna if you know who is responsible now would be a good time to tell me."

"Yes." Dudka placed the last piece of bread in his mouth and washed it down with the last of his tea. "So?" Varchenko questioned.

"I do know who is responsible. And I know exactly what I am going to do to stop him. But first I must get back to work and face the music. Valery, do not worry about your pocket change, I am on the case. I have a plan. I'll call you when I need your help."

"Need my help Genna? It is I who has been robbed!"

"Exactly." Dudka ended the call.

SBU Headquarters, Volodymyrska Street, Kyiv

Zlotnik was far from happy when Dudka arrived at his office. "I was expecting you earlier."

"Yes. Blazhevich gave me your message."

"Where have you been?"

"Late luncheon."

"Whilst you have been 'out to lunch', another interbank money transport has been attacked!"

"I know. We live in dangerous times. The owner of the bank telephoned me."

"The owner?"

"It is a very serious matter. General Varchenko's bank can now be added to the list of banks targeted."

"Varchenko? Dudka you have been misinformed. I am talking about the attempted robbery of the Imexbank shipment from Rivne to Kyiv."

"Attempted?" Dudka paused for a beat; he'd heard nothing from Major Bodaretski. "The criminals are in custody?"

"The duty of the crew was to protect the truck and its contents, and not apprehend their assailants."

"I see." Something did not add up. He was not going to mention the ALPHA mission. Zlotnik would find out soon enough, but Dudka needed time to investigate first.

"Now, tell me about General Varchenko." Zlotnik ordered.

"He informed me by telephone that one of his trucks had just been attacked."

"What!" Zlotnik reddened before Dudka's eyes. Dudka worried about the man's blood pressure.

"An interbank transport truck moving funds from one of his banks was attacked."

"Why was I not aware of that?" Zlotnik stabbed the air in Dudka's direction with his index finger. He was now crimson.

"I am telling you now, Yuri Ruslanovich."

Zlotnik started to shake with anger, before abruptly rising. When Zlotnik was angry he found it very hard to sit. Dudka remembered his daughter had been the same, when she was four. Zlotnik's nostrils flared. "I understood you had a team out on operations? I assumed incorrectly that you had made some progress!"

Dudka bit his tongue.

Zlotnik took a couple of steps, arrived at the wall and inspected at his antique Jungens clock. He had personally restored and installed it. It had been suggested as being therapeutic by his doctor. He traced a finger along the raised pattern on the case before turning back to face Dudka. His anger was now gone, replaced with exhaustion.

"The President will not be happy in the slightest. Tell me what I am supposed to do now Dudka? Am I to suspend you until we decide your fate?"

"There are other active operations underway, Director, and my not being there would almost certainly jeopardise them. But it is your decision." The older man did his best to look crestfallen.

"Are you asking me for another chance, is that it?"

Dudka saw a glint, a small glint of glee in Zlotnik's eye. Unfortunately he had to say yes. "Yes."

Zlotnik inclined his head and folded his arms, a sneer formed on his face. "I had anticipated this very situation which I why I have drafted in more manpower to assist you in your investigation."

"Thank you." Dudka said with disguised insincerity.

"They are both outstanding senior field agents from our Donetsk office."

"How delightful."

Zlotnik bent forward and pressed the intercom switch on his desk phone. "They may come in now."

Moments later two large men in suits joined the meeting. They stood to Dudka's left like a pair of gnarled gargoyles, in his opinion only a mother could love them.

"This is Senior Agent Poltavets and Senior Agent Kirkorov."

Dudka nodded at Kirkorov. "I've heard of you."

Zlotnik's nostrils flared. "Senior Agents Poltavets and Kirkorov are assigned to your directorate but will report directly to me."

Dudka nodded. "Is that it Yuri Ruslanovich?"

"For now, Gennady Stepanovich. I really want this to work. Do you understand?"

Dudka stood. "What is there to be misunderstood? We want the same result; we are on the same side. 'Transparency and Cooperation' - is that not the message that Interpol has given us and the Interior Ministry? And we are striving to achieve it before the conference. Thank you for my extra manpower, I am sure that with their help I can solve this nasty business."

Zlotnik sighed. "I hope you can Gennady Stepanovich. I sincerely hope you can."

Dudka bid the two men to follow him and left Zlotnik's office. They fell silently in step behind as he walked along the corridor to his corner office. Dudka's mind was whirring, two attacks in one day? Surely that would mean two groups of bandits, especially as the crime scenes were so far apart? But why had he heard nothing from ALPHA?

Dudka did not fear for his job, if he lost it he lost it, after all he would eventually retire. What concerned him more was the fate of the loyal agents in his directorate and Blazhevich in particular. This was another reason why he had ordered him away from the operation.

Dudka remained however surprised that Zlotnik had not suspended him on the spot. There had to be a reason, and a damn good one for Zlotnik to keep him on. He'd work it out, he always did, but first he had to induct his new agents. Dudka's secretary was at her desk. She smiled as he approached but her eyes constricted on seeing his entourage. Once in his office Dudka waved his two visitors into chairs.

"So, where shall we start? What are your suggestions?"

Poltavets and Kirkorov looked at each other before Poltavets spoke. "Should we not see if there is any pattern in the raids?"

Dudka nodded enthusiastically. "Good, very good. What is your first name?"

"Ruslan."

"Good Ruslan." He pointed at Kirkorov. "And you are Fillip?"

Poltavets looked down and Kirkorov remained stony faced, to him it was an old joke. He was nothing like the flamboyant Russian pop star with whom he shared a surname. "Oleg."

"Good. Ruslan and Oleg, solid Russian names." The pair bristled but Dudka carried on. "Now these banks that have been targeted, where are they based?"

Poltavets spoke again. "Two are based in Odessa, Odessa Bank and Imexbank. The other three are based in Western Ukraine."

"Hm." Said Dudka.

"What are you suggesting, Director?" Kirkorov asked.

"Just thinking aloud. There are banks all over our fine country. You would know this far better than me, coming from the Donbas region, but have any Donetsk banks received threats?"

"No." Poltavets said pointedly.

"Even though some of them are larger operations and by that token have more armoured CIT trucks on the road transporting cash and various high value items than say banks in other regions?"

"No." Kirkorov stated flatly.

"Good." Dudka stared at Kirkorov. Kirkorov stared back. Dudka ignored the hostility and asked cheerily. "Was there anything else Senior Agent Kirkorov?"

"Director Zlotnik briefed us to expect animosity from you; he told us that you had a severe, pathological disliking for Donetsk." Kirkorov replied whilst Poltavets nodded his agreement.

Dudka's eyes narrowed. "Now you listen to me, both of you, I have no specific prejudice or otherwise against Donetsk - your town and Donbas - your region. What I am against are the 'Bandits from Donetsk'. Today my directorate is combating a criminal element from the Donbas; tomorrow it may be investigating gangsters from Ternopol. Geography and party politics have no place within the SBU. You would both be wise to learn this."

There was a heavy silence in the room. Poltavets fixed his eyes on the desk and Kirkorov stared at Dudka.

"Good, well I think we are making some progress here. Now we know where not to look." Dudka leant back in his chair. "I suppose I'd better assign both of you with desks?"

"Yes Director." Poltavets replied.

Dudka nodded. "And of course you need to be up to date on the investigation."

"We are." Kirkorov folded his arms.

"Oh, but you have not read the files. You heard what Director Zlotnik said? You are to assist me with the investigation; you must therefore have a copy of the full investigation notes."

Kirkorov looked annoyed but logically could not argue. "We must."

"One moment." Dudka leaned forward and pressed the intercom button on his desk phone. "Olga Petrovna my two new agents are about to leave my office with a file. Can you kindly show them to the Zerox machine?"

"Of course, Gennady Stepanovich."

Dudka sauntered the few feet to his filing cabinet and removed a two inch thick file. It was heavy and his left hand trembled slightly as he shut the cabinet with his right. He stood in front of Poltavets and thrust the file at him. "Here we go."

Poltavets took the file and both men from the Donetsk office reluctantly stood before leaving the room.

As soon as they had left Dudka quickly scooted back around his desk, retrieved his mobile phone from his briefcase and used it to summon Major Bodaretski.

Shevchenko Park, Kyiv

The park and red-bricked University that overlooked it had been named in honour of the Ukrainian artist and poet Shevchenko and not as many Euro 2012 visitors had believed the footballer of the same name.

Varchenko and Dudka took a meandering path around the park before turning towards the chess tables. Knots of old men sat and played chess on purpose built tables amongst the falling autumn leaves whilst others looked on. The two former KGB officers were accompanied by four of Varchenko's men, two ahead and two behind. Dudka brushed a few blood red leaves from an empty bench and sat, reluctantly Varchenko joined him.

"My hotel is two minutes away, why did you insist on meeting me here?"

"So we could watch our cotemporaries play chess, Valery."

"What are you trying to say Genna?"

"That we are the lucky ones, the very lucky ones."

"Luck has nothing to do with it. It is hard work and vision that has put us where we are today."

"Is that what you get when you drink your Napoleon Brandy, visions?"

"Genna don't get flippant."

"This armoured truck of yours. What was it transporting?"

"I don't actually know."

"Really?"

"Yes really, Genna. I am a bank owner, not a bank manager. Do you expect me to know what each and every employee is doing? What each and every transport shipment consists of?"

"No." Dudka picked up a leaf and studied it for a moment. "They used a different modus operandi for the attack on your truck, more clinical, more deadly. Did you know the name of the man that was shot?"

"No, but I learnt it. He has a wife; they will be financially taken care of until he makes a recovery."

"Hm. I am just wondering why they changed the manner in which they attacked, if indeed it was the same robbers."

"Do you have any reason to believe that this was carried out by someone else?"

"They employed a sniper this time."

"And how many hundreds of thousands do we have of those in Ukraine?" Varchenko abruptly grew pale. "You think I may be personally targeted by a sniper?"

"Not at all, don't jump to conclusions. If they wanted you dead they would not have bothered with your truck."

"So what do they want?"

"Money?" Dudka now doubted this, there had to be a bigger reason but he was not about to share his ideas.

"Genna, I am being targeted and I don't like it."

"It is not the first time someone has attacked your bank."

"Thank you for reminding me." Varchenko looked around, still perturbed. "Why are we here? Are we hiding in plain sight, is that it?"

"Camouflage." Dudka noticed several of the assembled men had recognised Varchenko. He also noticed that Varchenko was now sitting up straighter as a direct result. "Where did you get your information from regarding the Imexbank robbery?

"The robbery that didn't happen?"

"It did."

"What?"

"According to the crew of the Imexbank truck, they were attacked but managed to escape due to their superior training and evasive driving skills."

"Two attacks in one day?"

"No."

"But you just said…"

"Valery, I know what I said. But there is a problem. Your truck was attacked…"

"Yes it was!"

Dudka continued. "We know that your vehicle was attacked, and we have been told by the crew of the Imexbank truck that they were attacked."

"Semantics."

"No. I had an ALPHA troop shadowing the Imexbank truck. Some behind, some ahead and they swear, on oath that the vehicle was not attacked or even challenged."

"Did the men inside the armoured truck know of ALPHA's presence?"

"Of course not."

Varchenko thought for a second. "They invented the robbery?"

"Yes."

"But why?"

Dudka tapped his nose.

"What is that supposed to mean Genna?"

"All in good time." Dudka went back to his earlier question. "Who tipped you off about the Imexbank robbery?"

Varchenko sighed and turned towards his old colleague and friend. "Someone who should have checked his facts."

"Has this person given you information before?"

"On certain business matters."

"And his information has been correct?"

"Always."

"How did he come to offer you this tip-off?"

"He approached me."

"Interesting."

"What do you mean?"

"Did you solicit his services?"

"I have never solicited his services. He is a business associate."

"Valery, stop being pompous, I understand that you are important. What was the context? Had you discussed security matters or the recent robberies?"

"I may have mentioned it in passing, over dinner."

Dudka looked up as he noticed two elderly men were approaching them. Varchenko's men advanced inwards from their lose perimeter. Varchenko stood and gave his security detail a visual command to stay where they were.

"General Varchenko." The first man said. "It would be an honour to shake your hand. I served but alas we never met."

"Where were you stationed?"

"Berlin station General."

Varchenko shook the old man's hand with the practiced grace of a public figure. "It is I who am honoured. And you?"

The second man cleared his throat. "At sea. The Far East."

Varchenko repeated his politician's handshake.

"Those were the good times." The first man said.

"I agree." Varchenko said.

"No bandits, real leaders." The second old man added.

Dudka smiled. "I agree."

"You do not like our President?" Varchenko asked the pensioner.

"I wish he was firmer."

"Oh?" Varchenko was surprised.

"Yes," the old man carried on. "He should just sign a Union agreement with Russian and Belarus and have done with it. We would be strong again."

"A post-Soviet Soviet Union?"

"Yes."

After they had all shaken hands again, Varchenko made his apologies and they walked away. The pair left the old men and their games of chess.

"You see, not everyone thinks like you Genna." Varchenko commented. "Most of our contemporaries want the Union back."

"True. They forget that at a time when everyone was equal, some were more equal than others. But I understand their position. Pensions would be higher and paid on time if we were still under the red star, and there would be less banditry."

"That much is true Genna."

"But we would not be independent." Dudka stopped walking. "Who was the source of your information?"

"A respected businessman from Kharkiv."

"Called?"

"Tatsenko."

"Andrey Tatsenko?"

"No, Victor Tatsenko. A cousin, I believe. Why have you heard of him?"

"Who has not, he is quite successful. And he gave you this piece of information?"

"That is what I have just said."

"So why was there no robbery this time?"

"I shall ask him!"

"Don't do that, I have an idea."

"Tell me then." They reached the edge of the park, Varchenko turned right to lead them back downhill towards the Premier Palace Hotel and comfort.

Lvivska Street, Kyiv, Ukraine

"I still don't understand what Dudka's up to." Nedilko said as he looked down the lens of the digital SLR.

"You'll get used to it." Replied Blazhevich.

"Has he told you why he wants us here again?"

"No. But if he didn't trust us he would have asked someone else, so take it as a complement."

"I'd rather be in bed, but that makes me feel better."

"Ok so Dudka said to expect some action at about seven."

Nedilko looked at his watch. "It's seven now."

"So then expect some action."

"From you?"

Blazhevich sighed. "Ivan perhaps that was how it worked in SOCOL and I am not condemning your 'practices', but I am a married man."

Nedilko chuckled and then became serious as he saw movement. "Mercedes, dark blue."

"Pastushak?"

"Confirmed as Pastushak."

As the two SBU agents looked on the main door to the bakery opened and the man Nedilko had filmed the previous day, Sergey the owner of 'Khlibko', stepped out. He was followed by Dudka.

"What's he doing here?"

"I don't know." Blazhevich replied, trying to mask his surprise.

Nedilko removed his Glock 19 from its holster. "We'd better be prepared."

"Don't you worry about Director Dudka, he can take care of himself."

Blazhevich flicked a switch on a control panel and both agents put on headsets. The audio feed sounded louder in their ears than it actually was.

"So this is your partner?" Pastushak asked as he walked towards the two elderly men.

Khlibko gestured. "This is Gennady Stepanovich."

"A pleasure to meet you." Pastushak said with a greedy smile.

"I imagine it is." Dudka said.

Pastushak frowned. "Sergey has explained the proposal to you?"

"He has."

"And have you signed the papers?"

"Yes. Here they are." Dudka reached into his jacket.

"Stop!" Pastushak took a step back and felt for his militia issue handgun.

"I am merely getting the papers." Dudka said in sing song.

"Slowly. No quick movements."

"Do you think I am capable of quick movements?"

The Militia Lieutenant Colonel laughed. "No perhaps not. I am sorry; there are so many unsavoury characters about. One can never be too careful." He pushed his side-arm back into concealment.

"That is quite all right. Here." Dudka extended his arm, papers in hand.

Pastushak's eyes tightened as he scanned the document. "What is this?"

"It is a warrant for your arrest, Lieutenant Colonel Pastushak, on charges of racketeering and corporate 'raiding'."

Pastushak scoffed. "Who are you old man?"

"I am Gennady Dudka, Director of the SBU's Anti-Corruption & Organised Crime Directorate. The two men behind you are my agents."

Pastushak twisted sideways, Blazhevich and Nedilko were approaching him tactically, weapons up.

"Place your gun on the ground! Now, Lieutenant Colonel." Blazhevich ordered.

"I'd do as he says, he's a great shot."

Pastushak dropped the papers then made a show of slowly reaching into his holster before he bent and placed the 9mm on the floor. Nedilko grabbed the militia officer's arms, drew them behind his back and plasticuffed him.

"You are making a grave mistake here. Do you think this stops with me?"

"No I don't." Dudka picked up the arrest warrant.

"I have a Krisha you SBU idiots!"

"The only 'roof' you will have for a while will be above a cell. Agent Blazhevich and agent Nedilko, take him away."

Zankovetskaya Street, Kyiv

Dudka ushered Blazhevich and Nedilko into the flat and once they had removed their shoes, directed the pair towards the kitchen. The room smelled of cabbage and boiled meat but above all fresh bread. The owner of 'Khlibko', Sergey sat at the table eating. "Good afternoon gentlemen."

Both SBU agents returned the greeting.

"Ivan, Vitaly, I'd like you to formally meet an old friend of mine, Sergey Alexandrovich Khlibko. He and his dear wife Zennia have been supplying me with the best bread in Kyiv for many years." Dudka said proudly.

"And he has been buying it." Khlibko replied with a smile.

There was an open bottle of vodka on the table with two shot glasses, Dudka collected a further pair from a cupboard and filled all four to the brim. He raised a toast. "To success!"

Khlibko drained his glass quickly, barley looking up from his food. Blazhevich and Nedilko hesitantly drank theirs.

Blazhevich deposited his empty glass on the worktop away from the table. "Gennady Stepanovich, you do know that Pastushak has been released?"

"Zlotnik did it personally." Nedilko added.

"I banked on it." Dudka smiled.

"I am sorry Director, but I am confused."

"Now young Ivan, let me explain. Sit both of you."

"Another toast first, Genna?"

"Quite right, Sergey."

When both agents were seated Dudka searched for Blazhevich's glass, found it, filled it, pointed at it then filled the other three. "You both have the afternoon off, my orders."

Khlibko lifted his glass. "To the fine agents of your directorate."

"Only the ones I have appointed."

"Of course, Genna."

Dudka picked up a piece of thickly cut Ukrainsky bread, sniffed it deeply, quickly drank, and then took a bite. "Khlib Invest Ltd..."

"Nothing to do with me." Khlibko pointed out.

Dudka continued. "Khlib Invest Ltd is a former state owned company that was appointed the exclusive grain supplier to the Agrarian Fund of Ukraine. Their first contract was worth approximately $8.5 million. However several weeks before Khlib Invest won their grain contract via closed tender, they sold a stake of the company to a private investor. The Ministry of Agriculture insists that the state owns 61% of Khlib Invest. This is a lie. A small grain trading company called Rozivka Ltd is the majority stakeholder." Dudka took more bread and gestured that his agents should do the same. "The founder of Rozivka is also the owner of a separate company which was once under investigation for selling $1 million worth of sugar to the Agrarian Fund of Ukraine at 10% above the market price."

"A sweet deal." Khlibko laughed.

"The founder of Rozivka, Andrey Tatsenko, is the son in law of the Head of the Donbas Council of Ministers and the cousin of Leonid Pastushak, the Lieutenant Colonel of the Militia."

"Have any laws been broken?" Nedilko asked.

"No, merely bent." Dudka tore a slice of bread in half and placed a piece in his mouth. He chewed before continuing. "Sergey approached me because someone had made him an offer out of the blue to purchase his business, including the bakery and distribution network."

Khlibko took over the explanation. "The man was at first professional and pleasant, but when I explained that the business would be inherited by my grandson he changed. He became impatient and insulting. He told me how the market was unstable and that we were entering difficult times. 'It would be much more prudent' he said, 'if you were to take my money whilst you can'. He then started to make thinly veiled threats."

Blazhevich nodded. "Let me guess. This man was very tall?"

"A giant." Sergey tapped his glass; Dudka shrugged and refilled all four. "This was when I decided to ask my old friend for his advice. To Gennady Stepanovich!"

Dudka drank. The others copied.

"I advised Sergey to keep the lines of communication open and then Pastushak appeared."

Blazhevich thought aloud. "So the giant – Krilov, was employed by Pastushak who was acting upon instructions from Andrey Tatsenko?"

"Follow the crumbs and you will find the loaf."

There was a silence as the two agents digested the information and the two old friends digested their bread.

"Why?" Nedilko asked.

"Why what?"

Nedilko stiffened. "Why Gennady Stepanovich?"

Dudka waved his hand as though batting away a fly. "That is not what I meant. I meant 'why what'. What are you questioning?"

"Why would Andrey Tatsenko be interested in Khlibko?"

"We make very tasty products."

"Ssh. Ivan it now looks as though our friends from Donetsk, and beyond, want to muscle in on all aspects of production, starting with the grain and ending with selling the bread to the end customers. A closed loop is the most lucrative business model."

Khlibko leaned forward conspiratorially. "I heard rumours, from business associates that Kyiv was soon to get a new enormous bakery and five hundred new smaller baking shops!"

"On Inter Channel news what do we see only two weeks ago?" Dudka asked. "Our President filmed eating Borodinsky bread at a colossal, new state of the art bakery in Kharkiv and talking about how great a thing it is that such a company will soon be expanding nationwide! The company that controls that bakery, who received a blatant presidential endorsement is again owned by Andrey Tatsenko."

There was a moment of silence, Nedilko spoke first. "I never knew that bread was such big business?"

"It is, believe me it is." Replied Khlibko.

"Andrey Tatsenko is looking to get rid of the local competition. One such competitor is my dear old friend Sergey Khlibko." Dudka lifted the vodka bottle, noticed that it was empty, frowned and placed it on the floor. "Director Zlotnik released Pastushak as damage limitation. Other than blood, we have no proven link between Pastushak and Andrey Tatsenko but if we question Pastushak who knows what he may say in order to save his own skin."

"He was adamant he had a Krisha." Nedilko said.

"He does have a roof above him, and a very powerful one." Dudka saw Blazhevich about to speak and held up his hand. "No Vitaly, very occasionally some things are better left unsaid so we are not obliged to act upon them. Thanks to your hard work we have fired a warning shot, if the bandits are mindful of the status quo they will retreat."

SBU Headquarters, Volodymyrska Street, Kyiv

Blazhevich closed the boot of his car. He heard footsteps behind him and turned as Senior Agent Kirkorov was about to tap his shoulder. The other new agent Poltavets stood by his side.

"Where is Dudka?" Kirkorov asked

"Director Dudka."

"That is what I said."

"I do not know, I am not Director Dudka's secretary. You could ask her."

"I asked his secretary," Poltavets added. "She said she did not know."

Blazhevich shrugged. "Leave him a voicemail."

"He has not given us his correct number."

"In that case I am sorry I cannot give it to you for security purposes."

Kirkorov stepped closer. "Listen to me. We work directly for Director Zlotnik. You understand?"

"I understand."

"So what is Dudka's number?"

"Ask your boss."

Kirkorov glared. "I have heard reports that you are a capable agent, but you would do well to afford Senior Agent Poltavets and I some respect. Things are not always going to be the way they are now. Some changes are going to happen, if you understand me?"

"I understand you."

Nedilko strode through the rear door of the SBU headquarters building and into the car park. "Are you coming too?"

Poltavets turned. "You are both leaving?"

"We are."

"Surveillance Op." Blazhevich stated.

"We are going to the cinema. I'll buy the pair of you an ice cream each."

Kirkorov pointed at Nedilko. "When I was as green as you I dared not speak to my betters, let alone make spurious jokes."

"I imagine you had a lot of betters?"

It took a moment for Kirkorov to understand Nedilko's insult. "You think you are very funny, eh? Village-boy."

Nedilko couldn't be bothered to point out that he actually came from a town. "Hilarious."

Kirkorov moved towards the young SBU agent. "I'd like to see just how funny you really are."

Nedilko stood relaxed with his arms at his side. "Did you hear the one about the hairdresser from Donetsk who became President?"

If they had been on a street corner somewhere and not in the official SBU car park, Blazhevich got the distinct feeling that Kirkorov would be trading fists and not words. His money however would still be on Nedilko and his Special Forces combat training.

Blazhevich tapped his watch. "Ivan, time to go."

Nedilko smiled at the two men from the East. "The offer is still open."

"What offer?" Poltavets frowned

"The ice cream." Nedilko said as he got into the passenger seat of the Passat.

Blazhevich tried not to laugh as he started the engine. They moved forward, Poltavets and Kirkorov were still staring at them as the guard on the exit opened the blast-proof gates. They turned left out of the car park, joined Volodymyrska Street and entered the flow of traffic.

Blazhevich shook his head. "Oafs. Who do they think they are throwing their weight around?"

"They have a lot of it."

"But not between the ears."

"What did they want, apart from a good slap?"

Blazhevich brought the car to a halt at the traffic lights opposite St Sofia's Cathedral.

"They were looking for Dudka."

"I see. Do you think Zlotnik knows about his plan?"

The lights changed to green and they moved off. "I don't see how he can. Dudka has kept the exact details a secret even from me. Don't worry about the clown brothers, it's a Friday afternoon, they'll make an excuse to knock-off early and get drunk."

"So what are we really doing?"

"Dudka wants us to check if a certain detention facility is ready to accept a few guests."

"Ok, now it all becomes clear. Where is this place?"

"I'll tell you when we get there."

"Is it that secret?"

"No, I can't remember the name of the street."

Odessa – Kyiv Highway, Kyiv Region, Ukraine

Dudka sat patiently in his old SBU Volga and watched the highway. They were parked fifty kilometres south of Kyiv and twenty north of the city of Bila Tserkva. The car had been motionless for an hour and the cold had seeped in.

Varchenko sat at his side, for once not complaining. The years had fallen away and both men were once again KGB officers awaiting an immediate action mission.

"Not long now," Dudka stated. "If your intelligence is correct."

"It is." Replied Varchenko.

Following Dudka's plan, Varchenko arranged a face to face meeting with his source and business associate - Victor Tatsenko.

Varchenko did not push him for the identity of his inside man, but according to Victor's informer another assault on Varchenko's business was imminent. That morning Victor received a text message confirming the details. As before Dudka had deployed the ALPHA unit, unlike the previous time he sincerely hoped that they would be able to prevent a real attack. Dudka's mobile phone chirped. "Tak?" 'Yes' he answered in Ukrainian and listened for half a minute before ending the call.

"It is happening?" His old chief asked.

"Bodaretski's team has picked up two car's tailing the van."

"How far away is the target?"

"Ten kilometres south. I shall give the command."

Varchenko sneered. "Give me a ballistic vest and a Makarov and I'll arrest them myself."

"The vests are in the boot, I can't give you a gun, now that you are a civilian."

"Maybe I brought my own." Varchenko quipped.

"I didn't hear that." Dudka said.

The pair climbed out of the Volga and went to the boot. Dudka nodded at Varchenko's men in the armour plated G Wagon that stood sentry over their position. He pulled a black kit bag out of the boot. The veteran intelligence officers removed their overcoats before shuffling into the vests now worn over autumn pullovers.

"Just like old times?" Varchenko stated.

"We did not have vests."

"You know what I mean."

"I do Valery." Dudka's phone chirped again. "Allo? Tak, tak. Ok do it."

"Time to go." Varchenko stated rather than asked.

Dudka did not reply as he was already opening the driver's door. The SBU Director engaged the ignition, a moment after the engine the heaters came to life. They waited a minute, then five.

The car was warm again before they saw Varchenko's armoured Mercedes Vario cruise by followed closely by two large BMW saloons. The BMW's were in turned tailed at a discreet distance by three VW Passats and two modified VW Transporters. Dudka put his Volga into gear and pulled onto the highway to join the convoy.

"Any minute now." Varchenko said.

"Now." Dudka said.

The plan was simple. They were going to offer the opposition an opportunity to attack, robbing them of the element of surprise and negating any sniper or pre-planned assault location.

Up ahead Dudka saw the Mercedes CIT truck slow and pull off onto the hard shoulder. The two BMWs closed and Dudka could almost hear the rapid conversation inside the cars leading to the decision to take the truck there and now.

The BMWs went into attack mode. One accelerated fast, arced swiftly and pulled in front of the stationary vehicle whilst the second BMW boxed the truck in from behind. A hundred yards back the Dudka overtook two Passats as they dropped away to block the highway. The remaining Passat overshot the target, stopping to form a cut-off ahead. The VW transporters slammed to a stop and ALPHA troops in full face masks and black nomex coveralls bomb-burst out of the side doors.

Seconds later men in balaclavas started to disgorge from the two BMWs directly into the path of the SBU's elite counter terrorist commandos. Two warning shots were fired and faced with superior firepower the assault was over. The gunmen were immediately forced to the ground by the ALPHA troops whereupon they were plasticuffed and searched.

Dudka brought the Volga to a stop, satisfied that the plan had worked thus far. They had dictated where the bandits attacked and caught them off guard.

"No sniper this time." Dudka noted as he scrambled out of the Volga.

Varchenko looked around. "Not yet."

Ahead the ALPHA commandos had the opposition face down on the wet grass as the search continued. Major Bodaretski saluted, for Varchenko's benefit, as the old-timers approached. Varchenko returned the salute, happy to receive the sign of respect. Dudka had never been bothered by such formality.

"Director Dudka, I've got something." An ALPHA commando handed him a wallet. "I took this from one of them."

"Thank you." Dudka looked inside. "A driving licence…a business card." Dudka removed the card and held it in front of his eyes whilst he attempted to focus.

"Let me see." Varchenko held out his hand.

"I was correct in my assumption, read the company name."

Varchenko's face flashed with anger. "How dare they!"

"They dared and this time they lost."

"Someone is going to pay for this." Varchenko bristled.

"Someone has already paid, that is the issue." Dudka stated.

Zankovetskaya Street, Kyiv

Zlotnik knocked on Dudka's front door with his left hand as he had a bottle of Vodka in his right.

Dudka opened the door and nodded. "You've come to confess your sins Yuri Ruslanovich?"

"No Gennady Stepanovich. We need to talk."

"You'd better come in then." Dudka pointed to a spare pair of slippers.

Suitably dressed, Zlotnik followed Dudka to the lounge. He noticed that since his last visit the Yeltsin era TV had been replaced, but the large redundant fish tank still remained as did the Soviet settee. In front of the window, at the far end of the dining room, the table was set out with four chairs. Dudka sat and pulled out another for Zlotnik.

"Here." Zlotnik handed Dudka the vodka.

Dudka nodded and removed two shot glasses from the built in drawer. He opened the bottle, filled both glasses and pushed one across the table. "What are we drinking to Yuri Ruslanovich?"

"To you, Gennady Stepanovich."

The men raised and then drained their glasses. Dudka folded his arms and looked at Zlotnik expectantly. Zlotnik nodded, closed his eyes briefly and grimaced as though he were the bearer of bad news. "You are the longest serving SBU Director, in fact the longest serving Director in the history of the SBU."

"So?" Dudka shrugged. The KGB had become the SBU and he'd been a Director in the KGB.

"What I have to say is quite delicate."

"Go ahead."

"I think we should have another drink."

"Why? Do you need it to steady your nerves?"

Anger momentarily flashed in Zlotnik's eyes before he regained control. "Gennady Stepanovich, there really is no easy way to say this, and in part this is why I asked to come to your home and discuss it with you, on a Saturday - one friend to another."

Dudka snorted. "Thank you, Yuri."

"Damn it Genna." Zlotnik took the bottle and raised it before he changed his mind. "After a long discussion between the President and I, after reviewing all the facts, the President has given me a direct order to terminate your position."

"I see."

"Do you? Do you really?"

"Yes."

"I now have no choice. If only you had listened to me."

"I did, Yuri." Dudka now took hold of the bottle and refilled the glasses. "To you, Yuri."

"Thank you." Zlotnik looked puzzled but drank nevertheless.

"You see I took your advice to heart. I carried out a complete investigation, my directorate compiled a rather full and shall we say shocking report."

"All this is good and I will be sure to pass it onto your successor."

"Who is?"

"Senior Agent Kirkorov."

"Ha ha, as I suspected one of your Donetsk stooges! He'll certainly sing your song."

Zlotnik folded his arms in an attempt to look magnanimous. "You are of course upset, which I understand."

"No I am amused." Dudka reached around and hefted his briefcase onto the table. He flicked the catches open and slapped a bundle of papers in front of Zlotnik. "My report. As his Director I think you should have a look at it before Kirkorov does."

"Very well." Zlotnik sighed and made a show of running his finger down the page. He abruptly stopped and his expression changed.

"Have you spotted a mistake? Or perhaps a Ukrainian word which you are unfamiliar with?"

The native Russian speaker from the East looked up, all trace of civility gone. "Do not mock me Dudka and do not think that this piece of defamatory fiction will ever see the light of day."

"Whatever do you mean, Zlotnik?"

Zlotnik looked back down at the report and turned the page. "You really have no idea of when to stop?"

"Not when the law is concerned." Zlotnik continued to read, Dudka addressed the top of his head, which at least was less repulsive that his nostrils. "I was not convinced by the motive of the criminal group conducting the robberies. They went to an awful lot of trouble and risk to steal what amounted to just over seven million American dollars."

"That is a great sum of money."

107

"I agree, but if they had simply attacked the destination banks and not the trucks their haul may have been tripled."

Zlotnik looked up. "And in addition the security risk would have been tripled."

Dudka shrugged. "Perhaps, but is it not harder to hit a moving target?"

"Maybe." Zlotnik continued to read.

"We are still talking about a life-changing sum but a lot less than they could have potentially taken. So that made me wonder, why? Why settle for less but with greater risk? My answer, they were ordered to by whoever was orchestrating their raids."

Zlotnik looked up again. He now appeared less angry and more concerned. He refilled both vodka glasses and knocked his back in one. "I'm listening."

Dudka mirrored Zlotnik and emptied his glass. "Five separate banks were attacked, some more than once. Now, only one of those raids failed. Three of the banks targeted use their own armoured vehicles, the other two use private security firms. Odessa Bank uses 'Hetman Security', which like the bank is owned by General Varchenko. Imexbank has a contract with a joint stock company called 'E7M'. The only raid that was unsuccessful was the attack on the Imexbank transport guarded by E7M."

"They must be better trained than the 'in-house' security teams."

Dudka smiled. "Perhaps they are, but it helps if the robbers you are repelling do not exist."

"What are you talking about Dudka?"

"We received a tip-off that an Imexbank transport was to be attacked. I had an ALPHA team covering the truck and the route. They report that no such attack took place." Dudka pointed to the papers. "Major Bodaretski's after action, or in this case 'after no action' report is included there."

Zlotnik looked back down and started flicking pages.

108

"Now," Dudka continued with his exposition. "When the Odessa Bank truck was attacked a different modus operandi was used. Why? Well the truck was newer and had a higher specification of armour, B6 ballistic protection, but this was not the reason. It was a message, a message to their clients that Hetman Security is vulnerable"

"Dudka, this is all hearsay."

"Then hear me say this, I looked at the state business register; Andrey Tatsenko is a shareholder in E7M. His cousin Victor Tatsenko is a minority shareholder in Hetman Security."

Zlotnik squeezed his eyes closed then opened them. "Dudka, are you telling me that all of this has been a family feud?"

"I am. There is a long history of rivalry between Andrey and Victor. Andrey Tatsenko has his fingers in many pies, but a year ago he placed his thumb in Victor's." Dudka folded his arms. "You may be unaware that there was another unsuccessful robbery yesterday afternoon on an Odessa Bank truck. This one was prevented by our ALPHA group. I have the robbers in custody at a secure location. Shall I let you guess who they say they work for?"

Zlotnik glowered at Dudka "What I really find unbelievable is the level of your naivety. Andrey Tatsenko is part of 'the family'. You understand me? He is part of the inner circle."

"Our President's inner circle."

"Dudka!" Zlotnik looked as though he was about to choke. "Have all these years taught you absolutely nothing?"

"Quite the contrary."

Zlotnik's neck snapped to the left, he heard a door close then footsteps and muffled voices. "Someone else is here?"

"Yes, did I forget to mention it? I believe they were on my balcony enjoying the evening air."

"They?" Zlotnik grabbed at the first few sheets of the report and screwed them up in anger. He got to his feet just as a tall, elegant, white haired figure appeared in the doorway.

"Ah, Director Zlotnik."

"General Varchenko." Zlotnik's eyes widened before he regained his composure.

"I am sure you know Mr. Bernstein, of Interpol?" Varchenko now spoke in English.

Zlotnik blanched and replied in the same. "Yes. Vice-President it is good to see you again."

The American beamed. "And it's good to see you too, Director."

"You are early for the conference?" Zlotnik now wore a wide fake smile.

"Yes, I arrived late last night so I could enjoy the weekend in Kyiv. General Varchenko was kind enough to lend me his driver."

Varchenko nudged the American. "Yuri has been praising Director Dudka on his exceptionally good work. Director Dudka has solved a major case and in doing so uncovered a far reaching trail of corruption!"

"That is indeed exceptional, Director Zlotnik."

"It was a delicate situation." Dudka now joined in, in albeit heavily accented English. His German was better. "Involving very nasty individuals."

"Has the investigation been completed?" Bernstein probed.

"I submitted my full report to Director Zlotnik for him to act upon personally."

The American nodded enthusiastically. "That is what we like to see at Interpol. Transparency and cooperation. Our bywords."

The three men looked at Zlotnik.

Zlotnik's smile was still on his face, and still fake. "Vice-President Bernstein, General, if you will excuse me, I must return to the office." Zlotnik jabbered hastily. He shook first Bernstein's and then Varchenko's hand before he swiftly exited the room.

Dudka waited a beat and followed him, clutching the report. On arriving in the hallway Zlotnik was already exchanging the slippers for his shoes.

"You have not heard the last of this." Zlotnik spat with venom.

"That is good news, I was hoping for a progress report, and I know that the President was."

"What?"

"Oh did I fail to tell you earlier? I passed my suspicions onto General Varchenko and he mentioned it to the President at a dinner party."

Zlotnik had one shoe on now and wobbled. He thrust his hand out against the wall for balance.

"You...you listen to me Dudka..."

"Yuri, it is you who has been plotting to remove me and not the President. You manipulated a situation to make it look as though I could no longer do my job. And you released Lieutenant Colonel Pastushak, without charge."

"I had no choice Dudka, he had a Krisha."

Dudka pointed skywards. "As have we all. But his was bulletproof, or so he thought."

Zlotnik straightened up and locked eyes with Dudka. He was about to speak again when there was a firm knock at the front door. Dudka brushed past Zlotnik to open it.

Blazhevich stood waiting to come in. "Director Zlotnik."

"Yes I am." Zlotnik stated bluntly as he pushed his way out of the flat. He hesitated and then turned back. "I underestimated you, Director Dudka. For that I am sincerely sorry."

Dudka nodded. "Donetsk may be calling, but I play by Kyiv Rules."

Zlotnik appeared deflated as he walked away, like an overstretched balloon Dudka mused. Blazhevich looked at Dudka, his Director, and awaited his orders.

"Vitaly Romanovich, please get me another bottle of vodka as I fear one will not be enough for my guests."

"Yes Gennady Stepanovich. Any particular one?"

Dudka allowed himself a wide smile. "Presidential Seal."

ABSOLUTION WITHHELD
J. H. Bográn

The thief sat inconspicuously in the second row pew when he saw his old friend Daniel Weiss, dressed in the traditional black cassock worn by Roman Catholic priests. The man of God walked towards the confessional, opened the front door of the booth and disappeared inside. What is he doing here? Alexander Beck, a.k.a. the Falcon wondered, his thoughts swept away by the sea of memories triggered by the chance sighting of a mere old school chum. As he drummed his fingers on the back of the front pew, he waited in line to take his turn in the confessional. After some time, he entered and knelt.

"Forgive me, Father, for I have sinned." He began with the prayer learned many years before.

The wooden window slid open, the priest's profile visible through the multiple small square holes of the grid.

"Tell me, my son." The voice was soft, benevolent, and still carried the unmistakable London accent.

Alexander lost his voice after the initial exchange. He had come to the church to do a job, not to practice confession of his sins, much less seek absolution. Now he felt his past catching up with him, and quite a past it was for a twenty-three-year-old man. Debating what to share, what to keep secret, he found himself barely able to mumble. It had not been by chance that he took that particular confessional, the third on the row of five positioned on the right side of the ample nave. Perhaps it was divine intervention that, while trying to pry something he had hidden beneath the booth only the night before, he had run into a man he used to know; a man who now happened to be a part of the Church. After a second's hesitation, he sighed and made up his mind.

"I am a sinner," his head down, "I steal from people."

"To steal is a grave sin, my son. Why do you do it?"

"Because I can," he stated in an even tone.

* * *

The night of his hit, Falcon sat on the edge of the single bed inside a nondescript hotel room in the heart of the United Kingdom's capitol. The television set, or telly as the locals called it, flickered every two seconds with the constant thumb clicking of the remote control.

A short double beep on his wristwatch broke his aimless channel surfing. Alex clicked off and stood up, casually dropping the remote on the bed.

He caught his reflection in the mirror: the fake moustache in its proper place although the itching was terrible, his natural jet-black hair now lightened to a dark blonde; his brown eyes hidden under blue contacts. He took a deep breath, squared his shoulders, and left the room.

Falcon covered the distance to the building, to the job. He entered its plush foyer. A solitary guard greeted him from behind the monitoring station.

"Good evening, Mr. Parker. The Christmas party is in full swing."

The real James Parker, tied-up and unconscious under heavy sedation, lay in Falcon's hotel room. The thief felt confident passing the first trial when the guard did not stop him. Still, his response was to flash a knowing smile to the guard while walking past him to the elevator doors on the right. The white cotton undershirt prevented his perspiration from soaking the black silk shirt he wore. He felt self-conscious about the rubber-soled shoes, thinking them out of place, even if they were the same color as his black linen two-piece suit.

The solitary bell announced his ride up had arrived. He stepped in and pushed the button to his destination. On the way up, he stood in the center of the cage, facing his reflection on the polished doors.

"Hi, I'm Parker, James Parker," he practiced then shook his head, "Fool! You won't be introducing yourself to anybody. They know you already."

He got off on his floor, turned left and walked all the way to the last door that stood on the center of the long well-lit heavily-carpeted corridor. The noises from the party managed to escape through the heavy wooden door, indistinct chatter and laughter mixed with Latin rhythms in the background.

"Full swing doesn't quite cover it, does it?"

He stared at the locked door. Affixed to the left wall, almost at chest level, a car reader controlled the entry. The device was similar to the ones used on commercial establishments to swipe credit cards.

Falcon withdrew James Parker's ID card from his inside jacket pocket and swiped it. A bright green light blinked on and, holding his breath, he pushed the door open. Once inside, he was surrounded by the loud music. He stood at the center of the short side of a spacious rectangle. A quartet played on a stage set up at the opposite end. He had studied the building's blueprints and knew the area, now occupied by half-drunk dancing and party-hard employees. The space usually held many secretaries' desks all crammed together.

Wouldn't it have been easier to rent a hall elsewhere instead of moving all the furniture? He shook his head in amazement, although he thanked the managers. Their idea made his job less hazardous. At least, it was easier to a certain degree since there were never any risk-free jobs.

He edged his way through the crowd and the remaining furniture, nodding and smiling at his co-workers, until he reached the base of the stage where the speakers rendered conversation impossible. Parker's office faced the left side of the stage; Falcon found it and entered.

Once inside, he moved around the wooden desk and made a cursory search through all the drawers. Nothing. He perused the walls and lifted each of the four frames. Nothing again. He returned to the chair behind the desk. He cursed his luck, showing the first sign of despair. Were he not to find the information he was hired to retrieve, this entire charade would have been worthless.

His mind raced over the possibilities as his gaze swept the room looking for nooks that might have escaped his first appraisal of the room. Every piece of furniture seemed to be mocking him, the couch by the door, the computer on the desk and the pair of visitor's chairs opposite him. Even the potted plant next to the bathroom door formed a smirk to him.

Sometimes panic gives the kind of clarity that sparks ingenious ideas. Another place to search took form at the front of his mind. He held his breath as he pulled the top drawer all the way out, his hand quickly inspecting the underside. Bingo! He retrieved the gray file folder that Parker had taped there.

Falcon browsed the contents with his penlight. Satisfied, he folded it in half, placed it in his inside jacket pocket, and headed toward the door.

115

When he was about to reach for the knob, a woman entered the room startling him. She was dressed in a cream silk jacket and matching skirt, a white silk blouse with a red ascot around the collar. Her long black wavy hair hung past her shoulders. She wasted no time putting her arms around his neck, as her caressing tongue parted his lips, probing. Almost stunned, he returned and deepened the kiss until she finally drew back. Her lips were soft, sweet but mixed with traces of alcohol.

"Oh, James! I've been waiting all evening. Why didn't you turn the light on as we agreed?" Her soft voice held no accusatory tone despite her protesting expressions.

"I..." He found himself at a loss for words.

The woman led him backwards through the dark office until he felt the couch behind his knees. She pushed him with her right index finger so he sat down. Without any haste, she removed her wedding band and pocketed it, then unbuttoned her jacket. The darkened office hid her features; still, her silhouette told the tale of a perfectly proportioned body, full breasts that seemed to defy gravity and a rounded derriere. She slipped out of her clothes with playful moves, teasing him, taunting until Falcon felt drunk with desire and ripped off his own garments.

When she drew near, in the nude, Falcon knew he was past the point of no return. He let himself be taken over by the passion of this chance encounter.

Twenty minutes later and dressed again, he heard her stirring on the couch as he grabbed the doorknob.

"I know you're not James," she said.

Falcon's muscles tensed. He turned to face her.

"What are you talking about?" he said forcing a smile.

She extended her hand reaching for her jacket on the table. Rummaging through it until she found what she was looking for. She pulled out a cigarette and lit it. She did not speak again until after she exhaled the first cloud of smoke.

"There's nothing better than a smoke after sex, don't you agree?"

Falcon tilted his head, watching her every move.

"You did a good job copying his hair style, even that annoying part in the middle. It's uncanny! Then, there is the moustache. I think it's a fake. By the way, does it itch too much?" The British accent seemed to envelop every uttered sound in velvet.

Falcon held her gaze feeling she enjoyed toying with him. His pulse ran faster than a few seconds before. His nostrils filling with the smell of her tobacco, the dimmed light partially hid her naked body. He could still taste her kisses, smell her perfume, feel her sweat on his own body.

He felt cornered, thinking of all the ways he could get out of the secured building should she raise the alarm.

"Do you want to know what gave you away?" she taunted.

Falcon grunted.

"First of all, James doesn't have those tight washboard abs," she flashed a smile, "or your vigour. No, he is rather shy in bed. But not you, my dear stranger."

"What do you want?" he said, fearing the worst.

"You already gave me what I wanted," she said laughing then turned serious and added, "The question is: do you have everything you came here for?"

"I don't know what you mean," he said.

"As a security measure, James kept only half of the data here. The rest is in his boss' office across the hall, my husband's. You must go there to get it. On the wall behind his desk hangs a woman's portrait. Look inside the vault hidden underneath."

"Why are you telling me this?"

"Consider it payment for services rendered." She crushed the butt of her cigarette in the ashtray. She rose from the couch, collected her clothes, blew him a kiss, then walked to the bathroom swaying her hips and locked herself in.

Falcon crossed the hall to the other office in the midst of noise. The band, having changed tempo, was now squeaking some rock ballads. He reached the locked door. Thinking he had nothing to lose he tried Parker's magnetic card, shocked with disbelief when the green light went on.

The office was an exact mirror image of Parker's office, the only noticeable difference being the plush executive chair behind the desk.

Falcon rushed around the desk, removed the painting to reveal a small vault. He grimaced eyeing the dial. Perhaps the task would prove complicated and time consuming, but not impossible.

He spotted a glass on top of the desk; he snatched it and placed it next to the dial, cupping the sound. He pressed his ear to the glass and turned the dial clockwise. A soft metallic click stopped him and he reversed direction straining his ear for a similar sound. A full minute and several turns later, a slightly higher click brought a smile to Falcon's face. He held his breath as he turned the handle to open the box. He half expected an alarm but nothing happened. He reached in to grab the sole content: a compact disk.

When he closed the vault door, a piercing alarm filled the office, overpowering the sounds of the band outside. Falcon fled the room knowing that the guard's security panel downstairs must be blinking like a Christmas tree. Having studied the company's security procedures, he knew the guard had already made the call to the police. His chances of escaping unscathed had diminished to a tad above zero.

* * *

"To say you do something simply because you can do it well is a fool's error, Alex."

"You remember me!"

"The moment you spoke, I knew. Are you the one the police came looking for last evening?"

"Yes, Father Daniel. Sorry about that," Falcon said.

"The parish priest had never seen so many officers enter the church at once, especially in the middle of the night. Quite a mess it was! They searched inside the living quarters in the back."

"I was trapped. The church was my only way to escape."

"Men always seek sanctuary in the House of God during desperate times." He paused. "But, why are you here today?"

"I came to retrieve what I left behind." His hand removed a loose panel on the confessional floor and grabbed the folder and compact disk.

Falcon did not know what he had stolen. He knew they were complicated formulas, but that was the extent of his knowledge. To him, getting the information was his mission, for which he received a handsome payment in advance.

"Is that all?"

"At first it was. Now I think fate put you in my path. How else do you explain this?"

Alexander went on to tell Father Daniel all the deeds of his life since they had parted ways after high school graduation. The account took over ten minutes and Father Daniel listened without interruption. Falcon felt like he had just dropped a heavy load. He was nothing even close to a puritan, but telling all his dark secrets to another man had a liberating effect.

"And now you seek forgiveness for these actions?" he asked with benevolence.

"That would mean that I never do it again, wouldn't it?"

"Of course! Don't you remember what Jesus told the woman caught committing adultery?"

"No," Falcon said.

"He said: 'Now go and sin no more.' Are you ready to sin no more?"

Falcon shook his head, unable to respond or even to hold eye contact anymore.

"Alexander, please!" he pleaded.

"I...I can't."

"Then I cannot give you absolution. Your sins are retained until you repent."

Falcon sighed. He had expected such an answer, but that didn't prevent the hurt of actually hearing it said.

"I must go. Will you give me away?"

"No. What you told me is a secret of confession and I cannot betray that trust. I can't condone it either."

"I see. Thank you. Perhaps in a few years..."

"In the line of work you do, you might not live those few years," Daniel cut in.

Falcon's face took on a sad look, a smile contradicted by the eyes which conveyed the lack of joy. He rose and walked down the aisle towards the main doors. At the threshold, he turned to face the line of confessionals. Daniel had exited the booth and stood looking at him.

"There might be something I can do in the meantime," murmured Alexander Beck, the Falcon, as he turned once again and walked out of the church.

THE PERFECT TONIC
Stephen Edger

1
A letter.

An item capable of bringing joy as often as it is to bringing distress.

The small white envelope that greeted Detective Orville Jameson looked harmless enough. It was neatly pressed and betrayed no obvious signs of scuff or damage. It was addressed to him by name, but there was no address or postage stamp, indicating it had been hand delivered to his desk. It was the first thing he saw as he entered the large room that he liked to refer to as his office, despite sharing it with a dozen other officers. The envelope was sat on a stack of manila folders and the contrast in tone, made it stand out. He couldn't help but look at it.

He had only just returned to the office, following a short supper down in the station's canteen. He had taken the requisite thirty minutes he was entitled to but had tagged on an additional ten minutes either side, to account for a nicotine fix and the fact that the lift was out of service. In all he had been gone for just short of an hour, and the envelope had certainly not been here when he had left. He sat down at his desk and surveyed the damage.

The stack of folders must have been ten deep at least, and he was coming under more pressure from the D.C.I. to clear the backlog. The truth was there were another fifteen folders, twice as thick, hidden in the bottom drawer of his desk, and these ten would have been hidden too, if he had the room. His priority should have been to open the first folder, devour the contents and to try and make some progress.

The files were a combination of burglaries, muggings and traffic violations. Not the 'sexy' work that he had imagined when he had signed up to join the force. Hollywood really didn't paint an accurate picture of the average policeman's life. He had expected a role where he would be speeding across the city in an unmarked squad car, fighting the scum that threatened to destabilise the justice system, tearing up the rule book along the way. He had pictured himself as the new Jack Regan or George Carter. He hated completing paperwork, particularly when the cases were likely to remain unsolved.

Jameson picked up the white envelope and turned it over in his hands. It was a good quality paper, not the usual thin, recycled rubbish he was used to. Definitely not a bill or a summons, he mused. He moved the edge of the envelope to his nose and sniffed, but there was no perfumed scent; not from an admirer, then. His name had not been printed, nor hand written, so whoever the sender was, they were computer literate.

He moved a stubby finger between the sealed edges and ripped the envelope open. As he squinted down at the contents, he found several pieces of A5 paper, neatly folded in half, poking out. It wasn't a card, as he had expected, but in fairness his birthday was a month away so that would have been odd anyway.

HARD TARGETS

Jameson removed the pages and opened them at the fold. He placed them in front of him on the desk, flattening them as he did. There was no name or correspondence address in the top corner, but he did see his name and today's date. He took a glance back at the manila folders, before turning to read the letter.

***

Detective Jameson,

Good afternoon. If I am correct, you are reading this letter, while sat at your desk in the Police Headquarters building on the edge of Millbrook in Southampton. If I'm not mistaken, there is a coffee-stained mug sat on the edge of your desk, still containing the remains of your last beverage. I am sure there are also half a dozen manila wallets with sheets of paper spewing from them, scattered in no particular order across the front of your desk. How do I know these things, I suppose you might be wondering? The truth is, Detective, I know a lot about you, and that is the reason I have chosen to write to you and not one of the other, more experienced, and ultimately better detectives in your team. I am aware of your poor successful-convictions rate and the fact that you have the worst track record in the whole of Hampshire for closing cases. I'm sure that's the real reason for the files on your desk, and not because you think it will make you look busier. Hopefully, you will now be satisfied that I have written to the right person and that I haven't confused you with another, useless, detective.

The reason I am contacting you is to report a murder, well, in fact, a double murder. The decision to write, instead of phoning you about it, is that I am the perpetrator of the crime. I should also warn you at this point that I believe you will not be able to bring a successful prosecution against me, which is why I am providing you with my written confession. It may be possible for you to save the victims, if you reach them in time, but you will need to read the whole letter if you are to discover their identities and whereabouts. Skipping to the final page of this letter will not help you find them any quicker, nor will scanning the letter for their names as I will mention several names during this piece.

***

Jameson counted the pages in his hands. Why did killers have to be so pretentious about their crimes, he thought to himself. Whoever had written the letter had clearly droned on and on about their motivation. Why couldn't they just have written 'I have killed some people, here are their names'? In fact, why even write, a phone call would have been so much quicker. It was just a waste of his time.

That's when the thought struck him. He looked around the office to see who was watching. It had to be a wind-up; one of his colleagues playing a cruel joke on him. Whoever the perpetrator they were bound to be watching him, to see his reaction when he read it; to see if he fell for their silly joke.

Nobody was looking even remotely in his direction. Two of the four officers in the room were stood by the far wall, deep in conversation, whilst pointing at the large map of the city hanging before them. The other two officers were sat with their backs to him, busy studying text on their monitors. Maybe whichever one it was, they had seen him putting the letter down and had looked away at the last minute. He decided to pick the letter back up, whilst using his peripheral vision to spot subtle movement.

He remained this way for five minutes but his four colleagues remained focused on what they were doing; it was as if he wasn't even in the room.

The references in the letter to his poor conviction record could only have come from somebody he worked with, but that didn't necessarily mean they were here right now. Maybe the perpetrator was smarter than that and would get his or her satisfaction at a later date. Jameson didn't know the names of half the team that worked out of this office, and in truth, it could have come from any of them. He knew he wasn't a popular figure in the department, but to send a false confession with stinging criticism of his detective-skills was a bit harsh, he thought.

Despite the guidance, he started to skim read the next couple of pages for names, but none were forthcoming. He glanced up at his colleagues again and noticed that the two who had been stood by the wall had departed. That left Molly, sat at her screen facing the window and the woman whose name he could not remember sat with her back to the window.

'Molly,' he said, 'you didn't see anyone leave a letter on my desk, did you?'

Molly looked irritated by the interruption, and as she turned to face him, she slid the glasses from the end of her nose.

'What letter?' she asked.

'When I got back from the canteen, there was a letter in a white envelope on my desk. You didn't notice anybody leave it there when I was away did you?'

He held up the pages and envelope to indicate what he was referring to, like it would jog her memory. She studied him for a moment, as if she was summoning the will to speak with him.

'No,' she replied and promptly turned back to her work.

Jameson tried to make eye contact with the other woman, hoping that she would have heard the brief exchange with Molly and was ready to offer an insight. She remained rooted where she was. Feeling too embarrassed to admit he had forgotten her name; he sighed and returned to reading the letter. Maybe the perpetrator would let slip their identity in something they had written.

2

It's probably an appropriate time for me to share some background details on myself with you. I am not psychologically disturbed and have no sociopathic tendencies that I am aware of. I wasn't abused as a child, either sexually or physically. I did not come from a broken home, have never spent any time in social care, and I am not a repressed homosexual. My decision to kill my victims was made rationally, while I was under no stress. It wasn't made on a whim and was very much pre-meditated. I knew where they would be, how I wanted to kill them and the reason why. They were not chosen at random, in fact I have known the victims all my life.

So why did I decide to kill them? I found earlier in the year that my life had reached something of a crossroads. I was in a decent job, not one I had imagined when I had been at school, but still one that paid a reasonable wage and allowed me to live a life that I had quickly become accustomed to. I had met a woman whom I felt I could settle down with. She wasn't local and we had discussed the possibility of moving away to start afresh. I was really keen on the idea, but found there was something holding me back: My parents.

My parents, whose names, I will withhold for the time being were entering the twilight time of their lives. They had both taken early retirement, some years ago, and were now spending the days in each other's company and taking exotic holidays abroad. That was until my father suffered a stroke and lost the ability to communicate fully. He could say some words, but not most, his speech was slurred at best and it had become a real struggle to understand what he wanted. The stroke had also reduced the motion down his right side, meaning he spent most of his time in a wheelchair, waiting to be ferried from one point to another.

My mother did not cope well with the change. She was suddenly required to care for him 24 hours a day and it wasn't something she was ready for or happy to do. This meant they became more reliant on me to help them. My brother lived further away, so as the nearest relative, my parents became ever more reliant on my support, financially, emotionally and physically. Every Tuesday, she would phone and say I was to pick them up and take them out to lunch. It was worse than it sounds! We would go to the same fish and chip restaurant each week and my parents would order the same meal. I say my parents, it was mother who ordered the food, without even consulting my father. When the food arrived, she would sit there and cut it into small pieces for him and then would sit and moan while he tried to scoop up the morsels of food onto his fork and failed miserably. I suggested several times that we could try a different restaurant but she would insist that "dad always liked fish" although I'm not totally convinced that he ever did like it.

***

Jameson casually placed the letter back on his desk and reached over to pick up the telephone receiver. He was about to dial, when he caught himself, and replaced the receiver. Was he being silly, he wondered. Surely, nobody was stupid enough to send their written confession to murder? Besides, the notion that the writer had bumped his parents off because they were infirm was pretty ludicrous. The letter had to be a wind-up!

Jameson glanced around the office. Molly had now gone too, so it was just him and the other woman. A thought struck him and he raised his eyes to the ceiling: CCTV.

The station had only been opened in the last eighteen months, and when it had been, security cameras had been installed in each of the offices and the interview suites, to monitor officer behaviour. Before the large station building had been opened, amalgamating several smaller, nearby stations, there had been concerns that officers wouldn't mix well from the neighbourhoods. The cameras had been fitted as a safety precaution. Jameson knew the feed from the cameras was visible on the screens in the custody suite where the Custody Sergeant could monitor comings and goings. What if they were all down there now, watching his reaction? It would make sense; it would be like watching the scene unfold in a television documentary.

Jameson calculated that it would take him at least three minutes to get down to the custody suite, if he ran, though 'jogged' would have been a more accurate description. If he was quick enough, the gathered throng wouldn't have time to disperse and find hiding places. To play along, Jameson lifted the letter again, before dropping it and dashing from the office, hoping to use the element of surprise to his advantage; they wouldn't pull the wool over his eyes!

He dashed down the hall, to the open staircase that would lead down two floors to ground level, where all arrestees were booked in. If the audience became aware that he might be on to them, he would surely spot some of them, making good their escape. As he reached the bottom stair, he bent over, wheezing. He hadn't anticipated how out of shape he was, and the adrenaline had forced him to move quicker than he was used to. Undeterred, he headed for the suite at the end of the corridor, pushing the door open, in a triumphant fashion.

'Can I help you?' questioned the Custody Sergeant, an arrogant man in his late twenties, whom Jameson had never cared for.

The room was empty, save for the man talking to him. Whilst he hadn't necessarily expected to see a large group hunched around the monitor, he had expected to see at least a couple of his colleagues in the near vicinity. There was no way they could have scarpered so fast!

'Just looking for someone,' Jameson replied, as casually as his wheezing would allow.

'It's after six, the day shift have all knocked off. I thought your lot would have gone home too,' came the response. Jameson knew that Daniels, the Custody Sergeant, despised C.I.D. but chose to ignore the comment, and instead turned on his heel and headed back towards the staircase.

As Jameson considered his options, it dawned on him that Daniels would never have allowed C.I.D. to hover around a monitor to watch a practical joke unfold. If only, he had considered that sooner, he wouldn't have needed to race downstairs and wouldn't be feeling so ill now. The other option, as ridiculous as the notion sounded, was that the letter was genuine. To satisfy his curiosity, Jameson headed for the control centre, the room where all radio communications with uniformed officers were managed. If there was any truth to the letter, potentially the deaths of an elderly couple may have been reported. He popped his head around the door and spotted his D.I. chatting with the sergeant on duty.

'Jameson, what are you doing down here?' quizzed D.I. Jack Vincent, glaring.

Great, he thought; the last thing he wanted was to explain to Vincent that he had received a possible hoax letter that he was taking more seriously than he should have been. Jameson was aware that Vincent hadn't been his biggest fan since his transfer to the squad.

'Just following up on a case,' he replied. 'Was wondering if there have been any reports of a murdered elderly couple?' The question was aimed at the room, even though all those stationed at desks were deep in conversation through the headsets they wore.

Vincent turned to the sergeant he was with, anticipating a response. The sergeant shook his head, causing Vincent to glare back at Jameson.

'What case are you on?' Vincent demanded.

'Just something that's come up,' Jameson replied vaguely. 'Not to worry,' he added as he disappeared back through the door and headed back up to his desk. If he was lucky, Vincent would quickly forget about the unusual encounter.

As Jameson sat back down and looked at the letter, he frowned. No murder had been reported as yet, which undermined the contents of what he was reading. He decided to continue reading, on the off chance, that the murders weren't local.

3

Usually, twice a week I would get a phone call advising that I needed to take one of them to the doctor or the dentist or to the pharmacy to collect a prescription. There just always seemed to be something. What made it worse, was knowing that this was just the beginning. They were going to get worse. Undoubtedly, dad's condition would worsen and he would become even less independent and mum would become frailer and less able to move of her own volition. Of course, 'Golden Boy' phoned every week and told them how he wished he could be closer to help them out, even though I knew this to be a lie. If he really wanted to help them, he could have done. But they didn't see it, of course. Instead, they just took pleasure in telling me how great he was and how he had such an important job. What a bastard!

So, this is where the crossroads arose; continue along this bleak road where more and more of my time would be taken up by them or...find another way.

I should say at this point that the decision to kill my parents is not one I made over night. I spent several weeks thinking non-stop about it. When the idea first popped into my head, I dismissed it immediately, and hated myself for even considering it. I mean, what kind of sick bastard imagines killing his parents? It's like some kind of twisted Oedipus-act.

But, I was under stress. Wait, no, that's not fair. I wasn't feeling stressed when I was making the decision. I just couldn't face a future with them running me down. I thought about my choices every morning, afternoon and night. Whenever, I had a free moment or was on my own, I considered both possible futures: one with my parents alive and one without.

I reached the decision to kill them whilst watching an old black and white B-movie in the early hours of one morning. The film was about a man dreaming about killing his wife and trying to get away with it. Up until that point, I hadn't properly considered what would happen to me if I did kill them. I could totally relate to the husband in the movie, albeit the object of my murderous intentions wasn't a partner.

The lead character planned his crime so that somebody else would take the fall. He came so close to getting away with it, but like most made-for-television movies, good had to overcome evil and he was caught before he managed to carry out the deed. Still, it got me thinking; what if I pinned the crime on somebody else? That way I would be robbed of my problem without facing years behind bars. In 'Golden Boy' I found the perfect fall guy.

Once the decision was reached, I had expected my conscience to give me real hell over what I had chosen to do. But to be honest, I was thinking clearer than I had ever done before. I started to carry out research on the internet of ways to kill. I wasn't stupid enough just to type 'how to kill and get away with it' in a search engine; I'm aware that the security services are alerted when certain key words are entered into the internet and I didn't want my research to come back and haunt me. Instead, I started scanning newspaper websites, in particular, historic stories, focusing on the word 'death'. I figured there was still a minor chance that this action could still alert the security services but I doubted they would follow it up. At first, it was difficult to find any stories not relating to suicide or suicide attempts.

Eventually I managed to find a run of articles relating to murders and attempted murders and read everything I could find. The stories I found could be broken down into two categories: pre-meditated or crimes of passion. The former were those crimes where somebody had ultimately decided to go out and kill someone. The latter related to stories where death had resulted from alternative circumstances such as the outcome of a mugging or a serious car accident. I was able to quickly identify these stories, skim-read them and dismiss them. It was the stories about those who had gone to great lengths to plan and carry out their crimes that I spent time reading. I made pages and pages of notes. I hadn't done this much research since school!

The stories I was reading and studying were like plot lines from classic shows like Murder She Wrote and Columbo. The perpetrators all had simple motives for disposing of their victims and, where in the past, I would have been appalled by the crudity of their decisions, now, I found I was thrilled and excited by them. I am sure there was more than a hint of sensationalising on the part of the newspaper and magazine editors, but that didn't put me off my cause.

There were several articles, which tackled the theme of euthanasia, the lengths spouses would go to in order to ease the pain of their loved ones really moved me. I began to become impassioned by their cases and found myself questioning the law in this country that prevents a victim of circumstance from choosing somebody to help them to die. My situation was different, I realise, but I managed to convince myself that my parents would choose to die if they could truly see the inconvenience they had become to me. Looking back on it, now, they probably wouldn't have chosen to go out as soon as they did, but it's too late to change that now.

The tone of the letter was starting to concern Jameson and he could feel beads of sweat starting to form along his forehead. For the first time that evening, he was starting to contemplate the possibility that the letter could be true. He paused for a moment to consider what would happen if he chose to ignore the letter, and then it turned out to be true later down the line. What if the murderer was collared and subsequently advised that he had written to Jameson to tell all, but it had been ignored? Jameson's career would be finished, and he would be unceremoniously dismissed. His D.I. would love that!

Re-scanning the page he had just read, he was frustrated that he still had very little to go on. He still had no idea of the culprit's and victims' names, nor their location. He couldn't even confirm how they had been killed. There was something about the tone that was starting to ring true, and it was this that had him perplexed.

Jameson decided to bite the bullet, and dialled Detective Inspector Jack Vincent's mobile number. He answered after two rings.

'Yes.'

'Guv, it's Jameson,' he began. 'I need to speak to you about something. Can you pop up?'

'I've just got in my car,' sighed Vincent. 'Can it not wait till morning?'

'The thing is, Guv,' continued Jameson, ignoring the comment, 'I think I've got a double homicide to report.'

'Right, go on,' Vincent replied, sighing again, louder this time.

Jameson took a deep breath. 'I've received a letter, confessing to the crime. The perp claims to have bumped his parents off.'

'Okay, said Vincent, expecting more to follow. When he was greeted with silence, he added, 'What's the problem? Go and pick him up, leave him in cells overnight and we'll take a look at him first thing.'

'That's the thing, Guv; I don't know his name, yet.'

133

'What do you know?'

'I know he claims to have killed his parents, that one of them suffered a stroke some years ago. I think he is based in Southampton, but that's just what my gut is telling me.'

'What are the parents called? You can probably find the names of any offspring on the internet,' said Vincent.

'I'm not sure yet, Guv. I haven't got that far.'

'You haven't got that far? What's going on, Jameson?'

'I'm only about a third of the way through the letter, so far.'

'Then why the bloody hell are you phoning me now?' Vincent questioned, losing his temper.

'I thought I should let you know as soon as I suspected something. It could be a big case.'

'Tell me, Jameson,' Vincent replied evenly, 'when did the crime happen?'

'I don't know, Guv.'

'So, you don't know who is dead, when they died, how they died or who killed them? How the hell can you be sure there is even a crime? Someone is having you on, and you have fallen for it hook, line and sinker! I knew you were slow, Jameson, but this takes the biscuit. Can you even be sure the killer is a man?' Vincent paused, before adding, 'I'm going home now. I want to see you in my office first thing tomorrow morning so we can have a review of your recent performance. Do you understand me? Do not disturb me again tonight, with your Scooby-Doo theories!'

With that, Vincent hung up the phone; leaving Jameson sat in the office, staring down at the letter. Vincent had reacted the same way he had when he had first started reading the letter, but there was still something in his mind that rang true, despite what his D.I. had said. If Vincent had read the letter, he probably would have felt the same, Jameson thought to himself. Embarrassed by his stupidity in phoning his boss, before he had anything concrete to share, he returned to reading the letter.

4

'Golden Boy' will never understand the decision I took or my motive for killing our parents, but then he really isn't in touch with the reality of the situation. He left home several years ago to pursue what he described as his 'calling in life'. I always questioned how he could be achieving his 'calling in life' when he was so bad at it, but then my parents would scowl at me and accuse me of jealousy. Usually when parents have two children, each parent tends to be closer to one child, whilst the other tends to share more with the remaining child. It isn't through choosing, it is just the way the world works. I mean, ask any parent if they have a favourite child, and they will deny it vehemently. Put a gun to both children's heads and ask them which one should survive and they soon narrow the selection down. As with anything, there are exceptions to the rule and my parents were such a case; they both preferred 'Golden Boy' to me. I am not looking for your pity, I have come to accept their choice, and do not require sympathy. I suppose their hand was forced. 'Golden Boy' arrived first and I suppose they never quite accepted the accidental arrival, which grew into the man writing you this letter.

They used to claim that I was a planned addition to the clan, but given that they were already living on the bread-line and mother had only just returned to the job she loved, it is hard to accept their claims. I remember my grandmother once referring to me as 'the accident' one afternoon when I was playing with my toys, and shouldn't have been listening to the adult conversation. Mum had told her to be quiet but it was too late, I knew the truth.

I don't deny that my parents loved me, in some way; it was just a love borne out of necessity, rather than devotion and perhaps on some subconscious level, their bias towards my brother altered their every decision.

135

'Golden Boy' was into building model planes, a pastime shared by my father. They would spend hours together every weekend, gluing small bits of plastic together until they had created a scaled model of some bomber or fighter I had never heard of. And when they weren't at home doing that, they were out at the model shop choosing what they would build next.

Mother didn't care for the model building but her common interest with 'Golden Boy' was baking. She loved to bake cakes at the weekend, and when his hands weren't covered in glue, 'Golden Boy' would be stood at mother's side, whisking and sieving. He was exactly what a parent wanted as a child; it was no wonder he became the favourite.

I, on the other hand, enjoyed reading and learning. When I was growing up, in my plight to find a happier childhood, I would read of Pratchett's and Tolkein's alternative universes. The more I was ignored and condemned, the more I would read. As a result, the more I would be ignored and condemned; it was the most vicious of circles and I was at the epicentre. I tried to take an interest in both baking and modelling, but I would be told that my hands were too small to glue stuff to the plane, and there weren't enough whisks for two of us to help bake. And so, I would be told, 'Maybe next time,' week after week, until I just stopped trying and focused on the life I longed for.

This is how things continued through Primary and then Secondary school. My grades were much higher than 'Golden Boy's' but they didn't seem to care. Father would often remark that exams were getting easier as the years passed and as I was three years younger than 'Golden Boy' the exams would have been three times easier. I knew this was inaccurate but would they listen? Of course not!

'Golden Boy' moved away to go to university on the eve of my sixteenth birthday. That's when things began to change. Slightly. Father's eyes were already deteriorating so model-building became a less important aspect of his life. He began to read more, and you would have thought this would become our shared interest? No. He enjoyed reading biographies about people who had made big successes of their lives and would describe the fantasy novels I read as 'utter garbage'. Mother was diagnosed with type-2 diabetes and so her cake-baking days came to a brutal halt. I bought her a cookery book for Christmas, containing recipes for cakes and biscuits suitable for diabetics. I had hoped we could work together and produce a delicious, nutritious snack. Instead, a week after Christmas, I found the book in a bag with items she was planning to drop off at a local charity shop.

'Golden Boy' dropped out of university at the end of his first year, claiming his thinking was too advanced for the seasoned academics teaching his course and as a result his ideas had been poorly received. The fact that he had probably spent more of his time drinking than studying seemed to go unnoticed by my parents. Bizarrely, they bought him a car by way of apology for forcing him to attend the university course in the first place. The car wasn't brand new, but it only had ten thousand miles on the clock. I had just asked for driving lessons but was told they couldn't afford it.

Being the dutiful son that he was, he would take mother to the local supermarket once a week to collect the groceries and once a month he would drive dad to the docks, to watch the ships arriving into port. The rest of his time was spent searching for jobs, or at least that's what he claimed to be doing. I have no evidence, but I am pretty sure he spent more time driving around trying to pick up girls than job hunting.

As I entered sixth form, my English teacher saw something creative in me and encouraged me to express my thoughts through story-telling. I won several awards for the short stories I developed and the next obvious step would have been to go to university to study English Language and Literature and become a writer of some kind. My father told me University wouldn't be the right fit for me and I would be better off following in his footsteps and becoming an electrician or a plumber like his father before him. I appealed to my mother's sense of reason and she told me that I would be wasting my time at university, as the image of academic life painted by 'Golden Boy' had been pretty grim.

To spite them both, I took a job at a local bank. The hours were enough to pay the rent on a small flat as well as sending some housekeeping money back to them. Living on my own left me plenty of time to develop my fantasy writing. 'Golden Boy' of course, didn't contribute to the housekeeping pot as he 'hasn't found a job', even though he was still living under their roof. It made me sick to think that he was spending all day, wasting time and petrol, and I was the one having to help finance it!

***

Jameson smiled to himself; at last he had a lead to work from. The writer worked for a bank. Jameson, unlocked the screen on his computer and pulled up an internet search engine. He typed 'Southampton banks' into the search box and located a list of all the local bank branches in the city. His smile vanished when he saw that there were over thirty branches. It had narrowed his search, but not by as much as he had hoped. Assuming an average of 6 employees per branch, that would give him a list of 200 or so staff to speak with. Vincent had been right, though; he couldn't be sure he was reading the work of a man, so it would be too early to narrow down the sex. He decided that once he had finished reading, he would start trying to request lists of employees from all the local banks. He knew the killer had at least one brother, so that would rule out any employees without one. He would also be able to rule out those whose parents had already passed away. The smile started to return to his face, that would probably narrow his list further.

What else did he know, Jameson wondered. He reached out and picked up a pad of post-it notes and started to jot down what else he had learned. The brother, so-called 'Golden Boy' had attended university and dropped out. As he re-read the letter, he was frustrated that the university had not been named by the killer, but it was still something else to investigate. The mother was diabetic, so her name would probably appear on some kind of register at the hospital.

Jameson continued to jot down his notes and his smile broadened. It was like putting a jigsaw puzzle together, and this was why he had joined the force. It was this kind of work he enjoyed. Stuff Vincent, he thought to himself. This was his case now and he would solve it single-handedly and claim the credit. This could be the making of him!

Jameson picked up the letter again and continued, but made a note to continue jotting down what he learned as he read.

5

'Golden Boy' came home one day and declared that he had worked out what he wanted to do and would be leaving home to pursue his dream. My parents admitted they would be sad to see him go but didn't want to hold him back. In the same breath, they said they would be okay as I would be around to help them out whenever they needed. The cheek of it!

I suppose that is when I really grew to resent them. For years, they made me feel like I was second-best, and even now, when they finally needed me more than ever, they still only saw me as second choice.

At first, it was just the odd job they would ask me to come round and help with; a trip to the supermarket, a visit to the doctor's surgery, that kind of thing. Then the list of jobs grew. Suddenly I was expected round every other Sunday to mow the lawn, when the cobwebs needed removing from the corners of the high ceilings, a trip to the bank so they could collect their pension monies. I found I had to make excuses at work because they would phone and say there was a desperate situation that required my attention. I remember, six months after the phone calls started, my boss called me into his office and said he was disappointed with the amount of time I was taking off work on such a frequent basis. He asked me if I had an alcohol problem as he had witnessed similar behaviour in others in the past. I had to protest that I had never had an alcohol problem, unlike 'Golden Boy' but rather than going into detail to explain the issues I was having with my parents, I apologised and promised to try harder.

This forced me to change the routine with my parents. I had to sit them down and explain that they couldn't continue to phone me during work. They were hurt and made out that I was the ungrateful one for refusing to support them after all the years of support they had given me. I mean, I wanted to scream some home truths at them, but I resisted the urge, and offered the compromise that I would call round every evening after work to check if anything needed doing. It was additional hassle in my life, but at least it would mean that my job would be safer.

The routine continued unabated for the following twelve months and as the time passed, I found myself having to spend more and more time with them. At first, mother had offered to cook me dinner when I visited, but I had never been one who enjoyed eating supper before eight, so the offer of meat and two veg at five had never appealed. As her body weakened, it became less and less possible for her to lift heavy pans and the thought of using a microwave made her giddy. So, the routine changed, and I would go round straight after work and cook them their dinner. It was hard work. After eight hours of dealing with customers who were complaining about the low interest rate on their savings accounts or the high interest rate on their overdrafts, I then had to spend an hour cooking, followed by another hour or two of them moaning about this, that and the other.

Jameson dropped the pages as a thought struck him like a locomotive: what if the murderer had failed in their attempt? Instead of waiting for a murder report to hit his desk, he should check for recent admissions. He reached out and once again picked up the handset on the telephone and dialled the Emergency ward at Southampton's General Hospital.

'Admissions,' said a shrill voice after a dozen rings.

'This is Detective Jameson up at the police H.Q. Can you give me a rundown of all your recent patients?'

'What is this regarding, detective?' the shrill voice replied impatiently. 'It's very busy tonight. Are you looking for something in particular?'

All the telephone lines between the local hospitals, fire stations and police stations were linked so that internal calls could be made between departments, without the need for verifying the identity of the caller. The nurse he was speaking with would be able to see that he was ringing from the station. It was a time-saving initiative that extinguished those awkward moments of checking name and rank.

'I'm following up on an attempted murder. The victims should be between fifty and eighty years old and there would be something suspicious about the nature of their injuries.'

'Hold please.'

It wasn't a request, it was a statement. The voice disappeared and was replaced by an irritatingly slow piece of classical music that Jameson didn't recognise. After three minutes, the music stopped and the familiar hum of background noise returned.

'Detective, there have been no patients matching the description you mentioned. So far this evening we've had several cases of vomiting and the usual run of sports injuries, twisted ankles, that sort of thing. The oldest patient we've had was thirty-seven.'

Jameson wrinkled his nose in frustration.

'Thank you,' he replied. 'If you do receive anything suspicious tonight, can you give me call back?'

'No I can't. My shift is just ending.'

'Is there anyone you can leave a message with?' he persisted, despite her unhelpful attitude.

The voice sighed and said, 'Very well. I'll grab a pen and paper.' Jameson left his name and his extension number so the hospital could come straight through to his desk. He made a point of thanking the nurse, hoping she would feel guilty about how she had dealt with him. In truth, he doubted whether she had even written the message down. He accepted that he had given the nurse very little to go on, and one person's interpretation of a "suspicious" injury would be different to another's. The writer had yet to give an indication of how he had disposed of his victims and that would ultimately prove to be a valuable piece of information. It might also provide a hint to the killer's identity.

Picking the pieces of paper back up, he returned to the narrative.

6

Mother became obsessed with daytime chat shows, particularly the kind where family members argue with each other over who has had an affair with whom, or who the father of an unplanned baby was. She would tell me each night what she had seen; freely expressing her opinion on how disgusted she was that some people could be so selfish. Believe me; the irony was not lost on me. It was as if she thought she had been watching the news and that it was a searing depiction of real life. I would try to explain that it was just trash-television; that the guests were carefully selected to air their issues, but she would discuss it in the same tone as anybody else would discuss world politics.

Most of the time, I would allow my imagination to wander while she spoke, only occasionally looking up and nodding my head to acknowledge something she had said. I would picture the worlds in the fantasy stories I was still trying to write. To be honest, some of the best plot lines came from being stood by the small cooker in mother's kitchen, while she would be sat behind me at the small, wooden table, talking about D.N.A. test results from the latest edition of the show.

I found I would finish with them and arrive back at my place a little after nine o'clock. I would have barely enough time to jump in the shower before I would hear my bed calling me. My writing eventually had to stop and my frustration grew. What for everybody else was an eight hour day at work, mine was twelve hours, but I wasn't being paid when I was with them. Despite this, I continued to work hard and last year I earned a promotion at work, and with a two thousand pound bonus. I was over the moon. I saw this as my opportunity to upgrade my one bedroom flat to something a little more luxurious. Mother had different plans. To this day, I have no idea why I even told them about the promotion. I suppose I was excited and wanted to try and prove that I wasn't the failure they believed I was. I wanted them to look at me and think, 'maybe he didn't turn out too badly'.

When I told them my news, with a big, beaming grin on my face, mother's response was, 'That's nice, dear, the extra housekeeping will come in handy.' She only saw me as an additional source of income. At this point I was spending at least four hours at their house each night and my duties had extended to include bathing both of them. Not that either of them thanked me for this arduous task. It's not right seeing your parents naked, feeling their worn, wrinkly skin, sticking to my clothes, and carrying them from the bedroom to the bathroom, before lowering them in. And then would come the scrubbing...Father would complain that the water was too hot or too cold, that I was rubbing him too hard with the sponge or that I had allowed shampoo to wash into his eyes.

I found I wasn't getting home until eleven o'clock at night and then would be up again at five to wash and shave before work. It would have made more sense had I moved back in with them, as the flat I was renting was literally just a bed in a room to me, I certainly wasn't making the most of my independence. The problem was that mum and dad never offered me the chance to move back in, and I wasn't prepared to ask, as if I did they would see it as confirmation that I had failed to live my life without their support and then they would win.

'Golden Boy's' visits became less frequent, as he moved on with his life. Due to the odd hours he kept in his profession, mother was always so forgiving of the fact that she rarely saw him. When father spoke to the few friends he had left, he would speak proudly of his son "the public servant" and would barely offer a comment about me.

Two months ago, today, I finally had a night to myself. 'Golden Boy' came round to visit them and this meant I was not required for the evening. Sadly, I didn't go out anywhere, I didn't catch up with friends and I didn't write. I ordered a take away pizza and sat on the sofa, watching television. I soon grew bored and spent most of the evening channel-hopping, without finding anything I was remotely interested in. I went to bed early but tossed and turned for hours, before eventually dropping off just after midnight. I wasn't asleep for long, as I had to make a mad dash to the bathroom just before two, as the pizza reappeared. I spent the next three hours laid on my bed with the television just on in the background. I think I was dozing in and out of sleep during the time, as my memory of events is limited. I can recall there was a black and white movie on the screen, which is what I described to you earlier, about the man dreaming up the perfect way to kill his wife.

Whether it was the lack of sleep, the dodgy pizza or the relentless pressure of dealing with my parents' every whim, something inside of me really empathised with the protagonist on the screen. As I watched him planning his crime in intricate

144

detail, I could hear a voice in my head telling me that he was doing it wrong. The little voice suggested better ways he could have planned the event to successfully get away with it. The voice was definitely subconscious, but it continued to talk to me. It started to say how easy it would be to kill my parents and rid myself of the weight around my neck.

***

Jameson was growing frustrated with the elongated narrative. He had been in possession of the letter for half an hour already and was still no closer to identifying the culprit, victims or location of the murder. He still couldn't be a hundred percent certain that the letter was genuine, though deep down he suspected it probably was. The level of detail being shared was too considerable for it not to be true.

Jameson wasn't much of a film buff. He struggled to understand why films such as Citizen Kane and Spartacus received such wild acclaim, when he found them boring. He acknowledged that he lacked imagination and this was probably the reason why he generally avoided watching television and reading books; he certainly couldn't recall a film where a husband plotted to murder his wife. Jameson loaded up the internet search engine again and typed 'Movie Murder Husband Wife'. The search returned thousands of pages of results and he had to trawl through dozens of links before he actually found anything remotely linked to a film. There were various news stories about husbands and wives attempting to kill each other, mimicking what they had seen in movies.

Eventually he found a website listing film titles where a husband or wife had attempted to murder the other. The letter indicated that the movie in question was shot in black and white, so Jameson surmised that it probably wasn't recent. He found a Hitchcock picture from 1954 and then typed its title into the search engine with the words 'last aired UK'. After a further trawl, he identified that the film had been shown only once in the last year and it was indeed two months ago, to the day.

Jameson swallowed as the realisation hit him; the letter was genuine and probably written today. The letter now proved a real threat and his thoughts of practical joking were quickly replaced with the anxiety that his actions would be heavily scrutinised when the bodies surfaced.

Jameson re-scanned the last page, to make sure that the notes he was writing reflected the new jigsaw pieces. The writer had made reference to hearing voices. Jameson jotted down 'possible schizophrenia' with a big question mark. He then double-underlined the note, so that it would be clear to anyone subsequently reviewing the page, that he had considered all possibilities. It was too late in the day to speak with any local psychiatrists to see if they had any patients causing them grave concern, but that would be his first task in the morning. The writer had been very calculated so far, keeping Jameson's detective-skills on a tight leash; it suggested the writer could be a cold-blooded psychopath, but it was too early to confirm.

With a growing sense of dread, he returned to the letter.

7

I woke the next morning with a ravenous hunger; it was my body's way of telling me to replace the nutrients I had lost. As I munched down a third slice of toast, I remembered the film and what I believed was a dream. I could remember a man's voice telling me how to kill my parents. Initially, I felt awful. I felt guilty that I could have allowed my subconscious to dream about murdering the people who had given me life. I went to work, as usual, but whenever I had downtime during the day, in between customer enquiries, my mind would wander back to what the voice had told me. It became harder for me to ignore the memory, and where I had once imagined a fantasy world that I could live in, all I kept seeing was my life without them.

I would be able to afford to rent a nicer flat, maybe a bit closer to the city's nightlife. I would have the freedom to go out with colleagues. Most of the staff in the branch went to the pub after work on payday, and I had never been. I could become more involved with the group. I would be free to eat what I wanted, when I wanted. I would probably have enough money to buy a new car. Seeing my life as it could be, excited me. It was the same thrill as for someone who imagines what it would be like to see their lottery numbers earn them a share of the jackpot.

I had to chastise myself every time the images popped into my head. The thoughts made my hairs stand on end and caused goose-bumps to pop up on my arms. By the end of the day, when I drove over to their house, I felt so guilty. I forced myself to remember the good times that I had experienced with them. It was hard to remember too many, but I persevered. I resolved to try harder with them and that it was still possible to deal with their annoyances. As I put my key in the front door, I found a new purpose in life. I took a deep breath and entered the house. There was a determination in me that I had rarely experienced in my life; I was going to be the dutiful son because I wanted to be, not because they expected me to be.

I caught my breath as I turned the corner into the living room and saw that 'Golden Boy' was sat in the armchair, watching television with them both. They were laughing and smiling, and I saw there was a bottle of sherry open on the table. The sherry only ever came out at Christmas but this was mid-April. I could see mother had an empty glass in her hand, but 'Golden Boy' had a larger and considerably-fuller glass in his hand.

'Look what the cat dragged in,' I heard him remark, which made mother laugh and whisper, 'You are terrible,' as she guffawed at what she had interpreted as a joke. The look in 'Golden Boy's' eyes told me it was not meant as a joke, but he played along for her sake. I wanted to pick up the bottle of sherry and smash it over his head! Not once had they offered to get the sherry out for me, not even when I had gained my promotion. I was livid but I exuded as calm an exterior as I could. I was also angry that they hadn't told me I didn't need to come over this evening. Clare at work had invited me out for a drink and I had had to turn her down. I felt like she quite fancied me and I had to admit to having something of a crush on her. If I had known 'Golden Boy' would be there, I would have accepted her invitation in a flash. Now, it felt like I had blown my chances for no reason at all.

I asked 'Golden Boy' why he was there but before he could answer, mother said he had brought good news that required celebrating. I wondered what news he could possibly bring that warranted the description 'good'. It turned out he had decided to transfer to a more local office and would be returning to the city. I suppose I should have considered this good news, as it should have meant we would be able to share out our responsibilities more. But I knew that he would make up all sorts of excuses not to become lumbered with their frailty as I had. He even added the caveat that he would still keep odd hours, so would only be able to call around at weekends. This seemed to go over their heads as they were blinded by the fact he would be around to see them more regularly.

The Prodigal Son was back.

I felt deflated. Once again, 'Golden Boy' had scuppered my plans. I made my way out to the kitchen to prepare dinner but 'Golden Boy' shouted through that he was going to go to the local fish restaurant and bring takeaway in. Mum and dad practically applauded his suggestion and I'm sure dad muttered something about me never making such an effort. 'Golden Boy' took everybody's orders and headed out to the shop. I asked him to get me a beef and onion pie and some chips. I specified that I did not want steak and kidney as the flavour made me retch.

When he returned twenty minutes later, you've probably already guessed it, he handed me a steak and kidney pie. I demanded to know why and he claimed that it was what I had ordered. I reiterated what I had told him before he had left and he argued that I had not been clear enough and he had misheard me; he thought I had said I wanted steak and kidney. Whilst his response was plausible, I knew deep down he was lying. He was the ultimate stitch-up artist and I knew he had deliberately bought the wrong pie. Mother told me to stop making a fuss and to eat the pie. When I refused and said I would just eat the chips, father mumbled something about me wasting food and showing ingratitude to 'Golden Boy's' generosity.

I made my excuses as soon as I could and headed home. On the whole journey home I couldn't help but picture the three of them laughing and joking together in my absence. I don't think I had ever felt so undervalued and neglected.

***

Jameson wrote the words 'Golden Boy' in the centre of a fresh sheet of paper. It was the only angle he had yet to consider. He started to map out what he had learned of the killer's brother. A university drop-out, keeping strange hours in a role he deemed his "calling in life", now transferring to the area. Jameson jotted down 'soldier', 'doctor', 'reporter' and 'dock-worker'. Whatever career the brother currently undertook, it had to be one of greater standing than the bank role the writer undertook. He scribbled out 'dock-worker' but kept his list of three other possibles.

He knew the brother drove, though he had no idea what type of vehicle. It still wasn't enough to narrow the search; not until he managed to get a list of names, and started to filter out what he knew. Jameson was convinced that the killer would reveal himself through the information being solicited but the letter was still moving too slowly.

Jameson had to stop himself feeling some kind of empathy towards the writer. The life being painted was certainly not one Jameson wished for himself but it still didn't seem painful enough to warrant committing murder. He pitied the narrator in many ways; how could someone still be so desperate for a parent's attention at that age? Not that he knew the killer's age, but he assumed he was in his mid-twenties at least, given the information gleaned.

Returning to the spider-diagram he drew further spikes from the occupations to help his search criteria. There couldn't be too many doctors in Southampton, could there? That said, there were two hospitals in the city. A thought struck Jameson and he quickly scribbled out the word 'doctor'; the brother would have needed to study at university for six or seven years to be a doctor. The detective scowled at his stupidity. That left him with 'soldier' and 'reporter'. The nearest army barracks was in Aldershot, which was at least fifty miles from the city. At best it was an hour's journey down the M3 so would the brother really commute so regularly? The more Jameson considered the prospect, the less lucid it appeared. Scrawling a line through 'soldier', that left 'reporter' as the only option.

Jameson loaded up the Daily Echo's internet page and scanned the headlines, looking for journalists' names. Nothing leapt out at him; there was no obvious list of employees' names either. It would take an eagle eye to review each of the possible stories and track the names that appeared, and he just didn't have the time. He decided this angle wasn't helpful to his investigation and jotted down a note for an eager uniform to perform the exercise in the morning.

He was only half way through the letter and there were other more pressing case files on his desk that he should have been reviewing, but despite this, he couldn't tear himself away from reading it. It was the challenge the writer had laid down at the start: 'I believe you will not be able to bring a successful prosecution against me.' Want to bet, Jameson thought to himself.

8

Over the coming days, 'Golden Boy' went about finding himself a flat to live in and sorting out his transfer. I continued to go around after work to do the cooking and cleaning and every time mother started to drivel on about her trashy show, I imagined more extravagant ways of killing her and my father. My imagination created vivid depictions of death. When I lowered them into the bath, I pictured forcing their shoulders down under the shallow water and holding them there until they stopped struggling. When I tucked them into bed, I imagined holding a pillow over each of their frail bodies. When I was cooking, I saw myself grabbing hold of a chopping knife from the wooden block on the kitchen counter and slashing it across their throats, watching in glee as the thick crimson blood poured from their throats and spattered on the tiles.

It got to the point where I had to pinch myself, just to check that I hadn't actually acted upon my thoughts. When I did pay attention to what they were telling me, all they would talk about was how things were going to be when 'Golden Boy' completed his move. I hated the fact that they could not see how unhelpful he had been over the years and how I had stuck by them through thick and thin.

'Golden Boy' moved into his new flat a week later and as I had suspected, he claimed to be working an unconventional shift pattern so wouldn't be able to come around until the following weekend to see them. That week, they made me take time off work to decorate the inside of their house as they wanted it to be nice for 'Golden Boy's' return. As I painted, I imagined pouring paint into their mouths while they slept or covering their mouths and nostrils with yellow tape.

The first Saturday that 'Golden Boy' was with them, I made the most of my freedom and rented a copy of the black and white film where the man planned his wife's murder. I must have watched it three times, back-to-back, making copious notes about what he had done, why and what else he could have done to avoid getting caught. I began to listen to the little voice in my head.

You are probably thinking that the decision to kill them was a bit drastic? I disagree. It was already hard enough putting up with their ways, but I knew instinctively it would become a hundred times worse, having 'Golden Boy' popping around at the weekends; I knew they would spend the first three days of the week telling me how much fun they had had with him and the final couple of days explaining how excited they were about what they were planning to do the next weekend. I also knew that they wouldn't ask him to contribute towards the food and heating bills as I had to. He would continue to get away with giving nothing and receiving everything. I couldn't allow that to continue. I wouldn't allow that to continue.

**

Jameson tried to stop his hands trembling. What had started as a whimsical fantasist claiming responsibility for a murder had swiftly become something far more insidious. The tone of the letter was continuing to darken and like a rabbit trapped in the glare of headlights, he was unable to move. There was no way this was a practical joke, he knew that now. This was a very real confession to a double homicide. What he was holding in his hands was a valuable piece of evidence, clearly sent from somebody not right in the head.

Jameson loosened the tie around his collar.

'Why is it so hot in here?' he said to the now empty room, and then added, 'What would Vincent do?'

He needed help, he had never handled anything this big before. He was the person they went to with the shit cases that the more experienced detectives couldn't be bothered to deal with. But this could be the making of him; this could be the case that made his name and moved him up the office pecking order. It was a horrible dilemma to be faced with, particularly as he had no idea how to solve it. What would Vincent do, he asked himself again.

The truth was, he didn't know; he had already exhausted all the avenues available to him. Another ten minutes had passed since he had last checked the clock. The longer he dwelt on the letter, the greater the chance that the culprit would get away with it. Jameson banged his fist down on the desk, causing the telephone to shudder closer to the edge. Impetuously, he grabbed at the handset and dialled the Control Centre, hoping that somebody might have phoned in and reported two elderly deaths.

'Control,' said a gruff voice.

'Hi,' he replied as casually as possible. 'It's Jameson from C.I.D., have there been any homicides reported this evening?'

'Jameson?' replied the gruff voice, 'weren't you down here earlier, asking the same question?'

He realised the gruff voice must have belonged to the sergeant who had been talking with Vincent, when he had popped by after his visit to the custody suite.

'That's right,' he replied nonchalantly, 'have there been any new cases reported yet?'

'Are you so un-busy that you're trying to predict crime now?' chortled the sergeant.

Jameson laughed falsely back, trying to keep the real reason for the call under wraps.

'Not exactly,' he replied. 'I'm just following up on something. If you do hear of any double homicides, can you give me a call? It's really important.'

'Trying to improve your arrest targets, eh? I'm not one for fudging figures, Jameson. We'll continue to report crimes in the proper manner, do you understand me? I am not prepared to cherry-pick cases for any of you C.I.D. lot!'

With that, the line went dead. Jameson was tempted to phone the sergeant back, to defend himself, by explaining the real purpose of the call, but there was no point. There was an obvious divide between uniform and plain-clothes officers, and it stretched from his level, all the way to the top: they were different breeds.

The hospital hadn't phoned him back yet, and from that he could only draw to realistic conclusions: either the killer had yet to carry out the deed, or the bodies would never be found. It was a sobering thought to have and caused Jameson to swallow hard, before he continued with his reading.

9

The World Wide Web really is the greatest invention of our time, do you not agree, Detective Jameson? Anything that you want to know about life is there, in one convenient place. If you are looking for a particular type of knife, or a gun that fires a deadly blow, with the minimal amount of noise, it's all there; one step away; at the click of a button. Any method you choose to dispatch of your victim can be found online.

I wouldn't describe myself as a cold-blooded killer. I didn't want to inflict pain on my parents, I just wanted them to cease existing. For me, it was never about watching their blood spill, in spite of my ever-more-lurid visions, the most-recent of which saw me skewering mother with a cucumber while she rattled on about some nonsense or other.

HARD TARGETS

My internet search began with looking at the types of drugs that could be mixed in with their food and would cause them to slowly drift into a deep sleep, never to wake again. But what I found was that there are limitations to these types of drugs. For one thing, there would be insufficient time for the substances to leave the body before any kind of autopsy was performed, and inevitably there would be an autopsy; my brother would demand that! If only one of them passed away, the police might accept the conclusion of 'natural causes' but if they both died together, at the same time in the same house, 'foul play' would be suspected.

The other issue with sleep-inducing drugs was the propensity for them not to work properly. The last thing I wanted was to plan my new life and find one or both of them coming round and pointing the finger at me. No. If I was going to do this, it needed to work, without repercussions.

My search led me onto toxins. Did you know there are lists and lists of colourfully-named poisons on the internet? I found myself getting lost in the various names: abacavir, abamectin, acetone, aconitum. The list is endless and that was just the 'a's'. I am nothing, if not methodical, so I persevered and began to look up the side-effects of each and every poison, to identify what I would require to carry out the deadly deed. In the end, I had to take a couple of days off work just to complete my research. I didn't have the internet at home, but 'Golden Boy' did so I slyly borrowed the spare set of keys mother had hidden at her home, and let myself in when 'Golden Boy' was at work.

The secret to getting away with murder is covering your tracks, hiding your motive well and above all else, making sure you are not around when the smoking gun goes off. I knew that if I was the one to deliver their poisoned last supper, I would clearly be in the frame when the police investigation commenced. Even if I wasn't in the house, if I had been there in the recent past, I would still be in the frame and I knew 'Golden Boy' would be able to talk his way out of the limelight, leaving me firmly stood alone to take the blame.

This line of thought spurred me to find a mathematical answer to my problem. What if I began to taint their food with one type of poison, which on its own wouldn't be deadly, and then at the end countering it with a second poison, which, when mixed with the first, had grave consequences? One plus one equals two dead parents; simple mathematics!

Acrenatol is a toxin used by agricultural specialists to kill certain types of weeds. It is commercially used and as such is widely available if you know where to look. When fed to humans, in small quantities, it slowly starts to destroy the cells of major organs, in a similar way to plaque destroying tooth enamel. Over a couple of weeks, at the right dosage, those ingesting acrenatol will start to feel ill, like having a heavy cold. They will not realise there organs are decaying.

Dibrenocil is used by doctors to help fight cancerous cells in patients. It works by radiating decaying cells. Again, it is in full commercial use across the UK and is readily available if you know where to look.

In reality, so long as the two toxins were purchased through different sites, there was no reason for anyone to connect the dots, not until it was too late. Even if an experienced pathologist undertook a detailed and thorough post mortem procedure on both parents, all he would find would be decayed organs and inevitably would assume that both my parents had developed aggressive forms of cancer in their final weeks alive.

My plan was simple; I would slowly start to dose their food with the acrenatol for a fortnight and would deliver the dibrenocil as the final sucker punch. That brought me onto finding a suitable fall guy to take the flack, in the event that the police did become suspicious of my parents' untimely demise. If I'm honest, it didn't take me long to decide that 'Golden Boy' would be the perfect scapegoat. In fact, I had 'Golden Boy' in mind from the first moment I had contemplated killing them. For me, there was a poetic justice to it all.

***

Jameson dropped the letter and jotted down 'brother framed' on his note paper, before turning to his computer and looking up the two toxins the killer had described. The search for acrenatol was rapid. Various websites were listed as sources for the purchase of the item, and whilst there was the odd, chemical company listed, most of the sites sold farm equipment. Jameson viewed a couple of the sites and found one that had put together a small animation showing the effects of the toxin. The image was of a brown field, with an array of green plants, jutting from the mud. The image then displayed a man in dungarees and boots spraying the plants with the acrenatol. The green plants were seen to wither and turn brown before disappearing from the screen, leaving waves of corn, blowing gently in the breeze. The animation was crude and looked like it had been targeted at children, but it was effective; Jameson certainly felt he had learned how the poison worked. If the killer had indeed used this on his victims, they undoubtedly would have become quite ill.

His search for the dibrenocil was not as easy. He eventually found a bio-chemical company that was selling the substance under the name 'Renocil' and described it as the latest wonder drug in fighting cancer. This site didn't have a video, but gave a detailed and complex explanation of the effects of the drug. Jameson didn't understand half the words that were used but it did seem to concur with what the writer had claimed. Jameson swallowed hard again. The killer had clearly done his homework and the terrifying consequences of his actions shocked Jameson to the core.

157

Jameson removed a soiled handkerchief from his trouser pocket and dabbed at his moist brow. He found the telephone number for the bio-chemical company and dialled it. After half a dozen rings, an answerphone machine cut in and advised that business hours were nine a.m. till six p.m. Monday to Friday. Jameson glanced at the clock and saw that it was well after six. This line of enquiry would have to wait until morning. He would phone the company back in the morning and demand copies of their recent sales activity, to see if any new customers had made a purchase of the drug. If he carried out a similar call with the agricultural companies, he might be able to find a common name.

Jameson felt a jolt of excitement as he felt the web narrow around the killer. With renewed enthusiasm, he returned to the pages.

10

Devising a plan to frame somebody else for murder takes careful precision and can take weeks to achieve the goal. You have to be careful not to let the incumbent become aware of what you are up to. Too much sudden attention will make him or her suspicious of your new found interest in them. The problem is: you do need to get close to them, particularly if you plan to leave clues as to their guilt, in their property.

As I was already performing my internet-based research at 'Golden Boy's' flat, it seemed only fitting that I should order my potions from the same place. Paying for the goods was not quite so straight forward, as if I used my own credit card, it would be traced back to me. That meant laying my hands on 'Golden Boy's' credit card. I knew I couldn't ask to borrow the card from him, and if I waited until he was next due to visit the folks, I could be waiting several weeks before I could complete the purchases.

Despite nerves, I utilised the spare key for 'Golden Boy's' flat and let myself in during the early hours of one morning. I was taking a chance that he would actually be at home, when I arrived and even more so that he would be asleep. Luckily, my gamble paid off and the moment I opened the door, I could hear his heavy snoring emanating from the small bedroom at the far side of the flat. I had no idea where he stored his wallet and personal items during the night but I was pretty confident that he wasn't security-conscious enough to have a safe. It amused me to find he had left his wallet, mobile phone and house keys on a small, wooden coffee table, fewer than five feet away from the front door. Had I been an opportunistic thief, I could have poked a long wire through letter box and fish-hooked his keys from the table. If his car hadn't been such a piece of shit, I probably would have driven it off and abandoned it somewhere. But, I didn't want him to be aware that anybody had been near his flat, let alone that personal items may have been pilfered. I opened his wallet carefully, removed the card and quietly let myself out.

I returned the following afternoon, and was relieved to find him out. I logged on and bought my special ingredients. I also purchased a further item that I will tell you more about later. That night, to my surprise, he was around at our parents' house when I called in. I knew he was only there because he couldn't be bothered to cook and he knew that my parents wouldn't want to see him go hungry. To be honest, I was only too happy to make him an extra portion of supper as it gave me the opportunity to return the card when he was otherwise indisposed.

Then I had to wait; wait for the deliveries to arrive. It took three days. At any point, I could have changed my mind and decided not to go through with it. I could have sent the items back and requested a refund. I could have sat 'Golden Boy' down and explained my unhappiness, try to reason with him. I could have just accepted that this was my hand in life and put up with it. But I didn't.

The desire to proceed was too strong and the thought of what my life would be like if I continued with this course of action was all the motivation I needed.

The day before the items arrived, I was sat at work when Clare approached my desk in tears. I sat her down and asked what was wrong. She explained that she had been mugged on her way into work and was quite shaken. I put my arm around her and just listened as she explained what had happened and how she had felt. I went and spoke to the branch manager and told him what had happened and he told me to walk Clare home and make sure she was okay before I returned to the office. Clare was really appreciative of the support and offered me a cup of tea. We sat and chatted for over an hour on her sofa until I had to make my excuses and return to the office. As I left, she leaned in and kissed me. She told me she had always quite liked me and wanted to get to know me better. I said I liked her too and agreed to return that evening for dinner. I couldn't keep the grin from my face as I marched confidently back to work. It was a real struggle to keep myself from jumping up and punching the air as I went along. It really did feel like everything was going my way, and once I was rid of the ogres, my life would be so much better.

I made the parents a quick meal and told them I had to return to work afterwards, to take care of an on-going customer complaint. They made noises about me abandoning them and how 'Golden Boy' wouldn't leave them if he were there, but I allowed the comments to wash over me, knowing that their time was imminent now. I drove straight round to Clare's flat, where she had fixed a delicious Italian pasta dish. We talked for hours and hours. It was midnight before I knew it, and as I got up to leave, she kissed me again and pulled me into her bedroom. I wasn't a virgin, but my experiences with women were limited. Clare showed me things that blew my mind. It was a Friday night and when I went around to 'Golden Boy's' apartment the next morning, I saw that the postman had left a note in the letter box saying that there were three items for collection at the local sorting office. I took the note and headed straight there.

***

Every killer makes a mistake, Jameson thought to himself. They all think they have planned the perfect murder that will see them escape punishment, but they all slip up. This killer had been careful not to look at the toxins from his own computer and had gone to great lengths to steal the brother's credit card so that the payment wouldn't be under his own name. He hadn't thought that collecting the items from a sorting office might be his undoing.

There were several Royal Mail sorting offices in and around Southampton, but the largest was near the Northam bridge, less than a ten minute drive from where he was currently sat. They were bound to have CCTV cameras set up to monitor the passing clientele who entered the office. There was every chance that they may have captured an image of the killer collecting the parcels. It was the first real breakthrough in the case and Jameson was about to get up and head for his car when he stopped and returned to his seat.

Was it too early, he thought. The killer claimed to have collected the toxins on a Saturday but which Saturday? And what if the killer was lying and had collected them on a week day? He would spend hours trawling through Saturday CCTV footage only to find that the killer didn't appear. He didn't have hours right now. Besides, even if he did capture the face of the killer, what would he do with it? If the killer didn't have a criminal record, there would be no image of his face on file. The best

Jameson would be able to do was forward the image to the media and hope that an astute member of the public identified the face.

It was a good line of enquiry but ultimately a long-winded one. He needed something faster, something that would identify the killer now. Something that would give him a chance of finding the victims before it was too late. There was only one choice: he had to read on.

11

I returned home and examined the packages carefully. There were no instructions included with the vials of transparent liquid but I had already calculated how much of each I would need, to use to achieve my goals, before I had ordered them. I hid the dibrenocil in my sock drawer and carefully wrapped the acrenatol in some tissue paper and placed it in my pocket. The internet had told me that the liquids were flavourless but I decided, to be safe, I would use the acrenatol in a strong-flavoured dish just to be certain that my parents wouldn't notice it that evening.

I made them a beef and ale pie with a thin short-crust pastry. I knew father had always liked pies and mother would be happy with anything so long as a handful of green vegetables were served with it. I sat with them and nervously drank a cup of tea while they ate and droned on about how 'Golden Boy' was going to take them out for lunch the next day at their favourite fish restaurant. I ignored most of what she said, until she placed her knife and fork down on her empty plate and I asked her what she had thought of the meal.

'Too salty,' was her only comment, followed quickly by father's, 'Pastry was a bit wet still.' I had expected their usual criticism but was delighted they hadn't noticed the acrenatol. I left them watching Casualty on the television and headed around to Clare's house.

Over the next ten days I casually dosed their food with the acrenatol with them none the wiser. Inadvertently, I managed to damage 'Golden Boy's' health when he popped round for a couple of free meals. Clare and I grew closer and I found myself spending more and more time with her. On day ten, she told me her parents had agreed for her to fly out to Spain and stay at their holiday villa near Malaga. She asked if I would come with her. I was delighted and worried in equal measure. On the one hand, it was thrilling to be asked to go away on a naughty weekend with a lady that I desired so much. On the other hand, it clashed with my plan to deliver the dibrenocil instalment. I needed to think of a way that I could get the toxin into their diets without raising suspicion.

I knew that I could tell 'Golden Boy' I would be away for the weekend and that it would be his responsibility to look after the folks. He would make excuses about work and refuse to go and that would leave them berating me for putting a girlfriend ahead of family, but I knew if I managed to deposit the chemical, these would be the last complaints I ever heard.

The answer made itself apparent when Clare suggested making some chocolate truffles for her parents by way of saying 'thank you' for letting us stay in the villa. She knew that I enjoyed cookery and wanted my help to prepare the ingredients. I told her I would like to make some for my parents as well, which she accepted as a reasonable suggestion, as I had not told her of the misery they had inflicted on me. If anything, she saw me as the dutiful son, visiting them every night after work to cook their meals. I don't think she would understand my decisions, so I have no intention of telling her what I have done, despite the pride I have for my actions.

We made a dozen truffles, which we placed in two separate boxes; gold for her parents and bronze for mine. While Clare was busy in another room looking for ribbon, I splashed the dibrenocil on the truffles in the bronze box. It was hard to keep the grin off my face for the rest of the day.

Clare's parents lived down in Devon, so we arranged for their box to be sent Special Delivery so we knew they would receive them. I told Clare I would hand-deliver my box but secretly sent them by special delivery as well, with a note I forged from 'Golden Boy' claiming credit for the chocolates. I knew, if he were questioned by them, he would claim responsibility anyway. Clare booked flights for us both from Southampton airport to Malaga that left the next day.

***

Jameson glanced down at the telephone. The hospital had still not called him back. His last conversation had been a bit non-descript. He hadn't known how the killer had planned to kill his parents, but now he did. He reached out and picked up the handset and dialled the internal number once again.

'Emergency department,' crooned a camp and cheerful voice.

'Hi, it's detective Jameson, calling from Central H.Q. I need to speak with someone in admissions.'

'Certainly detective, I'm Josh and I'm on the desk tonight. What can I do for you?'

'I'm investigating a possible double homicide. Can you check the records to see if you have had any patients admitted, with an aggressive form of cancer?'

'Can you give me any other details? Age, sex, that kind of thing?'

'They would be over fifty and I would expect one man and one woman.'

'Okay, detective, hold the line and I'll have a look for you.'

The familiar, unknown piece of classical music started in the ear piece. Jameson placed the handset on his desk and turned the telephone's speaker on. The music filled the room as he stood up and started to pace around the office. A knot was growing in his stomach and he thought moving might ease it. It didn't.

'Right, detective,' hummed the camp voice, as the nurse returned to the line. 'We've had one patient admitted this evening with cancer. He is in his early sixties and was found by neighbours, collapsed outside his home in Bitterne…'

'What's his name?' shouted Jameson, interrupting him.

'Mr Ishaq.'

'Ishaq? He's not white then?'

'Detective, don't be so judgemental!' admonished the admissions clerk.

'Is he white or not?' shouted Jameson into the speaker.

'Mr Ishaq originates from Pakistan. What does that have to do with anything?'

'Nothing, nothing,' replied Jameson, thinking through the evening's events. 'Can you tell Mr Ishaq I'll be down to talk with him soon?'

'What's this all about, detective? Mr Ishaq is the victim of cancer, not a murderer.'

'Never you mind,' he replied, pressing the disconnect button.

Jameson continued to pace. He had assumed that the killer was British and had drawn up an image in his mind of what he looked like. At no point had he even considered that the killer might be from Pakistan. Not that it mattered in the long run; a killer is still a killer, regardless of skin colour.

He finally had a name and he also had a very real list to compare it to. Picking up the telephone he dialled a contact he had used before at Southampton airport.

'Murray, it's Orville Jameson, how's things good buddy?' he began as warmly as he could.

'Orville,' replied Murray who was head of security at the city's international airport. 'It seems like forever since we spoke. I am well, how are you?'

'I'm good Murray and I wish this was a social call, but I need some help with something. Can you spare me five minutes?'

'For an old school buddy, like you, I can. What do you need?'

'That's great, Murray, I appreciate it. I need the passenger lists for all flights to Malaga for the last week.'

'Jesus, Orville, do you realise how long that will take? Can you not give me a more precise date or time?'

'Why? How many flights are there?'

'There are two flights a day from here to Malaga, one around breakfast and the other just after lunch. With an average of eighty passengers per flight that's...nearly twelve hundred names.'

Jameson paused to consider his options. The killer had claimed to have travelled on a Wednesday. Could it be that it had been yesterday?

'Okay, Murray, send me over the lists for Wednesday's flights first but also start preparing the lists for today and last Wednesday, will you?'

'Sure, Orville. Hey, what's this all about? Not a terrorist attack is it?'

'Oh no, my friend, nothing that drastic. I'm hunting a killer. When can you get me those lists?'

'I'll start faxing them over in the next five minutes if you like?'

'Perfect, Murray. I owe you a pint, my friend.'

'Yes you do,' chortled Murray as he disconnected the line.

'I've got you, you son of a bitch, Jameson thought to himself. Once the list was faxed across, he would look for the name 'Ishaq' and find his killer. To pass the time, he decided to continue with his reading.

12

That left me with one last but vital action to take, and that's where you come in, Detective Jameson. I couldn't ably continue with my life without sharing the truth of what I have done with somebody. It is still early days with Clare, but I am hopeful that love could blossom from those few short moments we have had together so far; we enjoy each other's company and the sex is fantastic! I don't think it is too presumptive to suggest that we may marry one day; after all, neither of us is getting any younger. You can see my predicament; how could I tell Clare? It would surely be the end of our romance, and I am not prepared to do that.

Why tell anyone, you may be asking? My conscience would not sit idly by while I build a new life, knowing the murderous act that I committed on the people who gave me life's breath. I have never been religious so it isn't out of fear of answering to some higher authority. No, it is purely the guilt I would feel keeping such a secret buried. In my experience, keeping secret truths buried does not make for a happy life. You've heard my story and I'm sure you are thinking that I should have spoken up for myself at some point; challenged my parents over their inherent behaviour towards me. As it is, I didn't and now look at the outcome: they will soon be dead and won't understand why the reaper has come calling so soon.

But you will know Detective Jameson and I can take solace from that. I suppose by writing down my actions in this letter format, I am expunging myself from blame. If I have told a policeman what I have done and he takes no action against me, then it is as if forgiveness has been bestowed upon me and I will be able to move on, knowing that justice has finally been served.

I mentioned at the start of my letter that you wouldn't catch me and I suppose it is prevalent to explain why at this juncture. Let's consider the facts of the situation. You know I had a disillusioned childhood and that I grew up in Southampton. You know I had a brother, 'Golden Boy' who was everything my parents wanted him to be. You know that 'Golden Boy' attended Bristol University, before flunking out and finding an investigative job. You know I wanted to go to University, but I wasn't allowed to because of 'Golden Boy's flawed experience of student-life. You know that my father has been impaired since suffering a stroke many years ago. Does any of this not sound familiar to you, Detective Jameson?

Or should I refer to you as 'Golden Boy' or perhaps 'brother' would really hammer the nail home.

***

Jameson sat rock still as the papers dropped from his suddenly-numb fingers. His rib cage wasn't moving and the only clear sign that he was alive were his occasionally-blinking eye lids. He was staring at nothing and it was as if his whole body had shut down while his brain worked double-time to process everything he had just read.

His mouth involuntarily opened as the images in his memory darted past his mind's eye. The image of the killer that he had been picturing since the moment he had started reading the letter turned to face him and he saw that it was his brother's face. Passages from the letter rang out in his ears but suddenly it was his brother's unmistakeable voice saying them.

Jameson remained sat motionless for the best part of five minutes and his attention only returned to the room when he heard the fax machine bleeping in the corner of the room. Without a second's thought, his body rose from its chair and walked over to the machine, lifting the paper that had spewed from it. It was like he was watching his life story playing out on screen. He was aware that his body was moving but he wasn't in control of it. He returned to the chair and sat down before his eyes danced over the list of names on the manifest. He desperately wanted to see the name 'Ishaq' spring up from the page but of the one hundred and fifty or so names, only one stood out: Jameson, Simon.

The passenger had flown out just after seven yesterday morning, seated next to passenger 'Adams, Clare'. He wanted to rip the page to pieces but he was paralysed with fear. Feeling a tear drifting down his cheek, he wiped it away and decided there was only one thing he could do. He had to finish the letter.

13

I can imagine your eyes widening as you read on, the puzzle pieces slotting together in the jigsaw in your mind. You feel like you want to start the letter again and to re-read it, knowing that it has been sent by your own flesh and blood, but at the same time you can't stop reading; you need to know if I am telling the truth, if the parents you have suckled from for so many years are now at death's door.

Did you know the name 'Orville' means 'Gold Town'? I learnt that years ago. Mother told me she named you Orville because you were her golden child. I suppose that's why I started to refer to you as 'Golden Boy' behind your back.

According to the internet, the box of truffles was delivered to the matriarchal home at ten a.m. this morning. Mother will have told father that they should wait before opening them, so that they can share the truffles with you. They won't have even considered letting me have one. Father will have told her that they could have just one and she will have agreed, although they probably will have eaten at least two each, if not all six.

Within an hour of ingesting the dibrenocil they will have started to suffer stomach cramps and acid reflux. If mother has any sense, she will have reached for an antacid tablet, assuming heartburn is on its way. She would be right, in one respect. The radiating effect of dibrenocil will have attacked the blood system first, where the majority of the body's cells can be found. Travelling in the blood, will send it first to the heart. A heart that has been degraded by the effects of acrenatol will beat faster as it tries to maintain performance despite the decay it is feeling. This will send the now toxic blood to each of the other decaying organs in turn and will wipe out the decay and indirectly shut down those organs.

Within two hours of ingesting the tainted-truffles, mother and father will be laid out in their chairs, dead.

What time is it Detective Jameson?

Tick-tock, tick-tock.

Is it already too late?

***

Jameson's eyes diverted from the letter and instinctively glanced up at the clock on the wall. It was already after seven p.m. If the letter was true, if his brother really had poisoned their parents, they would be dead. It was like a bad dream. No, it was worse than that; it was like the worst nightmare he could ever have imagined.

The whole time he had been sat questioning the reality of what he was reading, he hadn't even imagined that he could know the killer, let alone be related to him. The picture the killer had painted had been one of exclusion, but he had never viewed Simon in that way. It was true that he had allowed his younger brother to take care of their parents when they had started to deteriorate but that was more fool him for not standing up for himself. Jameson had always viewed Simon as a weakling, and their interests had been so different when they had been children that he had not been prepared to spend any quality time with him. In fairness, he hadn't realised how much of a poor sibling he had been, but that still didn't give Simon a reason to kill.

The more Jameson considered his relationship with his brother, the angrier he became. So what if Simon had to care for their parents, he thought, he had never had much by way of prospects to begin with; it's not like he would have been a famous scientist or anything!

HARD TARGETS

Jameson looked at the phone on his desk. He knew he should phone an ambulance for his parents; get somebody there in case they hadn't eaten the truffles yet. There was a chance that they were still alive and it was his responsibility to try to save them. Yet he didn't move. He didn't reach out and call for an ambulance. Simon was right; they would have eaten the truffles by now and it was probably already too late.

The only thing he could do was to catch his brother and bring him to justice. He snatched up the letter with renewed determination.

14

As you continue to read this, you may be wondering where I am. Well, I am at Clare's parents' villa in Spain. I've been here for the last day and a bit. I am thinking about asking Clare to marry me. Undoubtedly there will be some inheritance on its way to me soon enough. They probably left everything to you in their will, but given that you will be soon found guilty of their murder, I am quietly confident that a claim by me for all of their assets will be welcomed by the court. It seems that murdering your parents negates the murderer's claims under testacy-rules.

Remember, both poisons were purchased over the internet from your computer, using your credit card and were delivered to your address. The box of truffles was sent special delivery, including a note to our parents saying the truffles were from you. I'm sure mother has already put the label to one side to treasure her 'Golden Boy's' gesture. As you are the only one of us named in the will, your motive to carry out the deed is far greater than mine, I am sure you would agree?

***

It felt like a cold knife had been plunged into his side, and Jameson felt temporarily winded. Once he had caught his breath, the true breadth of the situation dawned on him; he was the fall guy in the killer's plan. When the investigation into the murder commenced, it would be his name that was found on the list of dibrenocil and acrenatol purchasers. It was his IP address that would be seen as making the purchase. It would be his address that the item were delivered to. It was his name that would be on the gift card on the truffles. Everything pointed at him.

And what would happen when the events of today were examined. Would the hospital staff remember the conversations with the detective who kept pestering them for details of a murdered couple who met a suspicious end? Would the sergeant in the Control Centre remember the suspicious detective enquiring updates on double homicide cases?

Were his parents still alive? It was impossible to be sure. Any move he made now could be misconstrued if the worst truly had befallen them. If he phoned home, the C.P.S. would argue he was checking that the deed was done. If he drove to their house now, a neighbour might spot him and later put two and two together.

Jameson felt his bowels give way. There was no way out, he could tell. He had been stitched up good and proper by the one man he underestimated. He thought about running away, but he didn't have much by way of savings, and he wouldn't last long. But what was the alternative? Prison? Jameson wasn't naïve enough to think time behind bars for a former policeman would be easy; if anything it would be twice as hard.

There had to be a way out of this mess, he rationalised. He was a pretty smart guy; all he had to do was prove that he was set up. The CCTV footage at the sorting office might help, but there was no guarantee it would reveal Simon's face.

Jameson fished the soiled handkerchief from his pocket and wiped the puddle of sweat from his forehead. As he stared down at the letter, it dawned on him: the letter. So long as he held onto the letter, he had the proof he needed. How could Simon have been so careless?

15

Tick-tock, tick-tock.

What are you going to do, brother?

Dare you risk, rushing to the property to see if my plan has gone awry and that they haven't yet eaten the truffles? What if you're wrong? What if uniformed police arrive, while you're stood there, staring at their lifeless bodies? How are you going to be able to explain what happened?

Wait a minute. You have my letter, right? That's it! You have the real murderer's written confession. That is sure to get you out of trouble.

Phew!

But wait.

What if the letter was written using a thymolpthalein-based ink? Thymolphthalein, which is normally colourless, turns blue in solution with the base. As the base reacts with carbon dioxide, the pH drops below 10.5 and the colour disappears. Do you remember, I told you I ordered a third chemical on your credit card? Why not turn back to the first page of my letter?

***

Instinctively, Jameson flipped back to the first page of the letter. It was blank, as were the second and third pages. The fourth page still had writing but it was clear the colour was fading already. Jameson eyes blinked as he watched his life disappearing before his eyes. He desperately held a couple of the blank pages up to the light, hoping that a watermark or imprint of some kind remained, but there was nothing. He began to hyperventilate as he read the remainder of the letter and imagined what the future would bring.

16

Are you surprised to see that you are now holding blank pieces of paper? Oh dear. There goes your alibi.

I hear, prisons aren't friendly places for former serving police officers, so I would recommend you tread carefully.

I can't say that knowing you has brought me anything but displeasure, brother. I won't pretend that I will miss you or our parents. At least you now understand why I have acted as I have and that everything that you have coming to you is full retribution for the misery that I have suffered over the years. My new life is just about to begin and I make this promise to you now: I will live it to the full!

I don't expect to hear from you again, other than through our appointed legal representatives.

Regards,

A dutiful son.

THE COMMUTER
Liam Saville

Journal Entry 153 – Monday, July 15

So here I am, seated in the back row of carriage three on the 6:45am all stations to the city. The trip should take about an hour, I know that; it hasn't changed for the last six weeks, or is it seven? No, I think it's six. Anyway, it's the same journey I've been making every weekday since moving from my apartment in the city to a townhouse in the suburbs. In hindsight, it probably wasn't the best move, but hey, it's really too late to do anything about it now. Although, to be fair, I'm not sure it's the length of the trip that's the problem—more the fact that I need to get up so early—I am, after all, not a morning person.

Looking around, it seems that all the usual suspects are present: At the front of the carriage, the annoying group of giggling schoolgirls has spread themselves out as though the train is their private living room. No doubt on their way to an expensive private school on the north shore, yet all too busy texting each another or watching YouTube clips to even talk. Dumb, rich bitches. Scattered around and respectfully evenly spaced, so as not to be closer to anybody else than absolutely necessary, is a motley collection of blue-collar types—most dosing off in their seats, trying to cram in a little more shut-eye before starting their day, while others sit reading the Telegraph, back page first—sports really are the new religion. Mixed among them are the suits, people who look like me, heading into the office. Some stare blankly at the front wall, others gaze out the windows as the world rushes by, and a few who are so fixated on their laptops or tablets, they are lost in their own world. On the left, third row from the front, is the librarian; she actually said 'hello' last week, quite a strange woman, really. You know the type: middle-aged with frizzy hair and glasses so thick they could be made from the bottom of Coca-Cola bottles. I see she's finished the latest Dan Brown thriller and has moved on to something by Stephen Leather—at least she's not the pretentious type who only reads the classics.

 There are still plenty of empty seats; that's normal, but after a few stops, that will change. By the time we get halfway there it will be standing room only: a hundred plus people, jammed together like sardines in a mobile tin can; fucking ridiculous when you think about it.

Two stops down, twelve more to go—add a few more suits and two construction workers, both decked out in fluro-orange long sleeve tops.

Hey, hang on, what's this? Who are you, and why did you just sit down next to me? There are still plenty of empty seats; don't you know the rules about spacing?

Ah, I see, so you're a people watcher, too. You like to sit and see what is going on, watching the dynamics of the carriage. I can understand that; I think I'm the same, but must say, I'm really not a fan of you reading over my shoulder like that. Yes,

HARD TARGETS

I can see you, watching my screen as I type... It really is fucking annoying.

Another stop down, two more suits and somebody's grandma. Still reading, I see. Scanning what I type out of the corner of your eyes, checking back when you don't think I'm looking — your tactics don't fool me. OK. If you're going to read along, you might as well know what it is that you're reading; you see, I'm a writer. I write stories—novels, in fact—usually inspired by true crime. I use this time on the train to write my journal, and to record my thoughts, but just recently I've also started using it to draft my work. My current book, or work in progress, as it's known in the business, concerns a serial killer, so be aware, if you are going to keep reading along, it is quite violent. Now, I won't bore you with the background, let's get straight to it; with the killer hot on-the-heels of his fourth victim...

Terrified and confused, the killer's latest victim stumbled in the dark.
Out of breath, she kept moving, not daring to stop and assess herself despite the blood from the gaping wound on her head that dripped down her brow and into her eyes, blurring her vision. The deep scratches on her arms and legs, inflicted by the thorny undergrowth she'd run through to get away, barely registered. So desperate to escape was she that her mind had blanked out all feeling. The pain would come later, if she survived.
Behind her, she could hear him, crashing through the bush as he made his way down the hill, calmly following her as she moved further from her house, deeper into the trees, and further from any chance of help.
How had this happened, who was he, and why had he attacked her?

She'd been at home alone, preparing her evening meal, when all the power in the house had tripped. The lights had gone out, and it had only been the soft flicker of the flame on her gas stove that kept the room from plunging into total darkness. It was an old house, fuses blew all the time, but why did they always wait until her husband was away on business?

Across the room, in the bottom drawer, she'd found a small flashlight and flicked it on, then turned back to the stove and switched off the gas. Satisfied that her dinner wasn't going to burn, she walked over to the front window. There, she pulled back the blinds and looked at her neighbour's house. Their lights were on, as were the dim street lights, so a blown fuse it was, not a blackout.

Annoyed that she'd have to fix it, she slipped on her shoes, wrapped herself in a light jacket, and stepped out onto the front veranda. Her small torch in one hand, she walked quickly to the side of the building, lifted up the lid on the meter box, and switched off the mains power. Forgetting to turn off the power before pulling the fusses out could be fatal, so she checked the switch again just to be sure. It had been a lesson that her husband had drummed into her when he'd shown her how to change a fuse. In fact, he'd gone on about it so much that it had given her nightmares about electrocuting herself. Confident she was safe, she pulled out the first fuse and checked the wire. No, that wasn't it. The second, no, not that one either, and then she reached for the third.

'Hang on, where's the third fuse?' She thought to herself. 'It couldn't just have fallen out, could it?'

She let go of the meter box lid and was startled when it swung down and shut with a bang. Ignoring a growing sense of unease, she bent over and quickly scoured the ground—the missing fuse had to be there somewhere.

Hunched over, concentrating on her search, she didn't hear the killer approach, and it was only the unexpected appearance of his black boots in her peripheral vision that saved her. She reeled back and turned towards him just as he swung the metal pipe at her skull.

His vicious attack still connected, only more as a glancing strike than the intended knock-out blow he'd aimed at the back of her head.

Knocked to the ground, she screamed.

Realising that there was no time to wait for help, and not wanting to be hit again, she scrambled to her feet. Catching her attacker by surprise, with all her strength she pushed passed him and ran along the driveway. Reaching the street, she didn't stop, but ran into the thick bush on the other side leading down the valley and away from her house.

Seeing his victim fight back and run off surprised the killer. He was not prepared for an escape. Too much time and energy had gone into planning this night to simply let her go.

It had taken him almost two weeks to carefully, and methodically, follow her home from her office. On the first few days, he'd only stalked her to the train station. After her daily pattern was established, he'd turned to waiting on the train. She hadn't even noticed him as he sat, watching her every move until she got off, just a half dozen streets from her house. On the next day, he'd taken the train before her, waiting at the end of her trip, out of sight down the road. Once she'd left the station, he'd shadowed her again, just part of the way home. The key, he knew, was to remain hidden.

The following week, he'd been waiting again, biding his time on a park bench, across the road for where he'd left her last. Still, she hadn't seen him; she had no idea what he had planned, as finally he tracked her all the way home.

That had been three weeks ago. Since then, he had watched her house, first from the rental car he'd parked across the street, then closer through her windows. Her kitchen window was the best, concealed as it was from the street and the neighbour's house by a fence and some large bushes. She didn't live alone, but that just added to the challenge, the result would be the same.

A week ago, he'd visited her house, breaking in while both she and her husband were out at work. Posing as a contractor, he'd walked confidently around to the back yard where he'd slipped on some gloves and used a garden bench to reach a rear window. There hadn't even been a flyscreen, let alone a good lock on the old double-hung, timber-framed window, and it slid open with nothing more than a push. Once inside, he made a point of shutting the window; after all, there was no reason to let her know he'd been inside.

Walking through her house touching her things, all the while knowing that she'd never know he'd been there, was empowering. He didn't take anything—he wasn't a thief, nor had he felt the urge to sniff her knickers or jack-off on her bed as he knew some other sick fucks would do. These things didn't interest him; they never had. He just enjoyed the kill. It was during this visit that he'd learnt of her husband's trip. The plane ticket sat on the bench, and the dates confirmed with the calendar they had stuck on their fridge. She'd be alone for three nights, but he'd be ready on the first.

He liked to surprise his victims, hit them hard and fast, and take control before they had time to react. He'd used the same ruse three times before, turning off the power or the water at the mains, waiting for his victim to come out to investigate. It had worked every time—or at least it had until this bitch had seen him at the last second. He'd be more careful next time, but right now, the most important thing was to find her and finish the job.

He had no idea why she'd chosen to run downhill through thick scrub. She'd have been far better off heading for her neighbour's house; there, at least, she might have found refuge, a way to escape, but now it was only a matter of time. Despite the fact she'd moved, he'd still hit her hard, the amount of blood on the ground glistening in her torchlight told him that. She was never going to get far. Running across the road behind her, he used her discarded torch to navigate the hill. Down below, he could hear her stumbling in the dark; he was getting closer.

When the noise of breaking branches finally stopped, he knew he had her.

"You know you won't get away," he said flatly into the darkness. "I know where you are. It's only a matter of time."

Movement again, closer now.

He swung the beam of light around, and there, curled in a ball behind a large tree, was the woman. Bloodied and exhausted, he had her now. She saw him approach, reached for a large branch that was lying on the ground, and then pulled herself to her feet. As he stepped closer, she swung the branch wildly like a baseball bat, screaming again.

He leaned back slightly and let the branch go sailing by, then stepped in and hit her in the arm with a powerful strike from his metal pipe, shattering the bone instantly. The branch dropped; her last line of defence gone.

Not waiting for her to try something else, he swung the pipe again, connecting with the side of her head. Her skull cracked like an egg and collapsed under the pressure of the blow, but he wasn't done yet. He waited and watched her fall to the ground, and then stepped forward, and hit her again and again, over and over, until all that was left of her head was a bloodied pulp.

Satisfied, the killer took a deep breath and smiled, then calmly made his way back up the hill. In the victim's driveway, he collected the bag that he'd left earlier, peeled off his overalls, boots, and balaclava, then stuffed them all, along with the pipe, into his bag before removing his leather gloves—leaving on just the thin latex pair to conceal his prints. After stuffing those too into the bag, he zipped it shut.

DEATH TOLL 2

The killer looked around. Nobody had even noticed he was there. If any of the neighbours had heard her screams, they certainly hadn't done anything about it.

Sorry, I'm going to have to leave it there. I know you've been reading along as I've been typing, I have been watching, but I really do have to go. You see, it's my stop is next.
Oh, just one more thing. Would you like to know what it was that drew the killer to this particular victim? I guess it is only fair to tell you. Just five weeks ago, she sat here, on this very train, right where you are now, next to me, reading from my screen. You have a nice day now. Be sure think of me the next time your power goes out.

182

BANGKOK SHUFFLE
Harlan Wolff

It was the tail end of my Bangkok 'young and wild' decade and I, Carl Engel very late of London, had already been describing myself as a private detective for about a year. I'd picked up some work and my lean and hungry look was gradually changing into something more professional. The vodka vice had passed unnoticed into a habit, thanks to my new ability to keep up with my bar bills. So far, the work had been nothing to sing and dance about, the odd insurance caper, the occasional wandering son or daughter job. My roof in Bangkok was comfortable for the first time and came with hot and cold running women. I wasn't going anywhere, not without a fight anyway.

One morning I got a call from an unfamiliar English voice, 'Sarf London' and, by the sound of it, something of an aging 'spiv' who had left his best years behind him. It was one of those hushed 'I don't want to speak on the phone' conversations that private detectives get from time to time. He asked me to meet him at his office on Soi Nana as soon as possible. Soi Nana was

183

another of Bangkok's red light districts so I didn't need to ask for directions.

He was a large bull of a man in his late fifties and I immediately knew that I didn't like him. The spider's webs of red veins on his nose and cheeks were well established, so his reasons for being a minute's walk from the girlie bars did not require great deductive powers. He was dressed in the suit and tie uniform of his past life but unfortunately for him the rattling inefficient air conditioner was not blowing English weather. His office was sparse and behind the desk was a large framed picture of him, as a younger man, posing beside a Rolls Royce in front of a large detached house. The message he was pushing was that he had once been a success. I read him immediately as a small time London crook that had come to Bangkok to escape some trouble or other back home, possibly the police or an expensive divorce.

I played it cool as the sweat ran down my back, noted the pot of coffee on a cabinet and asked for a cup so he wouldn't feel I was overly eager to hear what he wouldn't tell me on the phone. He brought me a coffee and then we sat in silence. I sipped the much needed coffee, he remained silent. I eventually tried to break the ice by saying "Interesting car."

"It's a beauty. I had her from new. Special limited edition, you can tell by the colour." He proceeded to tell me the Rolls Royce's entire maintenance history and how he was planning to have one in Thailand one day. When he'd finished and I'd finished my coffee we sat in silence again. It was getting a little ridiculous.

"Tell me what it is that you would like my help with." I told him, reluctantly being first to break the silence again.

"I can't tell you, it's a secret," he said sweating heavily behind the desk.

Again silence. Was this a joke? Had my friends put him up to it? I didn't think it was funny at all, everybody knew that it was best to leave me alone until lunchtime. Vodka was a cruel mistress. Everybody knew that.

"This isn't going to work," I told him beginning to assume the whole thing was a complete waste of my time. I looked at him. He looked at me. Nothing happened. I made to get up to leave.

"I have a suitcase full of money hidden at my house and nobody can ever know it's there."

"That's wonderful for you, but what has it got to do with me? Is it stolen or something?"

"Of course not! Why would you think that?" He blurted with a hurt look on his face, shocked that I would think he could possibly be involved in something not totally above board.

"I can't help you if you don't tell me the problem."

"I need you to find two men. I paid for their hotel so I have their names but cannot guarantee the names I have are the same ones on their passports."

I frowned. I hoped this wasn't one of those sordid cases. The image of the Londoner naked with two other men was something I could live without. "Could you begin by describing them to me?"

He looked down in embarrassment as he spoke. Like he was searching for something he had dropped on the floor. "They said they were from Liberia. They are looked down on because of their skin colour, which is why they needed my help with their business dealings in Thailand. They even asked me to arrange their hotel rooms and say they were from New York, for fear of not being treated fairly if the hotel knew where they were really from. They are also very secretive you see, and they would be very angry if they knew I was talking to you. They are both good men but I must tell you that they are also dangerous."

"In what way dangerous?" I asked him.

"They are the agents of a famous warlord in Africa who cannot travel to Thailand so insists that everything is done through them. I really don't think I should be talking to you."

"I think you should. Tell me more." I was glad it wasn't sexual.

"The thing is they have done nothing wrong. The suitcase of money was delivered to me as promised, and the only hiccup is that the delivery from the American Embassy has been delayed through no fault of theirs. Their contact got cold feet and refused to bring them the goods even though we had paid for them. Then last week they just disappeared. I hope nothing has happened to them."

"What was this delivery from the American Embassy?"

He sighed heavily. "Alright, I'll let you in on a secret, but you must never tell anybody." He leaned forward conspiratorially. "The Yanks have had so many problems with payments to rebel groups falling into the wrong hands that they now have a 'foolproof' way of delivering funds. The Embassy in Bangkok has a secret liquid. They were paid one hundred and thirty thousand dollars to provide a bottle to me but the man tried to back out. This product is never supposed to pass into the public sector, you see."

"Oh dear," I did see and I realised what had happened, "so let me guess, you have a suitcase full of black paper that you have been told will turn into hundred dollar bills as soon as they are immersed in a very expensive and secret chemical that you have advanced one hundred and thirty thousand dollars for?"

"They are hundred dollar bills! I mean they will be as soon as I find the two Africans and they go to the Embassy and sort this out. It must be soon though, that was all the money I had."

I decided to be as gentle as possible in breaking the bad news to him. "I am sorry to tell you that you have been the victim of the 'Nigerian black money' scam."

"No I haven't!"

"Yes you have."

"No I haven't!"

"I'm afraid you have."

"You don't know what you're talking about!"

"Look, I didn't come here for an argument."

He waved his hand and gloatingly said. "You are wrong. I have seen it with my own eyes."

"Look, here's how it works; liquid iodine is set alight to burn off the ethanol. A real hundred-dollar bill is soaked in the black residue and hung up to dry. There is only one real hundred-dollar bill in the game and that bill is in their pocket. This piece of black paper is the one they switch with the piece of black paper that you so carefully select randomly from all of the others in the suitcase. This switch is well rehearsed, like a magician. They then soak this bill in ascorbic acid and you see a black piece of paper magically turn into a hundred dollars. It is called the Nigerian black money scam."

"You are talking bollocks." He said aggressively.

"You don't have to believe me, pick up a newspaper or a tourist magazine, there is plenty about it in the weekly news."

"Do you think I'm an idiot?" I didn't reply and he continued. "Of course I've seen the stories in the newspapers. But this is different! This time it's real."

I looked around the sparse office with no secretary for a moment to allow him to regain his composure. I then asked him, "What exactly do you do in Bangkok?"

"I'm a financial advisor," he told me.

There was no answer to that. I looked around the room some more and now saw brochures on life insurance and pension plans and knew it to be true. "Look I'm sorry." I said and I meant it. "There's really nothing I can do if you don't trust me."

Having angered and alienated him I left him with his absolute belief that the only thing that stood between him and millions of dollars was a bottle of liquid that would one day be delivered by an anonymous American civil servant that had received payment in full and would therefore eventually honour his venal obligation. I had heard some stories in my time but this one had left me annoyed and shocked. How could anybody be so foolish?

187

It was only whilst drinking my second vodka in a bar 'round the corner that I had an epiphany. The picture on the wall of past affluence, the humble sparse office, its location in the red light district, and his advancing age enabled me to piece it all together. It was then that it struck me; the foundation of the big con is always the sucker's total desperation.

The man I had just met had once had money and wanted it again, he had allowed himself the luxury of imagining the life he would have if he could just get back financially to where he had once been. Having a little money in England will get you a nice car and a big house but that's usually where it stops. The suburbs of London often have wide lawns and narrow minds and can be a lonely place. The thought of Bangkok and all the pretty young country girls in tight tiny clothes following him around and doing anything just to get the chance to drink his Champagne or sit in his Rolls Royce and get whisked away for a late night visit to his mansion had clouded his logic.

Once he had taken on the dream of being able to afford the cost of being the big man in the naughty red light district of Soi Nana he had become hooked. The friendly black African wide boys that had accidentally crossed his path and entered his life knew how to play a man with such a delusion. He had then been willing to pay any price to hold on to the dream of an end to his loneliness, even denial, even bankruptcy. Nothing could come between him and his wonderful vision of the future, certainly not me, a streetwise private detective in blue jeans.

I learnt a lot that day. I saw the inside of the 'big con' and understood the ways of the lost, lonely men that are the victims of their own greed, and by instinct I could smell the total indifference of the well-schooled perpetrators that had used their craft to escape from the absolute poverty that was their birthright. I had chosen to be on the side of the rabbits but I didn't have anything against the hounds either. It's simply that when you're a private detective you have to pick a side. There and then I decided that the next time I encountered a scam, I'd stop it. As it happens I didn't have too long to wait…

"I shouldn't have done it. If my husband finds out I don't know what he'll do."

It was almost a week later and the lady crying on my shoulder was Birgit Muller. She and her husband owned my favourite Swiss restaurant in Bangkok. It was where I went for my comfort food. Bangkok was finally becoming more cosmopolitan and their restaurant was on a par with anything you might have found in Europe. I whiled away my evenings sitting in the corner with a good book. It was my shelter from the storm and I didn't want anything bad to happen to it. Willy and Birgit had been married forever and were both in their late fifties. They had three grown up children back in Zurich around the same age as me.

"Tell me what happened and I'll see what I can do." I told her sternly.

"These men that come to the restaurant, they always eat the steak and drink the good wine. Such nice men; well dressed, well mannered. They sell investments and said they had a special opportunity for their friends. They told me to put money in something called Trance Productions. They said it was a new technology for the music industry and the stock was going to go up very high. They guaranteed I would double my money in two weeks. Now they say something has gone wrong and I need to invest more money or lose what I have already put in. I don't understand what's happening. If Willy finds out he'll divorce me. You know how careful he is with money."

"I'm sure Willy will do no such thing. How much did you give these men?"

"One hundred thousand dollars, I can't keep it a secret from Willy for much longer. I wanted to surprise him." She started to cry again.

"You gave them a hundred thousand?" I was shocked. That was a fortune in the early nineties. You could buy a big house with

189

it. Maybe Willy would divorce her when he found out. Like she said; he was very careful with money.

"They promised me it was only for two weeks." She looked away as her face confirmed the amount. Somebody had stitched her up well and good. Shit, a hundred thousand dollars! I didn't even know Willy and Birgit had that kind of money. I made a mental note to stop drinking so much kirsch from their top shelf.

"Here's what we are going to do," I told her. "You are going to give me all their details and you're not going to say anything to Willy. I'll see what I can do."

"I already spoke to a lawyer. He said there is nothing I can do. The paper I signed means all I can do is sue them in the civil court and that will take years. He told me to forget it as I would probably lose anyway."

"Wow, a lawyer that's not painting a pretty picture to get his hands on a retainer. You were lucky. Where do you find one like that, I heard they were extinct?"

"He's a customer at the restaurant."

"Of course he is. Don't worry. I'll see what I can do."

"But the lawyer said there is no chance."

"He is probably right. But fortunately for you I'm not a lawyer." She looked exhausted. Her greying hair that was always perfectly put up in a bun was hanging ragged and her eyes were red from crying. I got all the information she had and promised I would do whatever I could.

That afternoon I was on the pavement outside an office on Silom Road in Bangkok's business district. I knew what I was dealing with. Since I had arrived in Thailand, shortly after the Vietnam War, I'd met all kinds of crooks and con men. They had sold everything from whisky futures to pension plans and we all drank in the same bars. None of them stayed more than a couple of years as by then they had harvested the expat community and were starting to feel the heat as their victims began to compare notes.

190

HARD TARGETS

The Office was your typical fur coat and no knickers job. It looked professional and expensive but was really only a front of respectability for the shady foreign characters that were employed to float around the town and make as many gullible friends as quickly as they could. I'd seen it all before.

I stood on the pavement sweating and smoking. An hour later, thanks to Birgit's description, I saw the owner of the company come out onto the street and walk hurriedly in the direction of Patpong, where the bars were. I followed him and when he entered his chosen bar for the evening I followed him in and sat on the barstool next to him.

"You've been taking money from little old ladies. You really shouldn't do that." I told him as I ordered myself a vodka from a passing pretty waitress.

"Who the fuck are you?" He asked menacingly. He was a stocky middle-aged man who must have been long used to getting confronted by disgruntled investors when he ventured out in public.

I told him my name and saw by his reaction that he recognised it. He then tried to be charming in the way con men do, by talking to me as if he liked me and we had some sort of existing relationship. The only problem was I hadn't tried to be likeable, quite the opposite in fact. I became impatient with his pleasantries and interrupted him.

"Birgit's an old friend and I would appreciate it if she wasn't screwed over for her life savings." I told him with as little emotion as possible as I signaled for another drink.

"Who do you think you are to talk to me about my business dealings? No motherfucking gangster is going to scare me. You dare to talk to me like I'm some kind of criminal? Who the fucking hell do you think you are?" The pleasantries were over, thank God.

"I checked the stock," I told him, "it's a penny stock and totally worthless. Now you are playing the 'load up game' by telling her the only way out of her dilemma is to spend more money."

He raised his voice. "You know nothing, but I know who you are. What the fuck does a two bit PI like you know about proper business?"

"I think you should listen to my concerns. It's hard to run a business like yours when somebody like me is pissed off at you." I told him without raising my voice to the same level as his.

"You can't touch me. See?" He threw a general's name card on the bar. "Walk away, while you still can." Lots of foreigners carried around big shot's business cards and produced them for everything from illegal parking to manslaughter. All you had to do was attend the right wedding or cocktail party in those days and some general or politician would eventually sidle over and hand you his name card. It didn't impress me but I was always aware of the possibility that one day I would have an argument with a foreigner that actually knew the big shot on the business card in his wallet and that that probably wouldn't be a good day.

"If you change your mind here is my card." I placed my card on top of the general's and left. He was bright red and angry which is always a good sign. It meant I'd ruined his evening.

I went back to the office around the corner and waited for one of his employees to leave. I didn't have to wait long before I spotted a youth with a pudding bowl haircut, acne and a cheap suit. I followed him home, which wasn't easy as he also went straight to Patpong. He drank himself silly in every bar where the girls wore bikinis and sat on the customer's lap for a Coca-Cola. He was a clumsy, gangly, strange looking youth but his money looked the same as everybody else's to the girls on Patpong. He left around nine o'clock accompanied by a hard faced dancer with a nice body. I followed them to the main road and watched as they got in a taxi together. I jumped in another taxi and followed them to an apartment building about five minutes away. My work was done for the day so I went home.

Over the next couple of days I had my own 'police boys' go to the youth's apartment in their uniforms and ask lots of questions of the security guard and the apartment management. Not specific enough questions to embarrass the police into having to provide evidence of a real investigation, just enough so that 'pimple in polyester' would hear about it and get good and paranoid.

When the rest of the foreign staff went to the office the following day they were confronted by a uniformed policeman in front of their building asking them where they were going and what they did there? They obviously didn't have work permits and in spite of their claims that they sold legitimate investments, deep down they knew what they were. The youth with acne was a no show at the office and I can only imagine what he was saying to his boss and his work mates on the phone. He was probably hiding under a bed in some cheap hotel crying for his mother.

Within two days the office was empty and the motley crew of employees, convinced there was a serious interest in their nefarious activities, were getting ready to run to the airport to leave and never come back. Most foreigners find Bangkok a total enigma and are easy to shake up. For all intents and purposes, after forty-eight hours, I had put my target out of business. At least temporarily, which was all that I felt was required.

On the third day Birgit call me. The depression had left her voice and she sounded very excited.

"They called me and told me that they had found a buyer for my shares. They sent a boy over with a cashier's cheque for my investment plus an eight per cent profit. I feel terrible for thinking they were crooks. I can't wait to tell Willy how well I did."

193

"Birgit," I told her sternly. "You cash the cheque as soon as possible and put the money back where it came from. You never tell Willy and, most importantly, you never do business with people like that again."

"You mean?"

"Yes Birgit, they are con men and I just executed an aggressive takeover and then sold them their own business back."

"What do you mean?"

"Do you really want to know?"

She went silent for a while, then said, "The special tonight is your favourite. It's Stroganoff with roesti potatoes. I'll reserve your favourite table for you."

"That sounds wonderful," I told her, "I'll be there at the usual time."

These encounters, sometimes with victims and sometimes with criminals, would become more frequent and were the foundation on which was built the required cynical understanding of the 'shadow world' that a Bangkok private detective must inhabit. I was quickly provided with the ability to see the crime from both sides. Although I didn't know it then, it was the start of my journey through the Bangkok underbelly. I had never wanted trouble and I didn't seek it, it looked for me and had no trouble finding me.

THE FOUR SHADES OF BLACK
Milton Gray

One. Gramayre Street

Lord Eddlemere's driver looked in the mirror at his two passengers. Lady Eddlemere was held in the arms of her husband, tears now abated but her hands clearly clung to him and her head pressed against his chest.

John Eddlemere was no harder to read, his arms held his wife tightly for his own comfort as much as for hers, while his eyes, staring out into the evening's dying light, were full of despair and certainty that what was to come would leave them feeling worse than they did now.

Bill looked back to the road ahead and then about him. Edgelands. This was not a part of Londinium that he wanted to be. Long derelict areas of the city, broken places that had once been teeming with life but which were now just shadows of the past, places where you didn't go unless you had nowhere else – or just didn't know better.

It was not just the gangs and vagrants who resided there but pieces of history that would not let go of the present. The Edgelands bordered the Underearth, where the divide between our world and the darkness had worn thin. He had heard stories of these places, of fools who came in search of the dead, sometimes finding them, sometimes joining them. Just stories he told himself. Their business here was family and it was not the first time they had done this and not the first time he wished they would give her up to move on.

Gabby, their daughter, had died here. A party held close to Hades was not something to scare a bunch of students who thought they were invincible. But there was nothing supernatural about that night and nothing ghostly that claimed her life, just a bad vapour.

The little glass phials sold for vapour pipes usually contained just a little nicotine, perhaps with a flavouring. Sometimes they had a legal high like cannabis, or even a prescription drug of some kind, but more and more they were used for illicit drugs – almost undetectable without chemical analysis. The analysis of her vapour pipe revealed a reckless and illegal cocktail of chemicals, which mixed together were mind-altering - but for her, also fatal. Nor was it a quiet death. Whatever vision was shown to her in that state was something fearful, terrifying, sending her screaming through the ruins until her mind seemed to break and her heart stopped - while the party continued around her till dawn. Only then did a friend find her where she had seen her fall and assumed her to be unconscious.

This close to the edge, where the distance between here and there was so thin, it was no surprise that her mental trauma would create a shade, though there was no comfort in that.

He drew the car to a halt and looked in the mirror again but the darkness had all but obscured them from him.

"This is the spot sir."

"Thank you Oates. If you could give us a short while alone, then we'll head out to find her."

"Of course sir." He opened his door and stepped out into the cool air, walking across the crumbling asphalt to what was left of a wall. He lent behind it to give the couple the privacy they needed and took out his own bulky vapour pipe. Putting it to his lips he breathed in a nicotine heavy brew, laced with the flavours of tobacco and menthol. He closed his eyes but could not relax. The city was silent here, an unnatural state for a metropolis.

He heard a car door open and close and the footsteps of Lord Eddlemere as he walked to the other side to get the door for his wife. He was strangely old fashioned that way, though he carried it off without being patronising. No words passed between the couple as they made their way into the maze of old buildings and Bill didn't risk looking until he heard them pass. They walked slowly, arm in arm, their torchlight waving on the ground before them. Thrusting the pipe back into his pocket Bill went back to the car, turning the inside light on so that he could read and that the couple could find their way back.

***

John Eddlemere held Caroline's hand as they walked, it didn't take long to reach the place. What had once been an old redbrick warehouse was now shelled out, without a roof and one of its walls. Broken bricks and rubbish bags, torn with half seen contents spraying out, lay all about the place, while weeds grew up through the cracked concrete floor. They stepped inside and immediately felt the darkness draw a little closer. It was still early but that didn't seem to matter, though they had once thought her appearance dependent upon time.

"Gabby!" Caroline's voice called out, unsteady and desperate. "Gabby!" Her voice was joined by that of her husband and they called out together several more times before she rested her arm on his, silencing him. They looked on at the far doorway as the form of their daughter stumbled in from nowhere. Her clothing was dishevelled, her eyes wide, looking this way and that at people who were no longer there. "Gabby darling, please, sweetheart, please, it's mummy, please hear me..." But whatever she heard, it was not in the present.

Twice before however, she had heard them, looked at them even...before dying the same dreadful death that had taken her from them again, and again.

They had been warned not to do this, warned that this shade was so slight, so limited, that it comprehended little more than its own raw feelings, its ongoing experience of death. Perhaps it would be capable of more were it not for the drugs...but then, were it not for those, they wouldn't be there at all. But a bereaved parent may accept the transparent fakery of a thousand mediums before accepting that they had truly lost their child and the Eddlemeres were no different.

For a brief moment they thought that perhaps this time she had noticed them again but once more her eyes looked through them, further back at some imagined horror. As her face contorted with fear, Caroline turned into the arms of her husband who held her as the dreadful scream cut through the air before all was once more silent, the shade slipped away. The two held each other and wept as they always did.

"Touching!"

The unsympathetic voice startled them, though they could not tell where it came from. They looked about, peering into the shadows for the man who would interrupt their grief.

"I'm here." This time its direction was plain and they turned to see a figure step from the shadows as though from behind a curtain. Tall and well built, it advanced toward them purposefully before stopping to kneel, picking up one of the broken bricks. "Come now, John, you remember me, don't you?"

"Yes, I do. How dare you come here! Damn you for this."

"Damn me?"

"It's been years Byron, let it rest."

"Don't flatter yourself. I've gone to a lot of trouble but you're no longer important enough to warrant the effort by yourself. Your death is no more than proof of concept...but I grant, chosen because I still hate you for what you did to me."

"John, who is this, what does he mean?" Caroline was struggling to take in what was being said.

"Let me demonstrate." The man said, before hurling the brick with force and malice. It stuck her in the side of her head, with both a crack and a dull thud before it dropped to the ground.

John Eddlemere turned cold. One moment his wife was looking up at him and the next, her eyes were unseeing, her mouth hung open and her body limp, slipping from his grip. He struggled to stop her falling but was only able to keep her from hitting the ground too hard. As he knelt over her, he fought to control himself and motioned again and again to touch her, but the deep indentation where the rock had struck repelled his hand.

***

In the heart of Gramayre Street's wealthier quarter stood a row of town houses, larger than most, wider than most, and available only to the few who could afford such wealth and had the connections to know that they existed at all. Gramayre Street had a strange exclusivity that went far beyond mere money. One of these was the property of Byron Black, who stood leaning against the wall of the stairs hoping for a little respite from the party. His thumb found his temple and rubbed, while his finger sought out the start of the scar on his forehead and traced it across, over his eye, then his cheek, and back up

199

again. It was an old habit. Suddenly his eyes snapped open at the sound of a voice. Carl Moody had arrived, the fool from the Ministry of Defence who had pulled the plug on his project. An anger welled up in him as he stormed down, seeking the source of the greetings and laughter.

"Black! Good to see you man, you're looking well!" Moody smiled at him, his face was tanned but starting to show its age in little creases, and his blonde moustache would be flecked with a grey had he not dyed it, as would the fine wispy hair that was always a little too long for a man of his position. He held out a strong hand that shook Black's, though he could not withdraw it quickly enough.

"We need to talk."

"Alright old man."

"Now!" If it were possible, he looked even more pale that usual, his lips thin and bloodless. But he was not a man to disguise anger to anyone. Turning on his heel he began to weave between the guests milling around with drinks and finger food, ignoring any who tried to make contact with him. In the hall he stormed to his study, knowing that Moody would be with him shortly – he knew the way well enough.

Like most of the rest of the property, the study was decorated in Edwardian fashion, in keeping with the house itself. Red patterned wallpaper contrasted with lush green plants and the dark stained wood of the furniture. Moody shut the door quietly behind him and strode toward the desk where Black was already seated, his chin cradled on his fingers.

"Look here Byron, I thought we had gone over this...there was nothing for it."

"Nothing?! Do you understand how close we are?"

"We can't risk it, not with all that happened, not to mention how much that Amnesty bloke seemed to know. Someone was leaking..."

"Nothing happened to warrant the project's closure!"

200

"Nothing? What are you talking about man? Six people are dead."

Black looked confused for a moment but shook it off, feeling certain of his position. "This project was too valuable to the Crown to..."

"Was valuable, Black, now it's a liability that we're still trying to cover up. This discussion is over. It's clear that I made a mistake in attending tonight, so I'll take my leave. We can speak again when you're in a better state of mind."

***

Bill looked up from his book, alert to something terrible having occurred. He had heard Gabby's awful scream on previous visits and expecting it he had not been phased. But this was Lord Eddlemere, a wail of despair and like nothing he had heard from him before. He didn't pause and letting the book drop to the floor, he opened the door and leaving it open ran for the building where he knew them to be, slowing himself as he reached its threshold.

He stepped within the three walls, where the night seemed darker than it should and the shadows longer, reaching toward him in the moonlight. All was silent.

"Sir? Lord Eddlemere sir? Milady?" Nothing but the sound of Lord Eddlemere's torch rolling toward him, its light weaving across the wall. Bending cautiously, he picked it up and began to search out the room and almost immediately found them. "Gods! Oh Gods no!"

They lay beside one another, dark pools forming around their heads while over the prostrate form of his employer there crouched another form. It looked up at him and into the light. The man's features were pale and angular with a heavy scar cutting a line over forehead and eye and cheek. A sneer spreading over the thin mouth and in his hand was a brick, dripping with blood, blood that Bill realised was everywhere, spattered over the man's face and covered his hand and sleeve as though they had been dipped in it.

His own blood chilled and fearing for his life Bill dropped the torch, turned tail and ran for the car. He fair leaped through the open door which he slammed shut and locked before he turned the engine, sweaty fingers almost slipping over the keys and then the wheel as he steered a path to the road. His eyes shot first to the wing mirror, then up to the mirror above, the mirror still directed to the back seat where, in a flash of moonlight, he could see them there, in each other's arms, their faces misshapen and rivers of red flowing from the injuries. He slammed the breaks in a wild panic and then struggled to control the car which skidded and smashed into a post that had once supported phone lines.

***

Byron was still sat at his desk when his next visitor made an appearance. His anger had abated and seemed strangely distant now, along with the reasons for it. Though with the sight of Martin Pommeroy it reawakened.

He had not been invited, the ill will between the two was beyond repair - they had both done so much to earn the other's hatred.

"Not exactly dressed for a party, are we?"

Pommeroy closed the door behind him and stood regarding the man he had worked with for the last three years, the man who had taken his wife from him.

"You should leave now."

"No, I've ignored you for too long...what you've done."

"I've done nothing...without consent."

"You bastard! You fucking bastard...she could have died and you don't give a shit do you? It was your baby!"

"Perhaps...it's not as if you didn't turn your attentions toward my wife, is it? But then, she stayed with me while yours, well, preferred to try and end it all rather than go back to..." He didn't finish. Pommeroy had heard enough, more than he had intended, and now drew the hunting knife from its sheath hidden within the dark boiler suit he had worn.

Seeing the weapon, Black began to rise while opening his draw to reach for the old revolver kept there. But he was too slow for the former army man, who now sprang forward over the desk. The two men fell back to the floor and the chair toppled behind and desk contents scattered about them. Each saw red, wanting nothing more than the death of the other. Black had hold of the hand with the knife and fought to turn it as it was pushed down. Neither made any sound, neither wanted interruption, only a final resolution.

Two

Bill felt his lids held open and then the sharp pain of a light shone in, bringing him back to consciousness with a start. He struggled to regain some sense of where he was. The woman kneeling over him looked down with concern in her eyes.

"No, don't try to move yet. We'll get a stretcher, I think you've some broken ribs and if they hurt now, they'll hurt a lot more if you try to move about. All right?"

They did hurt. A lot. Bill could see now that she was in the green uniform of a paramedic and behind her was another opening the back of an ambulance.

"Yes...yes." His own voice was barely audible to even himself. There was the crunch of more footsteps and another figure knelt down in view.

The policeman looked young, too young really. "Sir, can you tell me what happened here?"

"Not now, it can wait until he's at the hospital."

"No...please...Lord Eddlemere...and his wife. They're back there. It killed them. Both of them...oh gods...they're back there..." and with that he slipped back to unconsciousness.

PC Richards stood and looked about him. Places like this gave him the willies and he wasn't that bothered to admit it – but only because it wasn't something that would keep him from doing his job – nor from taking a short cut when cycling home. That's how he came across the car. Standing up, he tilted his head to his radio and called in what the man had told him, stating that he was going to take a look around. There was no protest from the station, no suggestion that he should wait for back up, no comment that he was no longer on duty, and so he switched on his torch and tried to determine where the car was likely to have come from.

The search could have taken hours in the darkness but somehow he felt drawn to the building, into the shadows that seemed to have a depth to them, as if chasms opening into another place altogether. Seeing the bodies there, he backed out immediately, not wanting to interfere with any evidence, speaking again into the radio before returning to the main road to wait for company.

***

The first light of dawn was beginning to brighten the horizon when Detective Inspector Bryn Berkeley drew his car to a stop at the road block. A uniform approached, recognising the heap for whose it was.

"Good morning sir!" Constable James Williams strode up with a smile. He had always liked the old boy, though not everyone shared his sentiment.

"Morning Jim." Berkeley eased himself out of his seat and brushed himself down, more from habit than from need. "So, what's the story? I was told two dead and one injured."

"Yessir. That's about the sum of it, though it's a bit messy and the victims are gentry...a Lord and Lady Eddlemere."

"Gods! This one could be high profile. What the bloody hell am I doing on it?"

"Can't answer that sir. Your new sergeant might though."

"My what?!"

"Well, that's who she says she is. A DS Meadows."

"Is she? We'll see about that. Any chance of a tea from someone?"

"I'll see what I can find for you sir. She's at the scene over that way."

Berkeley didn't want a sergeant and for the most part over the last year he had been indulged, given simple little cases and left to deal about them unhindered.

At fifty-eight he was going through the motions until retirement and while there were many who looked forward to seeing him leave, who saw him now as dead weight, he had made enough friends with enough influence over the years to get his own way for the remainder of his career.

He ran his fingers back through thinning grey hair, the strands no longer hiding the bald patch at the back. He felt tired inside. His limbs ached, and his breathing strained, though it could be as much from his extra weight as from his age. He knew that he looked worn out too. His jowls had begun to hang a little, while heavy bags were the first anyone saw of his eyes, their once sharp green now faded, greyed, like his soul. Nor did his attire help. He was an old fashioned dresser when he was young and now he looked like a caricature of the past. His musty tweed jacket was patched at the elbows and fraying a little at the cuffs, his paisley tie was dulled, and his heavy brown leather boots were scuffed with the heals worn down to be point of being uncomfortable.

He thrust his hands into the pockets of his mac and made his way towards the crime scene in no particular hurry and untroubled by his surrounds. Edgelands often lost much of their disquieting aspect by daylight, though this could be deceptive. He and the other officers on the scene all knew not to allow themselves to be distracted by anything they were not there to see – which made searching for evidence a nightmare. A number of uniformed officers combed the rubble about the building in pairs, cautious of being waylaid by something otherworldly, something not quite there. Unfortunately, given the nature of the place, anything they did find could be subject to extra scrutiny in a court.

He stepped over the yellow tape unchallenged and inside felt a shiver. The morning light did little to dispel the shadows. Instead they clung to the space, a cold, cloying presence. A woman stood next to the bodies, she broke from her conversation with a PC to look up.

"Good morning sir!"

He frowned as he approached. "You Meadows?"

"Yessir, DS Daisy Meadows, transferred in from Brighton yesterday." She held out her hand, which he did not take.

He fought to stop himself saying something about her name. "I don't have sergeants."

"Sorry sir. The DDI assigned me to you, at least for a couple of months. He did say you might not be happy but it won't be for long."

"You're right, it won't. Nothing personal."

She withdrew her hand but instead of looking offended, she smiled. "Right you are sir."

He took a moment to consider her. She didn't look like police – a little too much of a sophisticated air about her, a little too well dressed. But then, times changed and so did The Service and those in it. He was the relic. In her early thirties, she had shoulder length dark hair with a curly perm. Her face was strong and while pleasant now, he could see that it could become steely and sharp. In her eyes, dark and penetrating, he could see something of himself – they were not just looking but observing and judging everything...everyone. But there was something else. There was a pricking of his thumbs.

"I can't see us being kept on this case long, so don't get too involved with it. It's a bit above my station these days. We'll go through the motions so that we've something to pass on - no reason not to be professional, after all."

"Well, SOCO have been taking plenty of photos, we could head back to the office and work from them. This place is a bit on the dark side, it's playing tricks on my eyes anyway. I've even seen condoms that weren't there."

Underearth detritus, as if the place were forcing its own memories into view. He had seen it before. "Rubbish. You need to know the scene. It may come to nothing but you can't make assumptions."

"But this place, the details we're looking for, I can't tell what's real and what isn't."

"Then go and see what happened to my cup of tea...and make sure it has plenty of milk in it. And sugar. I'll walk the scene myself."

"And how will you tell?"

"I'll know." Somehow he felt she already knew the answer. He watched her leave. "Constable. You know anything about this?"

"Yessir. I was first on the scene."

"You see anything other than this?"

"No sir, but there was the driver, he wasn't quite coherent but if he didn't do it himself, then he saw something...might have been what caused him to crash."

"Where's he been taken, do you know?"

"Collbourne General."

"Right, thanks." He looked down at the two bodies. They had been moved since their deaths, shuffled about in their blood and laid out side by side, and their heads, disfigured by their injuries, had been turned to face one another. On the man's chest had been placed a half brick, sticky with congealed blood,

207

along with a little flesh and hair. "Bloody hell, look at all the boot prints around here!"

"Sorry sir...there have been some..."

"Photos, yes I know. Still, I would have preferred to see it myself." It came again, the pricking of his thumbs...his eyes cast about and found them, a set of prints unlike the others, deep and yet lacking detail – they were just shoe shaped. And they stopped at the bodies. He traced them back, watched by the constable, back to a wall, still somehow in shadow where they went no further. "Bugger." He hoped it didn't mean what he thought it might.

"There a problem?" Meadows had returned with his tea.

"I hope not. Come on, you're driving." He took the tea and strode past her.

"Driving where?"

"Collbourne General apparently."

***

Clarissa looked at her husband struggling beside her, she had never known him to have such disturbed sleep. She had tried waking him but to no avail, and now his head turned this way and that, his face glistening, his scar a deep red line across his face. Suddenly he tensed, his back arched and head thrown back. His hand clutched at his chest as he cried out, eyes wide open. He collapsed back into the bed and turned to face her with fearful eyes.

"Byron, are you...? You've been so...all night..." She ventured a hand to his face, her fingers caressing his cheek, finding it cold and wet.

His look become more intense, his hand covered hers and gripped it, pulling her to him, embracing her. "I'm sorry, it's alright now. It was just a dream."

But it was unlike him to suffer that way. He had been unlike himself for over a week now. His mood swings had made him difficult to manage, but his affection for her had been as it was when they first become lovers and she had begun to believe that his claimed desire for reconciliation might actually be sincere. She let herself believe it, let herself be held, and allowed herself to hope.

The embrace gave way to a kiss and the kiss led to another embrace, this time longing and passionate.

Three

Divisional Detective Inspector Kurland checked himself in his office mirror, a full length affair that he justified with his rank and station and the need for smart presentation to senior officers. He had been in the post for a little under two years, having received the promotion at just forty-one. He turned to one side, making sure that his shirt was tucked in neatly at the front and admiring his own trim figure before putting on his jacket. It was a good suit, navy blue and tailored to a standard that his job alone could not pay for. He leant forward to examine his hair, thick, black and brushed back and without a speck of grey, albeit thanks to a dye. He checked his little moustache too, smoothing it with a finger before stepping back again with a satisfied smile.

He didn't know much about the new sergeant, save that he had been told to put her with Berkeley for a while and to give them the Edgelands killing – which of course he had questioned when he learned of the victim but he had been over-ruled. Still, he was sure that he could find a better post for Meadows soon enough, along with the chance to know her better. Since his divorce earlier that year, he felt free to pursue the women liked

– without dreaming that they might not want to be pursued – and it wasn't as if he had controlled his urges when married anyway.

There was a bit of a walk through the corridors to Berkeley's office, tucked away in a windowless corner where it was intended to have been a storage cupboard. He knocked twice and didn't wait for an invitation before letting himself in.

It was a dingy affair lit by a simple overhead bulb. The two desks faced one another, each piled up with folders, trays and bits of paper that threatened to cascade over the eBrains and coffee cups. Meadows was stood between at the tiny sink washing a teapot, she looked around as he entered and smiled, though more to herself than to him.

"Ah, Meadows, getting settled in?"

"Yessir, thank you."

"He hasn't got you doing the housekeeping has he, making the tea and such? A bit of a dinosaur when it comes to women I think."

It wasn't her voice that answered. "Yes he has and no he isn't." Berkeley's grumpy voice came from behind his large eBrain screen. "She's a new sergeant, that means housekeeping and tea. Being a woman has nothing to do with it. It's called hierarchy."

"Yes, well, still, it doesn't seem quite the attitude in this day and age."

"Ah, the voice of progress from a divorced skirt chaser. I'll be sure to take it on board."

"Now listen Bryn..."

"Must I? Is it something to do with the case?"

Kurland straightened himself and decided to get to the point, pretence or not. He didn't like Berkeley and didn't like that he had to humour him. "I need something preliminary to give the brass, this one's a little more high profile than you're used to..."

"No, it's a little more high profile than I've dealt with of late. I'm plenty used to it."

"The point is that I need..."

"There's an artist's impression from the driver's description, that's all there is so far."

"Was he the only witness?"

"Yes, it's on the...on sergeant Meadow's desk there."

"You sure the driver isn't a fit?"

"Not sure of anything yet."

"Well, you're out of luck if this is the suspect."

"Why?"

"It's a good rendition but the scar makes it certain. This is Byron Black."

"You know him?"

"Know him? Yes and there was no love lost between him and the victim but then, I was at his party last night. I'd call that a cast iron alibi. You'll need to question that driver again. Means and opportunity and such."

"Means and opportunity and no forensics." Meadows spoke while spooning leaves into the pot. "There should have been blood spatter everywhere but he was clean."

"Then at least his concussion has done for his evidence." Dropping the picture into the bin he turned on his heels for the door. "Bring me something when you have it, as you get it, alright? The brass seem serious about this one."

"Should I worry about my future in The Service then?" But he went unanswered as Kurland shut the door loudly behind him.

"Gods he's prick. Look forward to some more attention from him sergeant." He reached down and around his desk for the waste bin and fished out the picture, pausing to look at it. "You know who this Byron Black is?"

"Yes, I think. He's some sort of industrialist. I seem to remember something about financial problems or a scandal. Want me to fish out his address?"

"Yes. It'll annoy the DDI." There came a chime from the eBrain that claimed his attention for a moment. "Hmmm. Looks like the photos are available, they should be on your account as well if you want to look at 'em."

"What did you make of the scene? The driver was terrified, called it a...spectre, was it?"

"Yes, the supernaturalists wouldn't like it though, a 'shade' is the term they like. I always liked 'apparition' myself but I suppose that doesn't allow for..."

"Interaction. You think there was any? They were looking for some. He said they wanted their daughter to recognise them."

"Yes, well, there was something at the scene, I'm sure of that."

"How?"

"Call it the pricking of my thumbs."

"You get that a lot?" She didn't seem surprised but again made one of her little smiles that Berkeley was beginning to find disconcerting.

"It wouldn't help us if I did, if this is clearly Black...and I'll want to see that for myself...then unless he's dead, it can't be a shade. Anyway, it's far too early to jump to conclusions."

"I hear you used to enjoy solving this sort of thing."

He looked a little irritated at this, his right hand moved to a brass band worn on his wrist and began to fidget. "Don't listen to all the rumours you hear about me and frankly, being a good detective isn't always about solving anything. A lot of the time it's just about being a catalyst and observer, along with being at the right place at the right time. Sometimes you just have to let things play out and be there to make the collar when whoever it is has made themselves obvious. Remember that and you'll save yourself a lot of wasted effort. People like Kurland have grown up on too much television and pulp fiction, they think that they're the stars of the story but they're not. It's not their drama, we're somewhere between audience and the bloke who drops the stage curtain."

"Milk?"

"Yes, lots...nearly white. Six sugars."

"Six?"

"Six. We can look go through the photos with it. Ginger nut?"

"Please."

"Then we'll go and see this Black when you've found where he is."

***

Clarissa put her hand on Byron's arm. She was again concerned for him, his mood all morning had been swinging wildly from loving to anxious and distracted. She wasn't sure how to broach it, so she decided to be direct.

"Darling, what is it? You're troubled by something...is it Martin? Did something happen between you?"

His body suddenly tensed, his hand gripping his chest as if in pain. It took a moment for him to recover, looking at first confused and then angry. "Why the hell are you brining him up again? I thought you were over hankering for him?"

Now she became defensive, snapping back, "And when did you stop hankering after his wife? Before or after she lost your baby?" She regretted it instantly but instead of looking angry, Byron again looked confused, he head bent low and frowning he looked like he was struggling to recall something important. "I'm sorry, please. I know we said we would put it behind us but...it's...well, Katie Beddows, she said she saw him here...last night. Is that right?"

"No! Yes...I...yes, he was." His hand rubbed at his chest again, but now as if looking for something. "He...I think...we fought. Maybe. Perhaps I had too much to drink. I don't know." He turned to look at her and she reached out to him, her hand resting on his cheek.

She wanted so much to hold him again and to be held but the moment was broken by a knock on the door. The two of them straightened themselves before she called out, "come in."

Their maid, Emelda opened the door cautiously and, as was her habit, peered her head around to see inside before opening it fully. "I'm sorry ma'am, but there's policemen to see Mr Black."

"That's alright E, where are they?"

"They're in the drawing room downstairs sir."

"Did they say what it was about?"

"No sir, they just said that they would like to speak with you."

"Very well, tell them that I'll be with them in a moment and offer them some tea or something."

"Yes sir."

As the little Filipino girl closed the door behind her, Byron stretched his back and again adjusted his clothes, always aware of his appearance. Clarissa, just as aware of it, adjusted his tie and smiled up at him before they kissed.

***

Berkeley didn't allow his coat to be taken, preferring to hold it under his arm. He asked for a cup of Earl Gray, specifying lots of milk and his six sugars before sitting himself down on a comfortable looking couch where Meadows joined him, sitting a little closer than he was comfortable with.

He looked about him, looked at all the ornaments, weighed up the prices and the taste behind them and kept it all to himself. "Hmmm. Nice place, this. The décor's a bit twee for my taste perhaps but still, not bad. I wonder what this must cost."

"I would guess more than we'll ever earn, I'm surprised he was able to buy it at all."

Bryn frowned. "Why? I thought you said he was loaded."

"He is...or was. No, it's Gramayre Street, it's not an easy place to buy into. Most of the properties are owned and leased by Gramayre House, and those that aren't are subject to local laws that give it right of veto over any proposed purchaser."

"Really? What's special about it? I've never heard of the place and I've lived here all my life. And Gramayre House, that's the huge place at the top of the roundabout, yes? How come I've never noticed that before?"

"You've not been looking for it. I've some friends who work there. This area of the city has some...unusual properties."

There was a pause as he took it in. "Are you saying that these are Edgelands?" To him, Edgelands meant largely uninhabited by anything other than the past.

"Yes, of a kind. I don't fully understand it I suppose but apparently you don't really notice the place unless you've business here. An invitation will do it but then, once your business is done, it just sort of fades from memory."

"Not yours though."

"We've business here."

"You had business here before?"

"Like I said, I have friends here."

The door opened and the tea service was wheeled in on a tray, followed by Byron Black and his wife. Although it was Black that Berkeley had come to see, even he couldn't help but notice Clarissa first. Obviously much younger in her late twenties, she was startlingly beautiful with something of the look of old Hollywood about her. Her blond hair was shoulder length and regularly styled, her clothing followed almost a 1950's modesty but had that chic which kept no secrets about her figure. She smiled warmly at her guests and then nodded to the maid to leave them.

Byron was no less striking in appearance but next to her was a man from a different movie. He was an imposing man, his dark eyes met Berkeley's gaze and bore through him. But he was not to be intimidated by body language and performance, if only because he was too old to care for it. Waiting for his hosts to sit opposite and seeing that they were not about to initiate the conversation, he unfolded the artist's sketch and handed it across to Black, who still without word, glanced down at it before showing it to his wife.

"It's a fair likeness." She said, "What is this regarding?"

"One of your husband's former colleagues, along with his wife, was murdered last night., That was drawn from the description given by the eye witness."

"Well, that's ridiculous, my husband was here last night... all night. There was a party here, with plenty of witnesses who can attest to it."

"If I'm to be a suspect, may I at least know who was murdered?"

"Lord and Lady Eddlemere," he noted no reaction from Black, while Clarissa only frowned a little, "apparently they were searching for their daughter's shade when someone, looking much like yourself, caved in their skulls with a brick. Messy, passionate... personal. Takes a lot of anger to do something like that."

"Or a psychopath." Black remained unmoved.

"The shrinks prefer sociopath these days."

"It doesn't matter, if I was here then this doesn't really concern me."

"I'm afraid it does, whether you had opportunity or not is something I have to establish yet, but from what little I've gleaned about you before coming here, you certainly had motive. He took your company from you."

"That was a long time ago."

"I don't think that you're the forgiving kind Mr. Black."

"I'm not. If it will save you wasting time, I'm sure that Clarissa can make out a list of guests from last night. They will verify that I was here."

"Thank you, and please, a complete list of everybody who was here." He saw Clarissa look uncertainly at her husband for a moment. "Not just those on the guest list, mind. There are always gate-crashes and unexpected partners. And any absentees as well."

"You don't need an exhaustive list just to eliminate me."

"With respect, this is my investigation and I'll decide what I do and do not require for it."

"Well, if that's all."

"Not really, no. When did you last have contact with the deceased?"

"I've never had dealing with his wife, only John."

"Never? You were partners for years."

"He kept his private and business lives separate."

"So, when did you..."

"Not for more than two years, closer to three. I severed any ties with him and my former company."

"All ties? Aren't you in the same line of work anymore? What line of work were you in? The files are a little...incomplete."

"Because it was...is...classified. We were defence contractors and much of our work was of a sensitive nature. I imagine it still is, as is mine. Keeping clear of John was not difficult."

"I will still need to know more about it however."

"Then you will need to go through the Ministry of Defence, I am bound not to discuss it. I really think that is all I have to say...unless you're going to arrest me?"

"No."

Black rose up and left the room without another word. Clarissa looked from one detective to the other, "I'm sorry, you must understand that my husband is under a lot of pressure at the moment but I can assure you, he has had nothing to do with this business. If you will excuse me, I should go to him." She stood, looking a little uncomfortable at the two faces whose attention she now held, "I...do you have some contact details?"

"Yes." Meadows smiled and handed her a card.

"Thank you, I'll send you the list shortly. Again, if you will excuse me, our maid will show you out."

"Yes, I'll finish my tea first. If you don't mind."

"Well, that was...brief." Berkeley noted now in the car.

"He's not telling the whole truth, is he?" Meadows pulled her seatbelt into place and looked at Berkeley and smiled disconcertingly. "Any thoughts then?"

"The tea wasn't bad."

"Oh, no pricking of your thumbs?"

He frowned, there had been something, but not a lie. "I won't dignify that."

"So, do we wait on this list with a view to dropping him?"

"No. This is Edgelands, right?"

"Yes. At least, that's my understanding."

"Edgelands have tears, don't they? The Underearth...distance isn't the same there, is it?"

"That sounds like a long-shot. A passage between here and there via the Underearth?"

"It's happened. Some of most heavily blitzed sites in the war bled into each other. You're too young to remember when the passages were still open but couple of them were still around when I was a boy and if you knew your way around the crap security of those days, you could hop from one side of Londinium to the other."

"True...but they have closed up somewhat. And Gramayre Street isn't really the site of anything very traumatic...we could ask at Gramayre House though."

"What's the deal with that?"

"Gramayre House? It isn't entirely clear...they seem to oversee what happens here. They also do a lot of research into the supernatural, deal out a lot of grants, and they have the most comprehensive library in the world on it."

"Except that not many people would know or remember that, right?"

"Right. Anyway, if you want to know more about it, then that's the place to ask."

"And you have friends there, right?"

"I know someone we can talk to."

218

Jean Herbin lowered his camera and watched the car pull away from outside Byron Black's town house. He frowned to himself and dug deep into his coat pocket for his phone, flipping it open and dialling with his thumb.

"It's me, I'm at Black's place now...no, it's in Gramayre St...GRAMAYRE...no it doesn't matter, I've contacts here. Anyway, my information was right, DI Bryn Berkeley is on it and he's connected Black...don't know...we can trust him but there's something odd, he's got a sergeant...never seen her before...no he doesn't, he's not had one for years, likes to work alone. If he's been given one now, it won't have been his choice and it must have been recent...Yeah, maybe. I'll try and contact him without her to be sure, meantime, I'll get myself to an eBrain and send you her picture. Ask around, see if she's one of them."

The phone closed with a satisfying snap and Herbin shut his eyes to think. As a rule, Berkeley didn't have much time for reporters but there were reporters and reporters and Herbin was an idealist, a crusader, fired from every paper that he had worked for. That was the price of scruples. Now he was freelance and still campaigning and Berkeley at least respected that and so, every now and then, they co-operated. It wasn't that they particularly liked each other but there was trust and that was enough for the both of them.

He wondered how the policeman would react to what was going on though, as the two of them had grown old in tandem, they each had changed. While Berkeley had let himself go, increasingly losing interest and conviction, if not his integrity, Herbin had kept himself fit and smart, and only seemed to grow in passion and indignation.

He breathed in deeply before opening his eyes again. He would have to try and re-kindle a little of the old Berkeley. He was running short on friends he could count on and the direction this story was taking, he would need all he could find.

Four

There came the sound of huffing and then shuffling before the door opened a little too quickly. The woman stood looking startled, as if she hadn't expected anyone to be waiting there, despite Bryn's loud knocking. She looked to be in her early thirties, average height, with a fine figure that even he could discern beneath her rather prim outfit. Her blonde hair was tied back with plaits, and cold blue eyes looked back at him through sharp looking glasses. She looked like a 1940's librarian – or at least the way they looked in Humphrey Bogart films.

Her voice was as sharp as her appearance and cut with a heavy Bavarian accept. "Yes? This isn't a good time, I am very busy. Are you from the university?"

The two of them held up their ID's unrolling them from the little cylinders with their thumbs.

"DS Meadows, and this is Detective Inspector Berkeley. I'm a friend of Ted Ursine, he told me that you might be able to help us with an interesting problem."

Her demeanour changed noticeably. "How interesting?"

"Well, Miss..." Berkeley began.

"Doctor, Doctor Marchen."

"Yes, quite, well...we've got a man who might be in two places at once, a murder in Edgelands, at least two shades, and a bloke I don't like in Gramayre Street."

Meadows smirked. "Two shades sir?"

"Yes, I told you to walk the scene."

"I did...did you get a..."

"Leave it sergeant. Can we come in? Thank you." He strode in past the woman leaving Meadows to follow. "I'd love one thank you."

"One what?"

"Tea, anything strong but with a lot of milk and six sugars."

"I'll take mine black, one sugar, thanks."

"You're welcome, I'm sure." She closed the door behind them and paused to watch the mismatched pair as they settled in chairs in front of her desk. She walked to the back of the room picked up the electric kettle, swirling it about to gauge how much water was in there before flipping up the switch to start it. Wanting to re-assert herself a little, she leant back on the bench, forcing her guests to turn uncomfortably in their seats to face her. "Very well. Why don't you start at the beginning..."

***

"You don't have much do you? Just a vague suspicion. Why are you so sure of there being two shades?"

"The tracks."

"And you trust your senses in such a place?"

"Call it experience."

"It takes a little more than..."

"So I'm told but that doesn't lead anywhere. We're faced with this: There were two shades, the one that fits their daughter's behaviour and the one that came from the shadows, with ill-defined tracks and which was identified by the driver as Black."

"Could he not be mistaken?"

"Tricky, Black is fairly distinctive, especially with the scar."

"Then an impersonation."

"I think it was a shade. Or if not, then Black. There was something not quite right about him."

"You said. A doppelgänger perhaps?"

"Are there such things?"

She shrugged. "Not that I know of. I'm just speculating. After all, your Byron Black is alive, yah?"

"Yah."

"So, you also wonder if he might have moved via a tear between worlds and navigated the Underearth to reach the place. It would be harder than you imagine, given that there doesn't seem to be any obvious link between the locations, though it would not be impossible. Still, I suspect you would have known. Its marks looked like a shade's. So, I wonder about some kind of projection."

Meadows frowned and looked up from her thoughts. "I've only heard of apparitions being projected."

"The projection of force is both rare and limited."

"You're talking about telekinesis. I thought that was a fad in the seventies."

"Yah, but cases have been reliably recorded. What would be unprecedented would be the combination and extent. It is, yes, a more promising line of thought than a man who is and is not a shade, who navigates the Underearth. In any case, we'll need a Sensitive with us and there is no shortage of them working here. It would help to have a priestess perhaps but I'm not sure if one will be available."

"A priestess? For the love of gods, we're holding an investigation, not a religious ceremony, I need something that will hold up in court." Bryn all but refrained from rolling his eyes and began to doubt the wisdom of asking her.

"You don't understand. Gramayre House is home to the largest temple of Hecate, a goddess associated with the Underearth and more significantly perhaps, with doorways. These tears as you call them, are easily found by her worshippers and sometimes can be closed by them. Although, that's not so easy to do."

"Alright. I take it that you're game for this, when do you think you can have someone to see the crime scene?"

She looked at the clock, brows furrowed. "Give me twenty minutes – I'll have a Sensitive to come with us at least."

"Oh, that quick." He seemed a little dismayed.

Meadows on the other hand just smiled. "Time enough for another cup then. Do you have any biscuits?"

"Yah, in the draw."

Berkeley looked less sure. "And the loo?"

***

222

HARD TARGETS

It was a tight fit in the back of Berkeley's car and Dr Marchen looked singularly uncomfortable in her struggle for personal space against the bulk of the oversized Sensitive. He was too young for his shape, which was decidedly squidgy and spread out alarmingly behind and beneath him. Wisps of black hair clung to his sweaty round face still red with the exertion of getting into the vehicle. He had begun perspiring as soon as he got in and now his white shirt stuck uncomfortably to his chest and back. He seemed oblivious to all that and droned on about being sensitive to what he called the veil between worlds, talking of it as a fabric with folds and creases, wears and tears. Analogies that didn't always make sense.

Berkeley glanced back at Marchen in the mirror. She looked bored and about ready to sulk. He shook his head, glad that she couldn't seem him fighting back a little laughter. After forty minutes, the lad was all she could find – and he seemed to be more talk than experience. But he was all they had, so he wasn't going to complain.

It was late afternoon as they slowed to a halt in the old car park. There was still a patrol car and at the scene itself a couple of bobbies would be posted to keep the public out. It was a relief to get outside and breathe a little fresh air which they took a moment to enjoy while their passenger eased himself out through the door.

"Right, Kevin, isn't it? Follow us and you can do your thing. Meanwhile, I assume you know to stay focussed on where we're going – don't get distracted by anything else."

"It's alright Mr Berkeley, I am a professional."

"Yes, you said, but you're also too young to get indignant with me, so don't. Instead, do as I say, which is stay focussed." He marched onwards, leading the group through a ruined maze of red brick walls and doorways that no longer led to anything but hollowed out foundations.

A single PC stood outside of the yellow tape surrounding the scene. She held up a hand as the group approached.

"I'm sorry but..."

"It's alright," he held up his ID, "what's your name Constable?"

"Oh, sorry sir, PC Kate Belling."

"Shouldn't there be two of you?"

"Yessir, PC Cole is just...relieving himself."

"Well, I suppose we can allow that. This is my Sergeant and two consultants, we're going to take a look around the scene again. Stay out here and when this Cole of yours turns up, let him know to keep the noise down."

"Yessir." Without being asked, she lifted the tape up for the party, who all still had to duck to get past.

"Oh." Kevin's face paled despite his exertions, his eyes fixed on the dark spread of dried blood in the middle of the space.

Marchen however, seemed untroubled and suddenly more alive. "This really is a thin spot, isn't it! Too many shadows, too deep. Where do you think the shade came from?"

Berkeley pointed. "Over there, that dark space."

She walked toward it and extended a hand into the darkness. "Yah, goosebumps!"

"Um...if you don't mind." Kevin had pulled himself together and was now seeking to assert himself as the consultant they had asked for. "I think that we should start with the shade the couple had come to see. Everything in its proper order, you see."

"Alright lad, what do you suggest?"

"Well, I should...I should be...roughly where they were st..."

"Yes, well, don't stand in it, you can stand just in front of it."

"Oh, yes." He stepped gingerly around and stood with his back to all that remained of the victims. "They were calling for their daughter, what was her name?"

"Gabby."

"What are you going to do?" Meadows had her arms wrapped around her as if cold, though she didn't feel it.

"Call for her."

"And that will do?"

"Anything that will recreate what happened that night will help me get a feel for what was here."

"Shouldn't we come back later then?"

"You're not paying me enough for that."

"We're not paying anyway."

"I'm not going to tempt anything here at night. Not in a place like this."

Feeling impatient, Berkeley began looking around at them all. "Well, in that case, there are too many of us in here."

"You are right." Dr Marchen made her way over to where Kevin stood but Meadows got there first.

"Sorry Doctor but one of us should be in here for this."

"Fair enough. Detective, I guess we get to be the spectators." She and Berkeley made their way out, almost feeling some of the light leave with them but it was only when they turned to look back that they could see how much the light had faded within.

"Sir?"

"Constable. Feeling prickly?"

"Yessir." The young PC looked as spooked as she sounded.

"Your other half not back yet?"

"No sir."

"Why don't you go and find him. Tell him to keep quiet when you do." She looked grateful as she left.

"Gabby!" Kevin called out, "are you here Gabby?"

There was something wrong, his voice didn't sound as loud as it should, muffled somehow. The air cooled a little more and yet became close and heavy, as if it had acquired a degree of viscosity.

"Gabby!"

She didn't appear but the shadows lengthened against the light that was left.

"Gabby! Please Gabby, won't you come to us?"

And there she was. She just popped into existence before them, looking so real, so solid that Berkeley thought he should be able to take her hand and lead her away. He wanted to, her face so full of fear and confusion, her eyes red and swollen with tears. Then they widened with terror as she screamed, her frail hands clutching her chest, her heart, chemically weakened, failing against the intensity of the drug induced nightmare. She died before them, as she had many times before for her parents. For a moment he felt a little of their pain and wondered at how they had managed to endure such an ordeal time and time again. He knew the answer. Hope.

Meadows looked back at them, frowning, unaffected and for a moment he felt angry at her for that but then he saw something else, a moving shadow, a voice that should have been clearer.

"Touching!"

Kevin's shoulder's stiffened. "Who is there? Show yourself to us."

Idiot, Berkeley thought. "Meadows, both of you get back from there. Out! NOW!"

The shadow became clearer now, the scar obvious, its shape solid along with the object in its hand.

"Meadows! Now!"

The brick was thrown toward them and with one hand Meadows pushed Kevin aside with all the force she could muster while ducking down in time for it to miss her head.

Such was his bulk that Kevin hadn't been moved far but stumbled, a little disorientated, his face confused as he looked to see Meadows spring to her feet in time to dodge another projectile.

"Get out man!"

"What? We should try to talk..." He was cut off when a brick cracked against his skull, as it did the figure leapt forward at the falling man, grasping at the ground for a new weapon which it raised and brought down with fatal force. With that, sound became liberated from whatever had restrained it, the smashing of Kevin's skull echoed around and out of the room as the grinning shade of Byron Black retreated back into the darkness.

Five

The two round glass towers of Bow Street station came into view, brightly lit against the night they reached up above the surrounding buildings, modern beacons of modern policing. Bryn looked up at them and flinched. The three of them sat in silence, Meadows driving, seemingly less affected by the trauma of Kevin's death. She focused on the road while Bryn focused on his guilt and Ute Marchen on her horror. Perhaps it was all the worse because the car still smelled of Kevin's sweaty presence.

The death of a civilian in these circumstances, helping the police and placed in mortal danger by doing so, was no light matter. There would be repercussions that could well lead to an end to his career, although at this point he wouldn't mind. Still, he couldn't let himself be distracted by that, it was a bridge to cross after he had solved this. This was no longer a case he was waiting to hand over, it was unfinished business.

His phone startled him and he opened it only half paying attention as DDI Kurland barked in his ear.

"Yes sir...No, I need to speak to a witness first...I'll not have anything to tell you until I do...yes, right after sir." He snapped it shut, disinterested in what had been said.

His eyes went back to the road as it dipped into the underground parking, light flooding the car from the well-lit space. He turned back. "Are you sure you're okay to do this now?"

Marchen nodded. She was in shock but her now determined expression told him she was plenty strong enough to deal with what had happened.

Ten minutes later they sat at a small table in a small conference room, too brightly lit, and too cold to be comfortable.

"Alright, I've never seen or heard of anything like what just happened. Meadows?"

"No, nothing in my experience."

"What's your take on it then doctor?"

Her hands wrapped around the hot mug of tea to steady them but her voice remained strong. "That was no projection, nobody has ever managed to project an apparition with that much definition. It was a shade. I am certain of it."

"But Black is alive."

"Yes, and yet...it is still possible, in theory."

"I don't get you, a shade is created by the trauma of death, like an emotional impression on the world."

"Not quite. And not on the world – the Underearth. Shades, what people used to think of as ghosts or lingering souls, are created by the trauma of death, that is right. There are different accounts of what the Underearth is and how it works. I can give you the account that I subscribe to. With such intense experience, there is a bleed of information into the Underearth, there, this information can coalesce into something tangible, with form but the detail of that form is limited and governed by the information which gave rise to it."

"Hence the constant replay of Gabby's death."

"Exactly, her trauma only included that limited information, its focus was simply her fear and her death, so that is all we really have of her. But others can be more detailed, they can include some personality, knowledge, and the ability to interact meaningfully."

"But not always physically."

"No, that depends upon the state of the divide between our world and the Underearth. We suspect that shades are

228

commonly created but that the conditions for them to be experienced here are relatively rare. But the point is that the trauma of their creation does not, in principle, require a person's death. Near death experiences have been known to leave traces of their occurrence."

"So the shade we saw, that killed Kevin, may have been created from Black if he came close to experiencing death? That still leaves too many questions. Why would it be there? – shades tend to be tied to locations. And there's its behaviour, the sheer violence of it."

"Could Black have been there before?" Meadows offered. "I mean it seems too much of a coincidence not to be related to the shade of Gabby."

"That is a question for your investigation. However, I think that what we saw was a repeating pattern of behaviour and it clearly occurred in response to a trigger."

"To calling for Gabby? We re-created the conditions to trigger the response for the killing?"

"I think so. Which raises another question for you."

"If the Eddlemere's had been through this before so many times, why did they only trigger the event when they did?"

"Indeed. It must have been created only since their last attempt to reach her."

Meadows leaned back and looked up at the ceiling, her eyebrows raised and something close to, though not quite a smile. "And created with purpose."

Berkeley leaned forward to his tea and stared down at it. "Defence contractor. It's something to do with what he's doing for the MOD."

Marchen shook her head, "That sounds like something I should stay out of."

"Yes, the three of us need to keep that line of speculation to ourselves for now, and I'll keep your name out of it as much as I can."

"I appreciate that."

229

"We are still going to need some help though."

"Of course. I said that it was something that I should stay out of but I prefer curiosity over prudence."

"In the meantime, we need to do something about the shade, to make it safe. I don't know how that works – there are ways to exorcise them, aren't there?"

"Not exactly, but where the space between worlds is so thin it can be physically breached, it is possible to seal up that breach. That is why I mentioned Hecate. But this isn't just a small room or building, you can't just seal up Edgelands that vast."

"I'll put in for a quarantine order then. For now though, you two go home. I'll handle the brass waiting upstairs."

It was late when Bryn arrived and paused at the door both glad to be home and at once saddened at the thought of what awaited him there. Kurland had tried to give him a hard time but the Commissioner had been sympathetic – more than the situation warranted and the more he thought about that, the more that troubled him.

He turned the key and stepped into the dark hallway of the little terraced cottage. "Hello?"

The light clicked on and Melanie Poule smiled at him. "Long day?"

"Yes – and thank you for popping in like this, you're a life saver. When did her nurse leave?"

"A few hours ago. And it's okay. She's been quiet and I've a lot of course work to do." Melanie was a full figured woman in her mid-forties, divorced for another woman but who didn't miss married life at all. She made sure that she had the home and then free of his overbearing and sometimes threatening influence, she had started courses with the Open University. Community nurses provided some care for his wife, his own wages and savings some more again, but he knew that without Melanie filling in the gaps in care, he would never cope.

"I put something in the oven for you after you phoned, give it another ten minutes and it'll be ready."

"Thank you again. I'll just pop up and see her before I get settled."

"Sure, I'll let myself out. You take care and call again if you need anything."

He smiled and nodded before heading up the narrow stairway. They had known each other long enough that he didn't need to say more. He paused at the top and waited to hear the front door before he opened the one to his wife's room.

The curtains had been drawn and the small bedside lamp cast an almost orange glow from its fabric shade. The only sounds were the hum of traffic outside and the slow and steady breaths from his wife as she slept. She mostly slept now and selfishly he preferred that, this way he could imagine that she were still the same. When she was awake she was confused and, without her memory, always in the presence of strangers.

Falling into a chair in the corner of the room, Bryn told her of his day, his concerns, his fears, and closing his eyes he nearly fell asleep before he remembered the food cooking for him.

***

Wanting an early start Bryn had again imposed a little on Melanie. He had expected to be able to settle down to some quiet and uninterrupted research and not to find a man sitting on his office floor with the casing of his eBrain opened up before him.

"Can I help mate?" The man said with a quizzical smile.

"I don't know, are you helping?"

"Oh, you're...um DI Berkeley then?"

"Um, yes."

"Sorry mate, wasn't expecting anyone to be in yet, we like to get these things done when you're out. You know, to minimise disruption."

"You know, I don't. What exactly are you doing?"

"Checking the outside Neuro-Net connections and ethics sub-routines."

"Why?"

He picked up the clipboard lying next to him and flipped a couple of pages with a little too much flourish. Everyone seemed to be a performer to Bryn these days. "Yeah, here it is, you reported behavioural problems. Apparently it was being...er...rude?"

"Yeeees. I remember now. It didn't come to me right away because that was about four months ago."

"Little behind on checking the minor issues."

"Well, you might have checked if it was still an issue before you dismantled everything and, as you say, caused disruption."

"Is it not a problem now?"

"No, it isn't."

"You corrected its behaviour yourself then?"

"Yes, well, given four months to do it in, I didn't really need a degree in A.I. Psych. Personally, I preferred it when they didn't pretend to talk to us."

"Pretend?"

"Pretend, though I suppose it's us that do the pretending," he gingerly stepped over the mess on the floor to reach the sink and clean his cup and pot, "like parrots, they're just mimics."

"No, mate, not for at least three generations of 'em."

"They're just machines."

"So are we, the difference is chemistry, that's all."

"Wonderful, well put your chemistry set back together will you, I have work to do."

"Right you are."

When the man left, Bryn sat back in his desk and surveyed the little changes, things not quite put back as they should. Like the phone. He looked across at Meadow's desk. Nothing had moved. He rubbed his still twitching thumb and frowned before getting up again when the electric kettle rumbled to a boil, rattling the spoons on its tray. An hour later the phone rang and at the same time Meadows opened the door, mouthing a 'good morning' as he answered it, and set her things down.

"DI Berkeley, Bow Street...gods, I've not heard from you for...no, wait a minute Jean, I think there's something wrong with this phone...can I ring you back on my mobile? Thanks, I'll just be a jiffy."

Meadows peered up from behind her screen to see him reach not for his coat but for the grey filing cabinet that stood behind his desk. He pulled open the top draw, riffled through the files and then beneath them to pull out an old mobile phone in an evidence bag. He did nothing to hide what he was doing. Pulling it out he dialled the number from memory.

"Jean, that's much better. How have you been, not getting into too much trouble over that dockworker business I hope?...good...riiiight...no, that should be fine, it will be good to catch up again...that's right...oh, nothing I can't deal with. Keeping your head down? OK, your usual spot then?...fine, half an hour?...I'm on my way."

Meadows stood expectantly. "Where are we off to?"

"We aren't. I'm meeting an old friend. You however, are going to fill in that quarantine request and take it to Kurland – he doesn't like doing them at the best of times, and given what went down yesterday, I think it will be better coming from you. Smile at him. But don't do more or you'll never shake him off." He didn't give her time to reply but grabbed his coat and was gone. However, he didn't head directly to the car park but to arrange the use of an unmarked car from the pool which he reached via the fire escape.

The man watching Bryn's own car, still wearing the technician's overalls, never saw him drive past and out.

***

Jean Herbin was a creature of habit. He always met his contacts in the same small bakery which afforded a good view of the street outside and whose owners he knew well enough for them not to mind if he made use of the rear exit which opened feet away from the entrance to the tube station. Not that that was how he got there, he was always loath to be without his car and the arsenal of equipment that he kept in it, so he parked two streets away and made his way on foot, which gave him the chance to check out the area and shop window first. It was not that he was paranoid as such, just a cautious man after stepping on so many toes in his line of work.

Sitting in the window with a cup of tea in one hand and a jam doughnut in the other, Bryn looked out at the busy street, knowing where Herbin would come from. There he was, approaching the crossroads. He saw him stop and press the button and wait for the lights to change, wearing his old cords, brown jacket, and tatty scarf. Looking towards Bryn and waving as he always did when he thought it was safe. Bryn waved back to confirm it as Herbin liked and then watched in horror as the shape of Byron Black appeared next to the journalist, giving him a sharp shove into the oncoming traffic. Herbin bounced over the top of a car, rolling over onto the other side where a van slammed into him, breaks screeching.

Bryn dropped what he was holding, the cup clashing against the saucer as the contents flew out over the table and floor. He ran out the door, running, hoping, but knowing what the outcome was likely to be. Cars had piled into each other, bent bumper to bent bumper, some at odd angles as drivers' instincts had told them to try and avoid the inevitable collisions. He held out his ID and shouted at people to move aside and knelt down beside the broken body.

"Jean! Jean? Oh gods no." He looked up to tell someone to call for an ambulance and saw that someone was already doing so. Looking back down, he saw Herbin's eyes open a little.

"Bryn?" His voice was barely a whisper and distorted by the blood that flowed out from his mouth.

"Yes, it's me. Help is coming. You just hold on."

"Don't be an arse...It was him, wasn't it?"

"Black? Yeah. I saw him."

"It's...nineteen...they...torture..." The whisper faded, blood bubbled up from internal injuries and then his eyes rolled.

***

He didn't wait for the ambulance. He couldn't help and he could file a statement later – it was his case anyway. But more than anything, he was angry, deeply angry. He chanted 'nineteen' over and over as he marched to the car until the piece fit with another piece and then another. He missed getting the key in the door twice before he finally managed it and getting in, slammed it closed with almost shattering force. He knew that he needed to take some time, to calm down, think straight and make a decision – a good one.

The drive back was slow and deliberate, the walk to his office, direct and focused. Meadows was standing against the sink, phone in hand. Looking up at him, she finished her call, her face suddenly tightened as she noticed the blood over his coat and arm.

"Are you okay? Is that yours?"

"I'm fine and no, it isn't mine."

"Something's wrong..."

"Do you think?"

"What's happened? Whose blood is it?" She was calm and curious, and the concern she showed, somewhat business-like.

235

"We'll get to that. What does the nineteen mean to you?"

"University, alcohol, bad sex."

"'Nineteen' and 'torture'"

"University, alcohol, bad..."

"Cut the pissing games Meadows, or whatever your name is. I'm done with them."

"You were such fun up until now. But I am who I say."

"Your hand."

"What about it?"

"Let me see it."

"Are you going to read my palm?"

"Would you like me to?"

She held out her hand, smiling now, ever curious. He reached out slowly, so as not to alarm and griped her wrist. Now she looked puzzled. "And?"

"And now you start telling me the truth."

"What truth would you like?"

"Let's start with your name."

"You know my name, it's Three." Her face changed. "How...?" It changed again, surprise became concern.

"Trying to move?"

"How? That isn't possible without..." She smiled again. "Without...something...? A gift from the Gods? This is a rare power." Her gaze turned to his arm. "The copper band? I'm not sure powerful little toys like that are legal, at least not for use by the police. I wondered how you had made so many difficult collars in your day. Can you extract confessions?"

"No, just tease out the truth sometimes – but that takes a little concentration on my part. I'll make a special effort for you. And no, not really legal but then, who would know? Like that Gramayre Street, you'll sort of forget about it soon after I let go. That's why nobody tries to take it."

"And does it give you that pricking in your thumbs?"

"No, that's something different. Three? That doesn't sound like much of a name."

"Because you're a free man, not a number?"

"Do you ever tire of being facetious?"

"No."

"An old associate of mine is dead, another shade of Black, another trigger I would guess, he had enough habits to base one on."

"Sorry, were you close?"

"Before he died, he said two words: 'nineteen' and 'torture'."

"And?"

"And in the context of the MOD, those two add up to MI19, the interrogation unit. I thought they were wrapped up after the last scandal – what was it, five or six years ago? Are they still around, still using a heavy hand?"

"Why would I know?"

"You're MI:Something." MI:Something did not mean that he didn't know, it was the colloquial name used by the few who knew or guessed of its existence. It was a department that grew out from Londinium Controlling Section whose role in the war was to deceive and befuddle the enemy. But as the supernatural became better recognised, it was clear that states would attempt to employ it in espionage and so MI:Something was born. Bryn could sense another question coming and so tightened his grip and focussed his mind. Two wills fought for a moment and his nearly lost.

"Yes. But it isn't good for you to know that."

"I'm too old and too tired to care. What's your interest? Why are you here?"

"I suppose we're at a stage where it might help for you to know something. But I'd prefer to volunteer it."

He nodded and released her. "Spill it, or as much as you can."

She paused to move her arms and shoulders before flexing her legs, reassuring herself that she had control back. "We've information suggesting that Black was working on something with a supernatural twist for MI19. That's our business. We don't like other departments meddling in that sort of thing without our sanction, control, or confidence. They have none. We know that some of Black's team is missing, we presume dead, and that the project was shut down after that. So we want to know what the project was and to secure any technology that resulted from it."

"I've spent my life catching crooks and killers, outside of that, I've no interest in tricksters and traitors. I want my man, be it Black or whoever may be framing him – if that end can work with your end, then so be it. I'll have my killer, you can have your toy."

"For what it's worth, that was always a preferred option."

"Fine, for the time being. Now, call your friend and have him undo whatever he's done to my phone and eBrain. And remind him that if he doesn't, I'll know it."

Six

It was in the small hours of the morning when she arrived. The city lights held back the darkness with a sodium yellow that glowed through the fog creeping in from the Thames. She pulled up outside of the police cordon a short distance from the crossroads and stepped out of her car.

She didn't look much like a priestess to Bryn's eyes, auburn hair cascaded over rather too much leather, which under the long coat looked all rather tight. He wondered if she carried a whip but did clock the large knife sheathed at her belt and knew she had a licence to carry it, along with semi-automatic firearms. She strode past the two constables on duty and made for Bryn, extending a hand as she did. As they shook hands he saw her gaze fall directly to the copper band on his other wrist.

"So, you're DI Berkeley."

"Elizabeth Rook."

"Queenie, please, nobody calls me Elizabeth. Ute...Doctor Marchen, has filled me in on the situation."

"And can you seal this up?"

"Yes, I can do that for you. I don't think that I'll be able to tell you anything about your shade though."

"If you can try, I'd appreciate it. Would I be wrong in thinking that this place can support such a shade because of the crossroads?"

"That's a fair assumption, crossroads are deeply tied to Hecate for that reason. There seems to be something about the constant crossing of paths that thins the space."

"And could this be the same shade, the one that we saw at the Edgelands?"

"It is possible for a single shade to cross the Underearth between locations but they need to be places closely associated with it. Ute wondered about the possibility of the shade being created somehow. I guess if someone could do it once, then they could do it twice. It isn't her most grounded speculation though. Can you tell me exactly where you saw the shade?"

"About four or five feet behind where we're standing."

"Right, I'll get my things and set up there. I'd appreciate it if you could keep everyone at a distance though. They wouldn't like what it involves."

"Should I know about that?"

"I can tell you if you want, but you'd prefer..."

"...if you didn't." He wasn't going to argue. He felt tired in his bones now, the damp air seeming to penetrate through to them. He left the cordon and led the constables a short distance from it.

Rook meanwhile, pulled from her car some poles and sheeting and a covered basket, from which Bryn thought he heard the yelp from an animal. The gods gave nothing for free and the usual price was sacrifice. He turned away as she set up the poles and sheets to surround the area where the shade had appeared, shielding the onlookers from what she had to do.

The ceremony lasted perhaps an hour and dawn had begun to break while impatient drivers sought to pass the cordon and drive through, held back by apologetic uniforms asking them to either take a detour or wait just a little longer. She pulled down the sheets and picked up the poles and basket, leaving behind a pool of blood that seeped along the lines of the paving. She paused beside Bryn. "Don't let anyone wash the blood away, let it dry there and fade over time. The space here will eventually thin again though, that's the nature of crossroads. I'll file this with Gramayre House as something that will need repeat attention in...let's say five years. They'll contact Bow Street then to make arrangements."

"Thank you."

"You're welcome."

***

Byron Black awoke to the sound of his own cries and of Clarissa trying to offer some comfort. He felt cold from the sweat that covered his body, making the sheets cling to his bare skin as he sat up and doubled up, his hands reaching for his head. Clarissa pulled the wet bedclothes from him and draped a clean blanket over his shivering shoulders before pressing herself against him, arms reaching under his to encircle his chest.

"It's alright, you're awake now, it was just a dream...a nightmare...it's over."

His hands moved down to cover hers and he lent back into her a little before they rolled together to lie on their sides. "I'm sorry...I'm so sorry, for so much. I've been selfish for so much of my life and forgotten how much I love you, how much I need you."

She closed her eyes and held him all the tighter. Their relationship had not been so intimate and caring for so very long and she had never felt so needed, something she had always wanted to feel and always felt denied by a husband who kept himself distant from everyone.

Seven

He had not yet made it to Bow Street when his phone rang. Keeping the steering wheel in one hand, he fumbled in his pocket to answer it with the other. "DI Berkeley...Where and when?...I'm on my way."

He slowed a little too quickly, provoking a driver behind him to beep him, he flicked the indicators and made a sharp turn. Twenty minutes later he was pulling up outside of a noodle bar a short distance from Hyde Park. A man waved to him from inside.

He was scruffy looking, in his early thirties, his black hair as unkempt as what passed for a beard, while the red tracksuit looked a little grubby and clearly hadn't been washed in a while.

"Are you Mr. Bowen then?"

"Yeah, pull up a pew. You want something to eat?"

"It's a bit early for that stuff, isn't it?"

"Nah, never too early for chow mein."

"I'll take your word for it. What do you have to tell me?"

"Herbin was working with us on a story..."

"And who is 'us'?"

"Amnesty...mostly. We've been certain that MI19 was never really disbanded but Herbin came to us with an informant who confirmed that. They've been backing research into a means of interrogation employing torture."

"Well, that's not news, it's what caused all the stir about them in the first place."

"Yes, but they've been using some new tech with a supernatural foundation, something that will enable them to torture victims who afterwards will recall nothing of their suffering and will have no physical scars to evidence it."

Bryn sat quietly for a moment, absorbing what he had just before smiling to himself. "You know, it might just be that they don't intend on torturing anyone. Not as such, anyway."

"What do you know?"

"Probably nothing. Give me a number and if it turns out to be something worth your while, I'll call you. I owe Jean that much. This informant, I'm going to need to know..."

The man passed a dog eared business card to him. "I wouldn't normally betray a confidence but he trusted you – the name's on the back. You know that you can't trust your sergeant, don't you? She's not who she says, though that's about all I can tell you."

"I know. Let's leave it that we've reached a modest understanding." He flipped over the card to read the name – Colonel Martin Pommeroy.

***

He was no sooner back in his car than the phone rang again. The call was short and unexpected. As soon as the call hung up, he dialled a number himself. "Meadows? Our friend Black just phoned – he says he wants to tell us everything. Meet me at his house asap! Oh, and bring that list of people from Black's party, I want to check a name."

***

Meadows was already waiting at the door when Bryn arrived and was ringing the bell as he climbed the few steps in time to charge in past the maid as she answered.

"No sir, please, you must wait."

"No need, we're expected. Where is he?"

"Mr Black is working, he's a busy man. You must wait here."

An old grandfather clock chimed loudly next to Bryn making him flinch and step back, he almost flinched again when he saw

242

Byron Black charging around the corner with a furious expression.

"What the devil do you think you are doing barging into my home? Your DDI instructed you to drop this – you were never even supposed to speak to me! Did you think that I wouldn't check up on you?"

"We're here now because you called us here."

"What are you talking about?"

"About twenty...no, you don't know do you?" Bryn looked puzzled. "But I would have known if it wasn't you." He turned back, "Meadows, you have that list?" Taking it from her he glanced down through the pages until he saw the name he was looking for. "Martin Pommeroy."

"What about the man? He's nothing to do with me now."

"He was here that night - but not as an invited guest."

Black looked distant for a moment, his hand moving to his chest as he stepped back, his hand taking his weight against the bannister. "We...argued. Briefly. There was bad business between us. A personal matter, it doesn't concern you."

"I think it does."

Regaining his composure, Black threw back his shoulders and looked down at them. "I say otherwise. Now, unless you are here with a warrant, or are about to arrest someone, then you are leaving."

***

"Come on, we'll take my car."

"Where to?"

"I want to talk to this Pommeroy bloke. He's tied up in it all somehow – between us, he's the man who led Herbin into all this."

"He was part of Black's project for Nineteen? And what was all that about? You said that he phoned you, that you would have known if it wasn't him?"

"Yes. I did. And I would have."

"You didn't seem to think that Black was lying to us back there though...you don't think that a shade would...could have phoned you? I don't think that makes sense. I'm not sure that they're capable of responding like that, not to original situations."

"Well, we're going to find out. But first things first. Pommeroy."

***

Margaret Pommeroy opened the door, her eyes puffy and red from tears which had not long stopped. She was an attractive woman, perhaps forty, with chestnut hair that surrounded a fearful expression which grew to horror when they identified themselves as police.

Barely able to stand and her voice unsteady, she had begun to speak when Bryn realised what she was thinking. "It's alright Mrs Pommeroy. We're not here with news...but we are looking for your husband. I can take it he's not here?"

She shook her head, her relief obvious.

"May we come in, please." He stepped in, taking Mrs Pommeroy's arm and leading her through the hall into what he guessed was the living room while Meadows followed, closing the doors behind them. The house was smart and a little chic but chic on a budget. He led her to a couch and sat beside her. "Now, clearly you think that something's happened to your husband and I'm going to guess that it has something to do with Byron Black. I know that he went to see Black a couple of nights ago, I know that there's bad blood between them, and pound to a penny, it wasn't a professional falling out."

"No. And it's my fault." Her voice was quiet but she had calmed herself now and looked at the policeman, pausing to think how she should continue.

"Your fault?"

"Yes. I had an affair, with him."

244

"With Black? When did it end? When did your husband find out?"

"He didn't tell me, not right away. He must have been so angry at me, so angry he turned to her, to Byron's wife. Revenge, he told me they wanted us to know how it felt, what we'd done to them."

"And that's when it ended?"

"No..." Tears seem to well up but she took a deep breath and held them back, wiping her eyes with the back of a hand. "I was pregnant...we hadn't been able to have children. Martin found the test, told me what he had done, how much I'd hurt him, called me things and left. I took an overdose and miscarried. I'm afraid that he's blamed himself for that. Himself and Byron."

"And why did you think something had happened to him?"

"Byron called and said that he wanted to meet him, to settle things between them."

"When was that?"

"At ten."

"Sir?"

"What?"

"At ten you were talking to Mr Black."

Bryn nodded. "When you say ten, do you mean around...?"

"No, at ten. I saw the clock."

"Where would they go? And why do you think something has happened?"

"It was Martin's reaction, he looked shocked. Since that night he's hardly left our spare room. Hardly eaten. When he took the phone from me, he didn't believe who it was, said he shouldn't be alive, that he didn't deserve to be..."

"And where?"

"I don't know...they spoke about the project, their lab."

"And do you have any idea where that was."

"Tyburn."

"Specifically...?"

"Tyburn, that's all I know. I probably wasn't supposed to know that much."

He stood up and straightened his coat. "Sergeant, time to make yourself useful. Call your people – I want to know what property Nineteen has at Tyburn. Double quick."

Eight

Martin closed the door behind him and stood in what had been an estate agents, which itself was just a cover. It was, he had always thought, a ridiculous place for the operation to be based but the property had been in MI19's possession since the last Great War and they had held on to it since, running odd businesses themselves to keep it looking legitimate. Now lit only by the little daylight that made it through the windows and remains of display stands, the deserted office was a strangely uncomfortable space. Desks and odd bits of remaining stationery littered the place and he carefully and quietly stepped over the odds and ends, photos of houses long sold, or broken staplers. It had once been so familiar, it was the entrance that he had used when the operation was in full swing. He smiled to himself as he remembered some of those he worked with, the smile fading as he recalled those he would never see again. In the back office, he needed a torch to see where he was going, finding the large wall of shelving and the discrete lever that allowed it to open as a door.

He looked at the stairs that led down into the darkness and felt a dread without fear. His breathing was shallow and his spirit weakened. There was a sense of inevitability, that he was about to face some sort of judgement for his actions. He had killed men before, but only from duty, only because he had too. He had hurt people too but had never really adjusted to that, never quite become cold to it. And now he had killed a man from

246

anger, personal hate, and before that he had overseen a failure that resulted in the deaths of people he was responsible for. Perhaps whatever awaited him was deserved.

"Byron?" His voice almost failed him, he tried to swallow and called out again, a little louder this time. "Byron?" He didn't expect an answer, he didn't know what to expect, he knew that Byron Black was dead...he'd killed him himself. He flinched inwardly as he recalled feeling the knife drive home during their struggle, the way the blade grated against a rib on its way into a lung and then back out. Free of resistance, his arm naturally drew the knife back while the need to finish what he had now committed to, sent it back with still more force. His victim beneath him was too occupied with the panic of breathing the blood which would have drowned him had he been allowed to die slowly. Instead the knife slipped effortlessly beneath the rib cage, finding the heart and bringing an end to the struggle.

The immediacy of the memory made Martin feel ill, he tasted bile as he fought to keep himself from vomiting. Whatever self-respect he had lost, a deeper instinct still sought to retain a little dignity in the face of his crime. He realised that he was shaking and sat upon the top stair, looking within for the strength and resolve to continue to whatever awaited him.

Tyburn, once a small town but long ago absorbed by the sprawling and unstoppable growth of Londinium, was home to many new monuments but still attracted the more morbid tourists who sought the famous Tyburn Tree. Or at least the current version of it, still true to the old three legged design, the eighteenth century re-build had been restored and maintained, and the gallows continued in use into the early twentieth century and then revived briefly for executing traitors in the Great Wars.

Bryn detested the sight of it, as black a thing as ever existed. As they drove past its dark shape, he wondered why it wasn't Edgelands, why it hadn't been quarantined. Perhaps its presence was part of the reason for Nineteen choosing to set up their research there.

"Pull up here." Meadows directed and he parked half onto the curb, ignoring an angry driver and some disapproving looks from pedestrians. "One of the properties on this side – but that's the best we have I'm afraid."

Getting out, Bryn felt it immediately, the pricking in his thumbs, and like a blood hound he turned to the empty property. "This one. Come on."

"Thumbs?"

"That and the obvious. Honestly, how long do you think a property in this area stays empty?" He reached straight for the door, instinct telling him it would be open. He felt where he should be going, a stronger feeling than he had ever had before and he went with it without hesitation. He charged through the half-light and abandoned furniture to reach the back and through there to the office behind. The secret doorway was still open but at the bottom there was a sliver of light through the bottom of a set of doors. "Come on, don't dawdle." He beckoned for Meadows to hurry, speaking in a loud whisper.

Their descent was quiet and with each step they listened intently for some sign of there being someone else present. At the doors it was too dark for Meadows to see him shrug to himself before his hands searched for the handles and swung them open.

The room was large and lit with low emergency lighting that hummed from the walls. What kind of workspace it had been intended to be was unclear as all that remained were the benches. The only clue to its purpose was in the line of old fashioned prison cell doors along the far wall. But more than that, there was blood, oxidised brown, splashed and smeared over one wall and the floor about it.

In the middle of it a lone figure spun around, dishevelled and clearly startled. "Who...who the devil are you?! You have to leave this place. Now – it isn't safe for you to be here."

"DI Berkeley...and its less safe than you know, at least for you. I think our friend Mr Black has something planned for you down here."

"He...he can't. Black is dead."

"Then who called you here?"

"He said it was him...Black. But it couldn't be. I killed him."

"At the party you crashed?"

"Yes."

"No. He's alive and well."

"That's not possible." He looked alarmed and almost unconsciously began to back away from them, moving further into the room.

"You need to come with us sir. I really mean it, you're not safe here."

"Sir..." Meadow's voice was a warning, the shadows were growing longer, the light as bright yet less penetrating.

He reached a hand into a coat pocket and pulled from it his police issue Bulldog, an old fashioned snub nosed revolver that still chambered only five shots.

"Sir?"

"If it's solid enough to hit something, it's solid enough to be hit back. We only need enough time to get him out and the doors closed."

"What are you talking about? This isn't right, it didn't happen like this. It felt different."

"What felt different Martin?"

"When we made them...shades...of prisoners..."

"But they were a little harder to control than you hoped, yes? Killed some people, yes?"

"Yes."

"And that's what Black has been doing, he's made shades of himself Martin, and he's using them to kill people."

249

Martin didn't get to answer, Bryn's eyes had been casting about for the first sign of his target, gun levelled and ready and when the figure appeared, he fired twice. The first shot missed, the second struck the shoulder. Instantly Meadows raced forward, grabbing Martin as he turned to watch Byron Black grasp at the injury, snarl and leap forward as if an animal. She pulled him with all her strength, as Bryn fired twice more, this time a glancing wound to the head sent him reeling to the ground with a wail of pain. Bryn took advantage of the moment to help his sergeant and between them they made it to the stairs, pulling the doors closed behind.

All became silent but for their breathing.

"Do you think it's still there? I mean, it's not as if you killed it."

"Probably not, now the conditions for its being there are gone, it's probably reset...or something like that."

"Shall we take a look?"

"No, we bloody won't." Reaching down to grab Martin by the arm, Bryn pulled him to his feet. "Come on sunshine, you can do some more explaining later but for now, I want to know who else Byron Black hated enough to kill."

"Hated more than me? Just his wife...he'll never forgive her."

"There didn't seem to be any animosity between them."

"Trust me, he hates her."

"No, really, I would know..." There was a pause. "Oh, bloody hell! Come on, get a move on." He raced up the stairs leaving the others to follow at speed.

He drove in silence, his hands gripping the steering wheel as he willed himself to be in time. He wanted to save this one. He dodged traffic, avoided pedestrians, taking every chance he had to, leaving Meadows to call in for some back up. As the car screeched to a halt in Gramayre street, a couple of uniform were waiting for them, one carrying a bright read battering ram. Bryn wasn't out of the car before he shouted out to them. "Get the door open! Now!"

They hesitated for a moment and Bryn's expression made clear that was a mistake, then they went to it, swinging the ram back and then into the door with enough force to send it crashing against the inside wall. Drawing his gun again, Bryn was first through the door to see Byron Black wavering on the staircase, a vague and uncertain look on his face.

"Where is she?"

"Who...why are you...?"

"Mrs Black! Where is she?"

"She's here..." He wavered again, his legs seeming unsteady. "She was right here...and then...I don't know."

He bounded up the steps to face him, as angry as frustrated. "Where would he take her?"

"Who, who would take her. She was here."

"Black, Byron Black, where would he take her?"

"Black...I'm Black."

"No, you're a memory, an alibi, a diversion, and appeasement for his wife until he was ready. Now think! Where would you take someone, to hide them, to be hidden?"

"I wouldn't..." He frowned, as if struggling to recall something, he eyes turning to the dark wood wainscotting that adorned the walls throughout the hall.

Then Bryn felt it, the pricking in this thumbs. He wasted no time, his fingers moving over the surface, following the beaded edge of the panels until he knew where to press. A large panel moved back and to the side, with a small stairway leading back and down into a lit room below. He could hear a shuffling, a muffled voice, a struggle. He descended as quickly as his footing would allow, Meadows now close behind him, as near to her own goal as he was to his.

Black looked up at them. Not the Black they had left on the stairs behind them but the Black they had seen murder and attempt to murder, one full of anger and malice. The long scar seemed almost crimson, his jaw clenched and in his hands, the neck of Clarissa, fighting for her life.

251

"Let her go Black." He raised his Bulldog and for perhaps only the third time in his life he wanted to use it, to take a life. "DI Berkeley, You don't get another warning."

Black seemed to relax for a moment, releasing his grip on Clarissa. She rolled over at his feet and immediately began to raise herself but that was a mistake, as soon as she was up Black pulled her back. Reacting, Bryn fired but in his concern for hitting Clarissa the shot went wide. He fired again only for the weapon to click harmlessly and he cursed himself for not reloading.

Now holding her in front of him, Black took from his pocket the knife he always kept there. It flicked open and hovered at her throat. "Back off. Whatever you think you have on me is worthless! You don't know what you're dealing with." He spat the words but even with the knowledge that Bryn's gun was empty, he couldn't quite hide the note of panic, his eyes casting about for something, anything that he might use.

"I'm dealing with an inventive murderer...but still just a murderer."

"No. You're dealing with a valuable asset."

"If you were that valuable why bother with the elaborate method, why not just kill them all openly? Or were you showing off how clever you are?"

"Showing off. And now that I think of it, I don't think that I have anything to lose. With that he pulled back Clarissa's head by her hair. She gasped as her throat was bared and the blade made contact with the taught skin. But Black paused, seeing something in the corner of his eye, something from the shadows behind him. And then he felt it, the cold steel tearing through cotton, skin, muscle, and organ alike. He turned his head as much as he could, his hands keeping a tight hold on his would be victim, his eyes widening as he looked upon his own face which whispered in his ear: "That's my wife!"

In quick succession, the blade was withdrawn and then forced back in, twice, three, four times, until Byron Black dropped to the floor perfectly dead.

Clarissa turned slowly, looking down at the body of the man who had tried to kill her with such anger and hatred, then up and the man who looked with the concern and love of the man she had married.

"It's alright, it's me. You're safe now."

"Bugger. I can't arrest a shade, not even legally a person. Still, I suppose we'll have to place a quarantine order on the house if it can't be sealed."

"NO!" Clarissa now stood beside the shade of her husband, his arm around her. "You'll do no such thing. He's no danger to anyone now, he never was. You have your murderer and if you want to have the technology he kept here, you'll leave us be."

Meadows took that as her cue. "And that is what I'm here for. Fair's fair – you have your man, I'll take what's left."

It wasn't the result that he wanted. It would all be covered up and Black would never answer for what he had done. He looked at the body and felt a little ashamed at having wanted him dead. He preferred his criminals to face justice and this was not his idea of it.

"I don't think that I get a choice in this, so fine. What you find is yours and I'll not bother with the quarantine notice – which will save someone having to ignore it. In fact, if you don't mind, I'll leave the report to you."

"I'll take care of it sir. I appreciate your help."

"Don't. I was doing my job."

The two of them walked back up and outside where Bryn took a deep breath and wondered at Clarissa Black, that she would recognise the truth so quickly and then settle for a dream. Perhaps deep down, she had always known something wasn't right, that he was a different Black. His phone rang and he answered without thinking and taking in the news he snapped it shut. "Meadows, drive me home please."

He wondered if she might know enough about him to know not to speak, to just drive without question. But of course she did, there was probably very little about him that she didn't know. He stared dispassionately out of the window, not certain of what he felt, what he should feel and when the car finally stopped, he took a few moments to notice, which she allowed him. Without a word, he got out and walked past the paramedic's car, his front door already being opened to him by his wife's nurse. He had hoped that it would be Melanie.

"Mr Berkeley, I'm so sorry but it was very peaceful. She didn't wake. The doctor has called for the...but...well, we thought you should have a few moments first."

"Thank you." He nodded as he walked on, not looking at her, not wanting to be looked at, to be pitied. The sound of his footsteps on the old stairs had never been so loud.

At the top the door was open and there his wife lay, just as he had left her but now without the shallow breaths. He sat in the chair and looked and realised that she had been long dead now, no more than a hollow shade that had finally faded. He didn't weep, his bereavement had already lasted years, and instead he felt a small release and a little guilt for it.

WIDOWS DANCE
Scott H Lewis

The courtyard that greeted Bohdan Mykhaylovych Siryk outside the entrance to his apartment building was a study in grayscale. The sun was just beginning to rise over Kyiv on this cool September morning, and its first weak rays mingled with the residual light cast from a few apartment windows and a forlorn streetlight to create a half-hearted, ineffectual illumination that left little real light, but rather merged dark shadows with shadows darker still.

In the courtyard – a rather fanciful way to describe what served as a parking lot for the building's tenants – water droplets remaining from last night's shower glistened on the assembled autos.

Bohdan closed the door and drew in a lungful of cool, crisp air. It was city air, not the fresher forest-scented air he preferred, but it was the best city air of the day, and that would do. The air had taken on a crispness that announced an imminent end to summer. He put a foot on the nearest car and stretched, preparing for his ritual early morning jog. The young police lieutenant liked to run along the bank of the Dnipro every morning before work and most nights after he finished, when he could. He enjoyed the exercise and took pride in maintaining his fitness. His desk job in the Interior Ministry's training directorate was a mixed blessing, he thought: While it was routine work that didn't allow him much exercise during the day, the hours were predictable, which allowed him to fit in a three-kilometer jog once or twice daily.

From his home in Podil, the Ukrainian capital's charming yet crumbling old Jewish neighborhood, Bohdan ran along Naberezhno-Khreschatyts'ka, often detouring from the sidewalk to run down steps to the moorage and back up again.
As he trotted along the riverbank, something unusual caught the young policeman's eye: An unnaturally round, white object floated in the algae-rich green water. He slowed to look closer, and then stopped before reaching into a pocket for his mobile phone to report the he had discovered a body.
Bohdan waited as the first policemen arrived, followed by an ambulance and a pair of detectives. He told them what he could and watched as the bloated corpse was pulled from the water and wrapped in a bag for transport to a city morgue. Bohdan could see that only part of the body remained, and that it was nude.

One of the detectives, a heavyset bald man in his 50s who had introduced himself as Pavlo, walked over to Bohdan.
"I'll take a wild guess that this wasn't suicide or an accident," he said. "No clothes, no documents, no hands and no head. Not much chance of identifying this fellow unless he had his name and address tattooed on his rump."
"Pretty strange," Bohdan replied.
"I have a high standard for 'strange' these days," the detective said. "Maybe this was a contract killing, I don't know. I do know

that whoever took this old man swimming didn't want him identified."

***

Borys Panchuk didn't love the accordion. He loved what he could do with it.

He remembered the way that his Uncle Sasha could make the box come alive with music, and how people's expressions changed when his uncle played.

When Borys was eight, his extended family had gathered to celebrate his mother's 30th birthday. His grandparents were there, as well as a coterie of aunts, uncles, cousins and friends. With dinner finished and the dishes swept into the apartment's tiny kitchen, Sasha opened the large black case that held his accordion and began to play. As Borys watched his uncle's fingers fly across the keys and buttons, his own fingers moved on his lap as he mimicked the man's movement. Though Borys wasn't aware of his mimicry, it hadn't escaped his uncle's eye. The next day, uncle and nephew became teacher and pupil, and the instrument's secrets slowly became known to the boy.

That party had ended almost 60 years ago. Most of those in attendance were now dead, Borys thought as he lugged the heavy black case off the Metro train at Hydropark. The people are gone, he thought, but the music would remain as long as he and his well-worn instrument were able to produce it.

It was Sunday afternoon, and the park was bustling with activity. Old women sold dried fish and snacks by the Metro as youngsters hurried past on their way to the beach. The cafes and bars were packed, young mothers pushed carriages and couples strolled. Borys headed to The Square, a small paved patch lined with benches that the park's elderly claimed as their own. Here, men sat playing chess and women congregated in twos and threes. There were few couples among them. Most of those who gathered in The Square once or twice a week did so for the companionship, having lost spouses to age, infirmity

257

and cruelties both natural and unnatural. Borys knew most of the regulars by name, and he knew the songs they preferred. He greeted a few as he took his customary seat on a red bench next to his old partner, Andriy Viktorovych, who was already playing his violin.

Borys began playing in The Square in 1997; a year after his Iryna had died. On warm summer days, as many as 100 retirees would gather there to listen, chat and dance. Some made the effort to thank him for coming.

Evgenia had been one of those people. As he was packing his accordion away five weeks earlier, she had approached him and thanked him for the music. Borys had noticed her earlier that day: She was well dressed and tidy, matronly and with the bearing indicative of a woman of culture and manners. Borys had been impressed with her even before she spoke.

That first encounter had spawned several more. They met several times a week for coffee or a glass of wine. They had gone to the opera on one occasion, and were finding that they seemed to genuinely enjoy each other's company. Borys found himself feeling guilty when he thought of Zhenia - homage to his dear Iryna, he supposed. At 67, Borys wondered whether he could be falling in love for the second time in his life.

***

Bohdan climbed the four flights of stairs to his apartment in the dark. The man was long past cursing ZhEK for not keeping the lights in the house in working order. Even when they did work, the alcoholics who entered the building at night to sleep in the stairwell broke them.

The policeman remembered the maxim: "Darkness is the friend of the young," to which he added, "and the criminal."

When he reached the fourth floor landing, Bohdan found a woman standing by his door.

"Can I help you?" he asked, trying to make out the woman's features in the low light.

"Bohdan?" the woman said, recognition registering in her voice. "I'm Natalia Chervachidze, Nikolai's daughter. Do you remember me?"

He inserted his key into the lock, opened his door and switched on a light. "Natasha, of course!" he said. "I haven't seen you for years. Please, come in."

Bohdan had grown up in the two-room apartment he now occupied alone. Nikolai Chervachidze had raised his family in an apartment one floor up. Now the old Georgian lived alone, his wife buried. He'd heard that Natalia had married an electrical engineer and was living in Donetsk. He hadn't seen her for some time.

He offered her a chair and slipped around the corner into the kitchen to put on the teakettle.

"How are your parents?" Natalia said after he had returned with the tea.

"They died three years ago last winter," Bohdan said. "There was an auto accident. They were driving back from the Carpathians."

It had been a long three years, Bohdan thought to himself. He had lived with his parents of necessity, as he could never have afforded a place of his own on his salary. Now he shared the flat only with ghosts. He'd continued to sleep on the divan in the living room for almost a year before he could bring himself to sleep in the room his parents had occupied.

"I'm sorry to say it, but I haven't spoken with your father for a while," he said. "Will you be visiting him for a few days?"

"I came to Kyiv to check on papa," she said. "A year ago, we had a fight, and I hadn't talked to him since. When I called last week, the phone had been disconnected." Her voice began to tremble. "I rang the bell tonight and a man answered the door. He said that he owned the apartment now, and didn't know anything about my father. I've been contacting neighbors to see if anyone knows anything, but he's just disappeared.

"I'm really worried." There was a catch in the young woman's voice, and Bohdan felt compelled to be reassuring.

"I'm sure someone knows something. People don't just disappear," he lied.

The policeman knew his statement wasn't true: People did disappear. It happened all the time. Some wanted to drop out of sight, to cut familial ties. Others went less willingly, victims of crime or mental instability. Some returned of their own accord, but many - like the man he had found in the river earlier that day - disappeared so completely that even the corpse might be denied a name.

"I wish I could tell you where Nikolai has gone," he said, and told her that he would make some inquiries. "I can check out the people in his apartment. Call me tomorrow evening."

Making what should have been routine inquiries turned out to be more frustrating and time-consuming than Bohdan had expected. He was a bureaucrat, not a detective, but his badge could still open doors - at least a little.

A clerk at the city's central property inventory office was able to tell him that Nikolai had transferred the apartment to Evgenia Stepanova, and that she subsequently had sold the flat to the current tenant, Ihor Markovich. There was no address for Stepanova, and no indication of why Nikolai would have sold or given the apartment to her.

He also learned that Stepanova had been involved in four similar transactions over the past two years. A bottle of Moldovan brandy helped persuade the clerk to promise to copy the transfer documents within a few days.

"I haven't got much information yet," Bohdan told Natasha when she telephoned the following evening. "I think I should talk to his friends. Do you know any of them?"

"I don't, I'm sorry," she said. "It's terrible for a daughter to say, but we weren't close. We argued, and as I told you, we hadn't spoken for a year. I wish..."

Her voice trailed off.

"He did go to Hydropark, to a place for pensioners there, and played chess," she said. "Maybe someone there would remember him?"

"Tomorrow is Saturday," Bohdan said. "I could go there in the afternoon. Would you come with me?"

"Of course," the woman said. "I need to get out of the hotel room anyway."

"Fine, then," Bohdan said. "Tomorrow."

The Kyivan sky was blue and cloudless and the air was cool. On the beach where a few weeks earlier hundreds of people had sunbathed, only a handful of hardy souls now lay. Bohdan and Natasha walked through the park to The Square, which was occupied by two dozen pensioners.

Natasha began showing a photograph of her father to people and asking if anyone knew him. Bohdan walked up to an elderly man unpacking an accordion and sat down.

Borys Panchuk looked at the young man beside him.

"You're a little young for this crowd," he said, smiling. "Are you a musician, or a lover of accordion music?"

"I'm not a musician," Bohdan said. "I'm a good audience, though."

"Not many people under 90 come here," Borys said with a chuckle. "But promise me that you won't steal our women and you can stay."

"Agreed," Bohdan said. "Actually, I'm looking for someone - Nikolai Chervachidze. I heard that he comes here."

"Came here," Boys said. "He left Kyiv a while ago. I heard that he went back to Georgia. Nice fellow. Came here for years, then nothing. Never even stopped to say farewell. That surprised me, because he was a one of the regulars, but people aren't like they used to be."

Borys had unpacked the accordion and had slung it over his shoulder. He played a few tentative notes and flexed his thin hands.

"What do you want with Nikolai?" he asked.

"His daughter lost contact with him," Bohdan said. "I'm trying to help her get in touch. Have you been playing here for a long time?"

"Almost every decent weekend for seven years," he said. "Since my wife died. I like to entertain, to bring a little real music to this park. Not like that disco music the kids play."

He looked around the square, expectantly. "I usually play with Andriy. Where is he anyway? He has only a violin to carry, not this elephant."

"The men listen to the music, and some sing along," he continued. "But the women feel the music, out here under the trees and beneath the sun. The women lose their inhibitions; they forget their aches and pains for a while. They forget their dead husbands and pair off with each other. The men appreciate the music, but the widows dance!"

An old musician with a violin case walked up and stood before Bohdan.

"Ah, Andriy!" Borys exclaimed. "We've been waiting for you." To Bohdan, he said. "Please allow my colleague to take a seat so we can begin. And remember our agreement."

"Your ladies are safe," Bohdan assured him, returning the old man's smile. Then he looked across the square and spied Natasha, talking with a clutch of 60-somethings.

"They know papa," Natasha said. "They say he went back to Georgia, but nobody knows anything specific. Only rumors."

"That's what I heard, too," Bohdan said.

"It doesn't make any sense," Natasha said. "Papa's family has been in Ukraine for two generations. We don't have any close ties to anyone in Georgia."

"It's convenient, isn't it? I wouldn't check the Tbilisi phone book just yet."

HARD TARGETS

Evgenia Stepanova sat on a bench in The Square, talking with two other women. She sipped a cup of kvas, and listened to the bore to her right describe her late husband's last agonizing days after a bout with emphysema.

"I know how you feel, dear," she said when the woman finally paused for breath. "I've buried three husbands, myself."

"Three! My God," said the woman sitting to Evgenia's left. "How awful!"

"The first one died after eating bad mushrooms," Evgenia said. "As did my second husband."

"How awful," the woman on her left repeated.

Stupid cow, Evgenia thought as she continued.

"How did the third husband die?" the gullible woman asked.

"He was beaten to death with a hammer," Evgenia deadpanned. "He just refused to eat the mushrooms!"

After a moment, the gullible woman giggled, but the other woman, whose husband had recently succumbed to lung disease, gave her a reproachful look. The joke had offended her, Evgenia supposed, but she didn't care in the least.

The two women on the bench with Evgenia could not have suspected that there was some truth to her black humor.

Life had not been kind to Evgenia, but it had made her strong. Other people lived for their families, their mates, their children and grandchildren. Evgenia lived for Evgenia, which was perfectly fine with her: she saw herself as an intelligent, strong and independent woman.

She had grown up in a communal apartment shared by four families in a building occupied by employees of the H. I. Makarov Rubber Plant. She had hated living next to the filthy factory in a house that reeked of tired bodies and burned rubber. The plant that produced gaskets and molds spewed rubber and polymers out its smokestack day and night. The fine particulates that filtered in through the apartment's windows and doors adhered to clothes, dishes, furniture, and even hair. Life in the communal flat was a dirty, noisy and cramped affair devoid of privacy. It was a joyless existence for Evgenia, and when she left the place for teachers' college, the 17-year old girl vowed never to set foot in the place again.

Evgenia still showered three times a day. Almost 50 years after she left the filthy communal flat by the factory, she still smelled burned rubber in her hair and on her clothes.

She had maintained only sporadic contact with her family since leaving for university. She detested her father, a fat, uncouth alcoholic who cleaned machinery at the plant until his death at age 54. She tolerated her mother, who had worked in the plant's cafeteria. She had been a gentle woman devoid of either ambition or curiosity, Evgenia felt. Ultimately, she had determined that they were undeserving of her concern.

She had similar ambiguity toward her brother, Ihor. Ten years her junior, she really hadn't known him growing up. Not until their parents were both gone and Ihor moved to Kyiv did she acquaint herself with little Ihor, the man. He had their mother's mouse-like timidity and their father's thirst for vodka. Between alcoholic binges, Ihor barely managed to make a living as a notary in one of the city's poorer districts.

Evgenia's one attempt at marriage had failed within a year. She liked the quiet boy she had met in university. He had been bright and funny and a hard worker, but even on two teachers' salaries, money was a problem. They had lived with his parents in Rivne for a short time, and then shared a one-room apartment. Evgenia had ended the relationship - she had always been in control - because she was ill-suited to cohabitation. She didn't need the companionship, the extra work, the clutter or the prospect of children that living with a husband entailed. One day she simply packed her things and left for Kyiv. As the door closed behind her, she put the man and the marriage out of her mind, forever. She moved on.

Over the years, she lived in a succession of apartments, always alone, though sometimes, of necessity, in one room of a communal. She vowed that the day would come when she would have a place of her own - large, airy and immaculately clean. This dream was near impossible for a divorced Soviet woman, though she spent hours imagining how she might attain it. She once considered buying counterfeit papers showing that she was married with three children so that she could qualify for a place of her own, but she eventually abandoned the idea, as the risk and expense of that proposition was too great.

It wasn't until many years had passed and the Soviet Union had collapsed that she found a way to achieve her dream, however delayed the gratification might be. She was almost there, she thought. Four steps had been taken. Two more steps and the dream would be fulfilled.

***

On Wednesday of the following week, Bohdan stopped by the property office to collect an envelope containing the documents pertaining to the transfer of Nikolai's apartment, and the other flats that had been sold by the mysterious Evgenia Stepanova.

That evening, he tore open the envelope and extracted a thick sheaf of documents. It looked like the bottle of brandy had been a good investment, he thought.

He examined the contract transferring Nikolai's flat to Stepanova, and the one transferring it to the current tenant. Everything looked in order, and each of the forms were neatly stamped and sealed. Nikolai's signature was there, as was Stepanova's.

None of the documents pertaining to Stepanova's other transfers were extraordinary, either, except that in each case, the seller was a single man, and the buyer was E. F. Stepanova.

Bohdan looked more closely at the documents: She had acquired, and then sold, four flats over less than 20 months.

Cumulatively, the flats were worth the equivalent of nearly 70,000 Euros.

The policeman was about to turn off the light and head to bed when he decided to shuffle through the documents one last time. Four acquisitions, four sales, 20 months. Too easy, he thought. And then he spotted an unusual commonality: each of the documents bore the stamp of the same notary. One man had prepared all of the documents. His address was on the documents, as required.

Bohdan decided that he would have to pay a visit to Ihor Filipovych Kyrylenko, Notary. But first, he picked up the telephone. It was time to tell Natasha what he had learned.

***

Kyrylenko's office was difficult to find. Only a small sign marked the door of an otherwise residential apartment house a few blocks from the Kharkivska Metro station. It was a bad house in a bad neighbourhood.

An old woman sat on a kitchen stool by the entrance to the building, mending a shirt.

"I'm looking for the notary," he said. "What room is he in, please?"

"The bar-room, probably," the woman said, looking across the street at a cafe-bar. She smiled at Bohdan, exposing a mouthful of stainless steel teeth.

"There's a notary three blocks that way," she motioned with the hand that clutched the sewing needle. "Don't waste your time on that alcoholic. Nobody else does."

"Thank you," Bohdan replied, "but I have to see Kyrylenko this time."

Kyrylenko sat alone in the small bar, a bottle of cheap vodka and a plate of pickles in front of him. Bohdan sat down and the watery-eyed notary watched him suspiciously.

"What do you want?" he said, taking a gulp of the vodka.

"I need to find Evgenia Stepanova," Bohdan said. "I have business with her. Police business."

Bohdan pulled out his wallet and showed his credentials to the man, whose eyes widened.

"I don't know anything," he stammered, pouring another 50 grams of vodka into his glass.

"Maybe you know these names," Bohdan said, removing the sheaf of documents from his briefcase and spreading them out on the table before the notary. He read the name of each person who had sold a flat to, or purchased a flat from Stepanova. He read eight names in all, plus Stepanova's and Kyrylenko's. "Maybe you know what they have in common?"

Kyrylenko looked at the documents, and shook his head.

"My sister," he said. "It was all her doing. I just did the legal work."

"You know, of course, that it is a violation of the law of Ukraine to notarize a document for a close relative?"

"I am more afraid of Evgenia Filipovna than I am of any law," he said. Then he asked Bohdan a question that surprised him: "She kills good men. Can it be over, now?"

As he finished what promised to be his last bottle of vodka for many years, Ihor explained that his sister targeted lonely retired men, befriended them and then coerced them into signing over their apartments to her. As Evgenia held them at knifepoint, Ihor would tie them up and leave for an hour. When he returned, the men were dead, bludgeoned by a hammer blow to the back of the head. They would remove the bodies at night and dispose of them in the forests outside Kyiv. Evgenia buried the clothes, hands and heads, and dumped the bodies, wrapped in blankets and weighted with rocks, in the river. The Dnipro was good at keeping secrets.

When the apartments sold, Ihor said, his sister would give him a small sum - $1,000 or $2,000. The rest she said she was saving to buy a flat of her own, in a new building, and with fine furniture.

267

"It was all she talked about," Ihor said. "It is her dream. It was a nightmare for me, though. I think about those men. All four of them. She promised, just two more times. Two more, then she'd have what she wanted from life and I'd never need to see her again."

It was early evening when the detectives knocked on Evgenia's door. She didn't answer at first - she seldom did. But the insistent banging continued, and when she angrily unlatched the door, it was quickly pushed open. She was arrested before she fully understood what was happening.

Natasha wept as Bohdan explained what he had learned. She knew that her father had been killed, and was coming to the realization that his body might never be found. She returned to her home in Donetsk. Kyiv now held nothing for her but bitterness.

***

The next Sunday was colder, crisper than the one before and there were fewer pensioners gathered at The Square. Bohdan walked past, watching the men play chess, and the woman talk in small groups. The sound of accordion music wafted over the voices, and the policeman saw old Borys on his bench, as usual.

Borys looked a bit sadder, perhaps. His friend Evgenia hadn't come by.

You have no idea how close you came to being victim number five, my friend, Bohdan thought. The sound of the accordion receded, yielding to recorded rock and the chatter of the Saturday crowd as Bohdan walked further down the path toward the Metro station.

Meet the DEATH TOLL 2 authors

Meet the DEATH TOLL 2 authors

Enjoyed their work in the anthology?
Visit Amazon to discover more bestselling titles from
these great authors.

Stephen Leather is one of the UK's most successful thriller writers. He was a journalist for more than ten years on newspapers such as *The Times*, the *Daily Mail* and the *South China Morning Post* in Hong Kong. Before that, he was employed as a biochemist for ICI, shoveled limestone in a quarry, worked as a baker, a petrol pump attendant, a barman, and worked for the Inland Revenue. He began writing full time in 1992. His bestsellers including the 'Spider Shepherd' and 'Jack Nightingale' series are published by Hodder & Stoughton and have been translated into more than ten languages. Stephen has sold in excess of 2 million paperbacks and is also one of the most successful eBook publishers. In 2011 and *The Bookseller* magazine named him as one of the Top 100 most influential people in publishing. He has also written for television shows such as *London's Burning*, *The Knock* and the BBC's *Murder in Mind* series. You can find out more from his website, www.stephenleather.com.

HARD TARGETS

Matt Hilton was a police officer with Cumbria Constabulary

 before leaving to launch his writing career. He writes tight, cinematic American-style thrillers and is the author of the 'Joe Hunter' thriller series, including his most recent novel 'Rules of Honour', published in February 2013 by Hodder and Stoughton. His debut novel, Dead Men's Dust, was shortlisted for the International Thriller Writers' Debut Book of 2009 Award, and was a Sunday Times bestseller, also being named as a 'thriller of the year 2009' by The Daily Telegraph. The Joe hunter series is widely published by Hodder and Stoughton in UK territories, and by William Morrow and Company in the USA, and has been translated into German, Italian, Romanian and Bulgarian. Matt is a high-ranking martial artist and has been a detective and private security specialist, all of which lend an authenticity to the action scenes in his books. www.matthiltonbooks.com

Alex Shaw spent the second half of the 1990s in Kyiv, Ukraine,

 teaching Drama and running his own business consultancy before being head-hunted for a division of Siemens. The next few years saw him doing business for the company across the former USSR, the Middle East, and Africa. He is the author of the #1 International Kindle Bestselling 'Aidan Snow SAS thrillers' HETMAN and COLD BLACK and the new DELTA FORCE VAMPIRE series of books. DANGEROUS, DEADLY, ELITE - The third Aidan Snow Thriller will be available in early 2014. Alex, his wife and their two sons divide their time between homes in Kyiv, Ukraine and West Sussex, England. You can follow Alex on twitter: @alexshawhetman or facebook: https://www.facebook.com/alex.shaw.982292 or contact him via his website: www.alexwshaw.com.

J.H. Bográn, J. H. Bográn was born and raised in Honduras. The

son of a journalist, he ironically prefers to write
fiction rather than fact. His debut novel
TREASURE HUNT was selected for the Top Ten
in Predators & Editor's Reader Poll. His second
novel *FIREFALL* was released in September
2013 by Rebel ePublishers. In his native
Spanish, he's collaborated in three TV series for and has penned
two screenplays; the latest for the movie *ONCE CIPOTES* which
will go on general released in 2013. His Spanish language novel
HEREDERO del MAL is published in Central America by Letra
Negra Editores. He's a member of the Short Fiction Writers
Guild & the International Thriller Writers where he also serves
as the Thriller Roundtable Coordinator and contributor editor
their official e-zine The Big Thrill. He lives in Honduras with
his wife and three sons. Follow Jose on twitter: @JHBogran or on
facebook http://on.fb.me/ZJwEq0 or visit his website:
www.jhbogran.com

Stephen Edger is one of Britain's up and coming new crime

writers, his novels including *INTEGRATION,*
REMORSE, REDEMPTION, SNATCHED and
SHADOW LINE. Stephen was born in
Darlington in NE England, raised in London and
now lives in Southampton after studying Law at
University there. Stephen works in corporate
finance and has used his experiences of the
industry in each of his books. Stephen was inspired to start
writing in 2010 after being burgled while on holiday in Spain.
The trauma this crime became the inspiration for his first novel.
For further information about Stephen and his works, visit
www.stephenedger.com or twitter: @StephenEdger or facebook:
https://www.facebook.com/pages/Author-Stephen-
Edger/170466706349526?fref=ts

Liam Saville lives in Sydney Australia with his wife, two

children, and their German Shepherd. He is a former member of the Australian Army and has studied at the Royal Military College Duntroon. Liam also served for several years as a police officer in his home state of New South Wales, and currently works full time in a regulatory and enforcement role with a public sector agency in Sydney. He is the author of the military crime novellas PREDATOR STRIKE and RESOLUTE ACTION featuring Australian Defence Force Investigator, Captain Sam Ryan. You can follow Liam on twitter @lssaville or connect with him on Facebook: www.facebook.com/LiamSavilleBooks Liam's official website can be found at: www.liamsaville.wordpress.com

Harlan Wolff left London for Bangkok in 1977 shortly after a

coup but in time for martial law and curfew. Overstaying his visa for seven years, he became the most wanted illegal alien in Thailand. Fluent in Thai he spent his days and nights with foreign businessmen, alcoholics, gangsters, imported gangsters, gamblers, whores, politicians, and policemen. By the 1990s Harlan became the person foreigners sought when they had problems. So began his life as a private detective and trouble-shooter, successfully concluding cases of theft, industrial espionage, extortion, kidnapping, and murder. The life of his fictional character 'Carl Engel' is not far removed from the author's own experiences. Harlan Wolff began writing after his 50th birthday. The bestselling *BANGKOK RULES* is his first novel. He hopes to spend the rest of his life writing and living a quieter, more sensible existence with his wife and three children in the Thailand he has grown to love. Follow him on twitter: @HarlanWolffBKK or friend him on facebook: https://www.facebook.com/harlan.wolff.3

Milton Gray spent a bookish childhood relishing flights of  fantasy, science fiction, and horror stories that were certainly not suitable for a child of his age. Eventually he sort of grew up, though not out of his past interests, instead just adding to them. He went on to study philosophy at university and graduated with keen new insights into how little he knew about anything, only to learn that the world preferred people to profess to know rather more about something. He lives a quiet, uneventful life at a seaside town in the South of England, composing frivolous novellas to entertain himself. These include the Blood Traffic trilogy; THE BOW STREET VAMPIRE, THE FOOD CHAIN and PEEL'S BLOODY GANG. He also writes long letters in cafés, drinks far too much tea, consumes far too much chocolate, and plays games with tarot cards (which he insists they were invented for). Follow him on twitter: @MiltonGrayBooks

Scott H Lewis is an accomplished speaker, corporate trainer  and PR counsellor. He is a former editor of the Kyiv Post newspaper, the Ukrainian Observer magazine, and a book editor for Vidalia House publishing. Lewis is a past adjunct faculty member at Peninsula College in Washington State, and has travelled extensively in the United States and Europe. His book for young readers, *A CROW'S DAY*, is an Amazon bestseller and has been translated into five languages. *THE WIDOWS DANCE* is included in his Ukrainian based fiction anthology by the same name. He regularly publishes articles on topics including PR, marketing, presentation skills, & the media. He is also the author of non-fiction works including: *60 SECONDS TO WOW!*, *THE KINDNESS CURE, and CRUISE POWER.*

Lewis lives with his wife, Natalie, in Kyiv, Ukraine.

***